That's Debatable

That's Debatable

JEN DOLL

FARRAR STRAUS GIROUX
NEW YORK

Farrar Straus Giroux Books for Young Readers
An imprint of Macmillan Publishing Group, LLC
120 Broadway, New York, NY 10271 • fiercereads.com

Our books may be purchased in bulk for promotional, educational, or
business use. Please contact your local bookseller or the Macmillan Corporate
and Premium Sales Department at (800) 221-7945 ext. 5442 or by email at
MacmillanSpecialMarkets@macmillan.com.

Library of Congress Cataloging-in-Publication Data

Names: Doll, Jen, author.
Title: That's debatable / Jen Doll.
Description: First edition. | New York : Farrar Straus Giroux Books for Young
    Readers, 2022. | Summary: Seventeen-year-old Millicent M. Chalmers is
    depending on a series of debating victories, culminating in winning
    Alabama's state debate tournament, to secure a college scholarship, but
    her singular focus is disrupted after a run-in with Taggart Strong, who
    seems equally dedicated to losing every debate as long as he says what he
    really believes.
Identifiers: LCCN 2021012485 | ISBN 978-0-374-30604-5 (hardcover)
Subjects: CYAC: Debates and debating—Fiction. | Winning and losing—
    Fiction. | Dating (Social customs)—Fiction. | Sexism—Fiction. | Sexual
    harassment—Fiction. | Alabama—Fiction. | LCGFT: Novels.
Classification: LCC PZ7.1.D638 Th 2022 | DDC [Fic]—dc23
LC record available at https://lccn.loc.gov/2021012485

First edition, 2022
Book design by Mallory Grigg
Printed in the United States of America

ISBN 978-0-374-30604-5 (hardcover)
10 9 8 7 6 5 4 3 2 1

This book is dedicated to the Decatur High School forensics team circa 1990–94 and, of course, the late, great Ellen Langford[1]

---

1 Who taught me everything I know about Lincoln-Douglas debate, speaking up and being heard, and the importance of dresses that cover your knees. (That last matter is itself debatable.)

We acknowledge that there is no
right way to debate and also that many
different styles of debate exist.

—DR. SETH HALVORSON & CHERIAN KOSHY,
Introduction to Lincoln-Douglas Debate

But what a weak barrier is truth when
it stands in the way of an hypothesis!

—MARY WOLLSTONECRAFT,
A Vindication of the Rights of Woman

PART ONE

October

Resolved: In the United States, private ownership of handguns ought to be banned.

WHAT: THE MONTGOMERY HILLS
ACADEMY FORENSICS TOURNAMENT
WHERE: MONTGOMERY HILLS, ALABAMA
WHEN: THE SECOND WEEKEND IN OCTOBER
WHY: TO DEBATE . . . AND TO WIN!

Hello, coaches and competitors!

Thank you for registering for the 10th Annual
Montgomery Hills Academy Forensics Tournament! You
probably know we're talking speech and debate, not
crime-scene investigations, but if you don't, check your
medical bag at the door! This is <u>NOT</u> *CSI*!

We're offering six robust rounds of policy, public
forum, and Lincoln-Douglas debate on Friday and
Saturday, and final rounds beginning with octofinals—
yes, that's sixteen skilled competitors vying for a top
slot—starting Saturday afternoon. We'll conclude with an
awards ceremony on Saturday evening.

This <u>IS</u> a Nationals qualifying tournament!

Please read on for rules and other important
information.

See you there,

Laura Lainey and Mark Grissom, Coaches
Montgomery Hills Academy Debate Team
"We're arguably the best"

MILLIE

I'm not saying this is right; I'm just saying it is: You play by the rules; you get what you want. The reverse of that: In order to get what you want, you pretty much have to play by the rules. Especially if you're a woman.

Reality isn't always fair. Reality can sometimes really suck.

Which is why it's so important to do everything you can to boost your advantage.

Enter high school debate. I've been competing for four years now, which means I've had plenty of time to get good. Really good. It's not bragging to say you're looking at the top seed in Alabama, the senior girl everyone expects to break records by winning the state tournament yet again, just like every other year I've competed. It's just a fact.

But let me backtrack, for those of you unfamiliar with the debate world.

Here's how it works. In the lead-up to a debate competition, we learn what the topic is. That's the *resolution*. Like, "Resolved: No one should ever eat pie again in their life because it would be healthier for the entire country." No matter that I love pie, particularly of the pizza variety, and am at least theoretically against the concept of limiting what you love—who gets enough of what they love in a lifetime? If it comes at you, you should grab a slice! You have to be able to argue both sides. That's the whole point.

I spend weeks preparing, writing affirmative and negative

arguments, like, for the pie example, that poor nutrition is rampant, and as a nation, getting rid of pie would lead to healthier eating across the board, or, on the converse, treating yourself leads to joy, which is inherently healthy and a value we believe in as Americans—it's "American as apple pie." And what about how pie sales stimulate the economy? I'm just riffing, but you get it. I work on my arguments until I could convince just about anyone of something they never would have believed they'd agree with in the first place. I practice having the toughest questions thrown at me, and answering them in a way that not only defeats the asker but also makes them want to put their tail between their legs and slink away like a dog that's just gotten yelled at.

But—and this is important—I never yell. I practice modulating my voice, because if you're a girl and you get "emotional," or "shrill," or you "uptalk," you're dead in the water. You have to be smooth and steady, always calm, always "ladylike." Better wear that pantyhose, because if you don't, some good-old-boy judge or middle-aged lady who wore pantyhose when *she* was a teenage debater and thinks because she did, you have to, too, is going to say something, and you're going to have to stand there and take it, thanking them for their opinion. They might even take points off for it.

Debaters talk about the burden of proof, which belongs to the affirmative, but as a girl debater, the burden of "proof" belongs to you: Does your skirt cover your knees? Are you *wearing* a skirt? Are you attractive, but not "too" attractive? When a boy comes at you hard, can you come back soft and still make your point? (Because coming back just as hard makes you "unappealing" or "rude" or "factually correct but abrasive.")[2] Can you deal with the jokes that aren't funny and the way that you're expected to laugh anyway to show you have a sense of humor? Can you avoid flinching, or drawing back, when the director who runs the tournament hugs you when he gives you your first-place trophy and holds on to you a little bit too long? Can you get up an hour earlier than every guy debater so you have time to do your hair and pull off your "no-makeup" look while they show up looking like they just rolled out of bed?

Can you make sure you never, ever cry, even when someone says something horrible to you, either right in front of you or behind your back? Even when you lose, because sometimes, you *will* lose.

There aren't that many of us on the circuit, probably one girl to every three dudes, and even fewer who make it to final rounds, not that we're not deserving. There were so many who might have been good. I have friends I made on the circuit who quit after feeling bullied or harassed or like the cards were just too stacked against them, even though they did everything right. I know girls who never started debating at all, just because they knew what would happen.

As one of the ones who stuck around, you can bet your butt I want to win.

And I do, most of the time.

I've even practiced getting hugged so I don't make a face, which wouldn't come off as "grateful" or "appreciative" or "award-worthy." My best friend, Carlos—he's a debater, too—we must have hugged fifty times in a row to get it right.

---

2 All comments I have actually gotten on the ballots that judges fill out and give to us after rounds.

Even when I think I've gotten it down, I repeat, repeat, repeat.

Topics change every couple of months, so once you've gotten really good at arguing one thing, you're on to the next. Last year I won state on *Resolved: The United States government ought to provide for the medical care of its citizens*. Easy-peasy, you're thinking? Who doesn't want health care? But I argued the negative, which means America *shouldn't* provide medical care for its citizens. (It was still easy-peasy. I can argue just about anything, which isn't to say I agree with it—that's beside the point.)

I do Lincoln-Douglas debate, which is named after Abraham Lincoln and Stephen A. Douglas and their famous series of debates about slavery and the future of America during the 1858 Illinois state election campaign. There are also policy and public forum debaters: We're usually at the same tournaments, but we exist in different worlds. Policy debaters, who operate in teams of two, get one resolution to work on all year, and they spend the entire debate reading "proof" of their point as fast as they can.[3] Public forum debaters also work in teams of two, and their topics change monthly, but they go less into theory and evidence than policy or L-D. Lincoln-Douglas debaters roll solo. Our topics change every two months, and, like Stephen A. Douglas and Abraham Lincoln, we present arguments based on values—like morality or justice or liberty or equality.[4] L-D debaters want to change minds, not just throw a bunch of facts at them.[5]

This tournament's resolution about what we "ought to"[6] do about guns was a little iffy, though, considering how many active

3 This is called *spreading*.
4 This is called the *value proposition*.
5 I'm an L-D debater, so I have to say that.
6 Implying a moral obligation

shooter drills I'd already been through by the age of seventeen. Don't get me wrong, it was definitely a topic people were talking about. And the point of debate is to come up with the best arguments for even the most seemingly impossible statement, regardless of your personal opinion. Most complicated topics do have another side to them that's worth listening to, even if it never changes your mind. But something felt wrong about this lofty discussion of gun ownership when kids were regularly being murdered with guns they didn't have any say in the legalization of and the NRA kept acting like it wasn't their problem.

Every time there's a shooting, more people buy guns. Did you know that?

The whole thing really pissed me off. So did the resolution's inherent construct of a country full of cops and military personnel who would still get to own guns when regular people didn't. That was the great argument on the negative side, in my opinion. If you took guns away from private citizens, you should take them away from everyone; otherwise you're slippery sloping to a complete and total police state. There was a part of me that wanted to yell "Abolish the cops and we'll all be safer!" when I was assigned the negative side in a debate round, and then start throwing out stats about police brutality.

For a second, I let myself really imagine it—changing the rules of the game, shocking everyone, and coming out differently on the other side.

But this was debate. This was Alabama. This was America, for better and worse. And I wanted to win. I hadn't put up with everything for this long to start losing based on some ridiculous desire to say what I *really* thought. I'd take home that state trophy knowing I was not only the only girl debater but the only high school student in the history of Alabama to have won every single state championship I'd competed in: freshman, sophomore, junior, and senior year. After state came Nationals, which you were invited to if you broke[7] at enough Nationals-qualifying tournaments—something I'd always done, and planned to do this year, too. And there were even bigger things on the line. Scholarships. You could have your entire college career paid for, no debt, free and clear. That would be everything to me and my mom.

It's like I said. To get what you want, you play by the rules.

---

7 Made it to the elimination rounds, which usually start with octofinals.

TAG

On the first morning of the Montgomery Hills Academy Forensics Tournament, as I got ready for an eight-hour day spent debating other high school students from the great state of Alabama and beyond, Millicent M. Chalmers didn't once cross my mind. Not then, or on the bus we took to the tournament, which was about an hour away from my own high school, or even after I set foot in Montgomery Hills Academy's cafeteria, where all the teams gathered to chug coffee and wait to find out who we would debate first.

Let's just say I had other things to worry about.

In debate lingo, *Resolved: Taggart Strong was having issues.*

Allow me to present my case.

1. The matter of college. At the beginning of the week, I'd been pulled into a meeting with my parents; the head of The Park School, Mr. Merwin; and our school's debate coach, Francine Cho, to talk about my future. I was a senior. Where was I thinking of applying? Would my debate record (so-so, with a few highs and an equal and growing number of lows) suffice to get me into a high-reach school? What about a safety?

That's when I said it. "I don't think I want to go to college at all," I told them, pushing my glasses up my nose while my parents gazed at me like I'd just suggested we eat babies for dinner.

Merwin hummed, as if that could cover up the diabolical

academic fart[8] I'd released into the room. Francine patted me on the shoulder. Thank God for Francine.

I go to this progressive school my parents pay a bundle for, so no one was going to yell at me, even though I could tell my dad wanted to. Instead, they were going to talk to me about my *feelings*.

"Why is that, exactly, Taggart?" Merwin asked, and my parents both leaned forward to hear.

"I just don't think it's useful in today's society," I said. "Student debt is a nightmare. And how is it remotely fair? Kids whose parents can pay are totally set while kids without that money end up paying the price for years. Also, there's plenty to learn outside of an academic institution."

My dad, a Park School graduate who'd won state in policy debate and gone on to law school, grunted. (The school had been a little different back then.) My mom put her hand on his knee and patted gently.

"We simply want to make sure you have each and every option you deserve," said Merwin soothingly. "What if you change your mind? College is a truly marvelous experience. We wouldn't want you to miss out . . ."

"You mean you wouldn't want The Park School to miss out on saying they had a one hundred percent acceptance rate into top-tier universities for their entire graduating class," I said.

My mom winced, but Merwin took it in stride.

"Ha!" he said. "That's the spirit we love in you, Tag. The Park School has given you the confidence to go against the grain! This is what we're all about! But also . . ."

"You're going to apply to college," my dad said in a low growl.

---

8 Not rhetorical, metaphorical

"Which brings me to your debate record," said Merwin. "You were doing great up through the middle of junior year, and then it seems that things just took a dive. What happened?"

2. The matter of debate. When I joined the team freshman year, things were different. It was fun learning how to put cases together, coming up with arguments that had philosophical and real-world backup, having thoughts on these important topics that impressed my parents and their friends. Everything felt theoretical.

Something happened along the way, though. There were so many lies out there in the world, and they weren't theoretical at all. They were the words that politicians and religious figures and celebrities and sometimes plain old citizens shouted from behind podiums or pulpits or microphones or their social media platforms to get what they wanted. Sometimes they'd say one thing and then immediately say the opposite, hoping to reap the benefits of whatever the prevailing opinion happened to be, claiming they'd never said the first thing, even though it had been coming out of their mouths minutes ago. They were sneaky. They used rhetoric. You couldn't blame society for being confused.

But debate was about having a voice. If *I* could say what I really believed, what I knew in my heart and mind to be true—I should say it, right? And keep saying it until people listened?

So that's what I started doing. If I didn't agree with the resolution, I said it. As negative, I argued the affirmative was right; on the affirmative side I recommended the negative get the judge's vote. My guiding principle wasn't winning the debate, or even the debate at all. Aren't some things just not debatable? Or they shouldn't be, anyway.

My school, my parents, they've always taught us that our voices matter—that what we say, and how we say it, can change the course of the universe. But here I was, saying what I meant, and no one around me, with the possible exception of my debate coach, seemed to think that what I was doing was actually important or meaningful or worthwhile.

Why did winning become more important than the truth?

"I just need to say what I really believe," I told them.

In the '90s, Francine had been an L-D debater at a school called Bronx Science in New York City. She'd won major tournaments like Yale, Emory, and Nationals. She even had her own slogan, CHO FOR THE WIN, that her friends back then had ironed onto a T-shirt for her (she showed it to us in class one day). She piped up to defend me: "Tag is wrestling with the heart of what makes debate debate: the need to interrogate both sides, even if one of those sides appears sorely lacking. Just because he isn't winning doesn't mean, one, it's not a valuable experience and, two, he's not learning." True to form, she still ticked off points on her fingers, and she knew how to speak the language Merwin loved. "To the contrary: He has embarked upon on a powerful educational journey." I wanted to high-five her, but instead I just futzed with the Kleenex I'd been slowly tearing apart in my lap. Stress relief.

"Just because I don't win that often doesn't mean I don't like it," I muttered. "Or that it's not good for me. Anyway, *I'm doing this for me. Not you.* And what's winning, anyway?"

"Speak up, son," my dad said. But if there's one thing I *had* learned from debate, it was that there were certain times you should stay quiet.

"We support you being you," added my mom. "But, honey, it seems like you're mocking the whole idea of debate, getting up there and arguing the wrong side when you don't like the side you've been given. Some of the other parents find it offensive. Some say you're hurting the other debaters' chances of getting into good schools by pulling down the overall record."

"When I was on the team . . . ," my dad began, but Mom shot him a look and he stopped talking. I'd heard it all before anyway.

Merwin cleared his throat. "It's one of the guiding principles at The Park School to give students space to explore and find their own truth. College applications aren't due for a few months, so we have a little time on that front. Debatewise, why don't we see how Tag does at the upcoming tournament"—he glanced down at the large calendar that sat across his desk with student events and appointments scrawled all over it—"Montgomery Hills Academy. Tag, it's your chance to show us what you're really about. We know you have it in you to do the very best you can!"

My mom nodded. My dad emitted a grunt that indicated acceptance.

"Francine, does that work for you?" asked Merwin.

"Sure," said Francine.

No one asked what I thought.

"Now, Tag, I'll also set up an appointment with Ms. Lalli in guidance to make sure you have all the information you need to get moving on your college applications." Merwin stood up and grinned at both of my parents, who rose as well. "I feel confident that we'll all get where we need to go, here," he said, shaking their hands. "Lovely to see you folks, as always. We do appreciate your generous donations to our school and to the debate program. I'm certain we're going to figure out the right fit for Tag, whether it's debate or something else."[9]

---

9 "Something else" = fitness walking or multivariate data analysis or show choir. I'd checked.

3. The matter of Rajesh. My parents and Merwin weren't the only ones giving me hell. My former best friend, the captain of our debate team, had a bone to pick. This morning, just after we got off the bus at Montgomery Hills, he'd motioned me over to a quiet section of the hall, where a series of trophies for football, baseball, and soccer mocked me from their glass cases, asking me why I wasn't doing them instead.

"Principles," I whispered. "You have yours. I have mine."

"Tag," Rajesh said, and grabbed my shoulders, giving me a shake.

"Yes?" I squinted at him, listening attentively. I got a lot of points for attentiveness on the ballots judges used to critique our performance, right before they said, "I'm not sure what you're doing up there."

"Remember: If you get the negative, *you argue the negative*. If you get the affirmative, *you argue the affirmative*. Act like you know what you're talking about! A rising tide lifts all boats, but no one wants to go down with the ship. That makes me look bad. And I don't have room to look bad. Harv—"

"I know," I said. Rajesh was applying early action to Harvard. He told us almost daily. He'd fallen in love with the school when his parents took him to visit Boston in fourth grade; he'd come back with a Harvard baseball cap he wore for nearly a year straight and a weird passion for the Red Sox. More recently, he couldn't stop talking about the Harvard College Debating Union, which was ranked number one in the entire United States. He had plans to join it. But first he had to get in.

"This is my future on the line," he said. "Our team winning—it matters. For me and for the rest of us, even if you can't understand that. This isn't the *Tag Show*. Could you take one thing seriously in your life? Play by the rules, dude. At least *try* to win."

He let go of my shoulders and wiped his hands on his khaki pants. His hands sweated a lot when he was nervous, which I knew because Rajesh and I used to be tight. In elementary school, we alternated between our houses to play, study (even back then Rajesh studied, so I did, too), and eat dinner (his dad's saag paneer is one of my top ten favorite meals). We survived middle school together, getting our braces on and off on the exact same days. Our parents threw a big party the first time we made honor roll (Rajesh had decided it was his job; I'd gone along because he was doing it). We joined the debate team together when we were freshmen (urged by my dad and Rajesh's mom, who thought speech and debate the perfect thing for her son, who she hoped would become a doctor, a lawyer, or, failing that, some kind of diplomat). "Though if he gets into Harvard," his dad liked to say, "he can be whatever he wants to be."

Everything was great between Rajesh and me. Until last year. After I introduced my new debate tactic, if you can call it that, at the Auburn Invitational and ended up losing to a guy who had to keep stopping to puke in a bucket due to food poisoning, Rajesh has gone from my best bud to avoiding me as much as he can. He takes my behavior as a personal affront, like I'm trying to bring him down. Maybe he thinks my failure is catching. And maybe I *am* hurting his chances to get into Harvard.

The truth is, I miss him. But I can't change what I feel in my gut is right.

"It's actually more complicated than that," I tried to explain, but he shook his head.

"Play the game!" He wiped his hands on his pants again, then turned and walked away. "That's why we're here. If you can't do that, maybe you shouldn't be here at all."

Ouch.

I guess that's why I remained blissfully ignorant to the presence of Millicent *Moot Point*[10] Chalmers until Rose Powell brought over the list of first-round assignments. Rose was new on the team, a junior who'd transferred from a high school near Columbus, Ohio. She'd done Model UN there, and our debate team was the closest thing she could find to it. She had a nose ring and a streak of purple in her hair and didn't seem to care much what anyone thought about that or anything else about her. I'd liked her immediately.

"Isn't this the girl everyone's terrified of?" she said, pointing to the name paired with my own. Which brings me to . . .

4. **The matter of Millicent Chalmers.** How lucky can one guy get?[11]

Her middle initial was *M*. If you believed the rumors, it stood for "Machete" or "Machine" or "Milkshake" or "Misandrist." Some of the lesser evolved of my male peers claimed it was for "Manboobs," and I'm pretty sure (1) that's not even a word that you use when referring to women, and (2) she did not have manboobs. Not that I'd looked. I'm not that kind of guy—at least, I try not to be.

---

10 A *moot point* is a fact that doesn't matter because it's not relevant to the current situation. Debating Millicent M. Chalmers made winning a moot point.

11 Not metaphorical, rhetorical: as in, intended for dramatic effect. I did not actually find myself lucky to be in this situation, in part because the year before, Millicent M. Chalmers had kicked my butt so hard I could still feel the sting. Better men than I had cried after a round with her, and, honestly, I was pretty comfortable crying.

Millicent M. Chalmers was the quintessential debate nerd, a robot created in a laboratory to do this thing we did after school and on weekends and, if we were really committed, at camps in the summer, too. (She was exactly that committed.) She was well spoken. Impeccably dressed: junior corporate associate at a law firm or high school debater, who could say?[12] She carried a briefcase while most of the rest of us slouched around with overstuffed backpacks. She was infinitely prepared: She didn't even use the prep time, four minutes to allocate as you needed, built into each debate. Her rebuttals were already prepped, and they were that good. This made her a darling to adults while super annoying to most of her peers on the circuit, who were jealous, sure, but also, she was *so damn smug.*

She had reason to be. She'd won state every year she'd competed, and about a million other debates in between. Probably had to rent a storage unit to keep all her trophies in.

It wasn't exactly fortuitous that the first round of the debate tournament where I'd been ordered to try my best—to win, that is, with a not completely veiled "or else" attached to it—would pair me against her.

Or that Millicent, who'd been assigned the affirmative, would be arguing the side I believed in.

---

12 What kind of teenage girl wore pantyhose? Again, a rhetorical question.

MILLIE

When I saw my opponent, this lanky kid in a wrinkled button-down and a pumpkin-patterned tie, he looked at me and he *smiled*. This big, goofy smile, like we were old friends and not about to debate each other in a Nationals-qualifying tournament.

I decided then and there I didn't just want to win. I wanted to destroy him. Win so hard he wouldn't know what had even happened. Not that he seemed to have a solid awareness of what was going on in the first place.

His dark hair swooped over his glasses and in front of his right eye, almost completely blocking his vision on that side—I was amazed he didn't bump into things as he walked around. He was from this progressive private school that's about forty-five minutes from my own public hellhole. I'd heard they let you roam free and create your own classes, which you could then grade yourself on. Perhaps that explained things.

His name was Taggart Strong, but the Strong felt ironic. I had a vague recollection of wiping the floor with him last year. Had he worn that tie then, too?

They have a great debate team at Taggart Strong's school, for the record. They're well funded, and a lot of them win regularly. There are a bunch of girls on the team, and their coach is a woman, this former debate star from up north.

Meanwhile, at my school, there's just me and "Coach Kargle, rhymes with gargle," the gym teacher/assistant football coach I convinced to take me on when I needed an adult to sponsor me for debate. I'm the only one on my team. He claims he's happy to do it, but sometimes I feel bad. He has to toggle between games and my tournaments. He'll leave one and go straight to the other. And there are a bunch of football players who don't like me very much because of it. It's like they never learned how to share in kindergarten. But then, neither did our school's administration: No matter how often Kargle and my mom ask, all our extracurricular funding goes to the boys' sports teams.

Most tournaments take place on weekends, and most debaters stay at hotels in the area so they don't have to go back and forth each night and get up at the crack of dawn to be there on time. But Kargle drives me home at the end of the day and then back the next morning, unless we're going to a super-far-away tournament, which only happens once in a blue moon because, again, money. I got a scholarship that sent me to Nationals last year, but Mom and I had to scrape together the cash for extras, like food at tournaments and my outfits. Luckily, I have an in at our local Goodwill: Ms. Cheney calls me whenever something debateworthy comes in.

This year, the stakes are even higher. Not only do I need to win debate, it's college time. You should see our den. It's like a serial killer lives there, only his murder victims are institutions of higher learning, mapped out on poster board: On one wall there's Yale, and everything we know about it, and the scholarships and financial aid that might let me go there. On the other, there's Alabama—a state school, sure, but a good one, and also, in-state tuition! Scattered throughout are a bevy of other options, from the small liberal arts colleges to the giant state universities, and notes on my best shot to get into each of them and actually pay for it.

There are sixteen scholarships I'm actively working on right now, but Mom and I are constantly updating our list. You never know when someone will decide they need to donate a chunk of money to a person just like me.

In the meantime, Mom works all the extra shifts she can get as an ER nurse at the hospital the next town over, and I work on debate and getting the best grades possible. We have a long-standing agreement that I won't get a job while I'm in school, so I can focus on the other stuff. At the beginning of the school year, the agreement got an addendum: No dating until my college plans are finalized. It sounds harsh, but then, it's not like there's anyone of interest at my school.

Don't get me wrong. It's not like I've never been kissed. I still got meandering emails about situational ethics from Riley Coffrey, who I met at debate camp freshman year. (He lives in Minnesota and I'll probably never see him again.) My flirtation from Nationals last year, this extemper[13] named Max Einhorn, still texted me **Sup** every so often, whether I wrote back or not. But there was no one yet who'd reached the level of love—what I thought it meant, what it was supposed to mean. Of course, I didn't have time for that, anyway. My mom is right: I have more important things to think about.

When I got up to present the affirmative case,[14] I poured it on. And the judge completely ate it up. From the first second I could tell he was completely and 100 percent on my side. He kept making check marks under my name on his ballot.

---

13 Extemp = extemporaneous speaking, in which participants are given several current events topics to choose from and then prepare a seven-minute speech about one that they deliver from memory to a judge. (I'll stick with L-D, thanks.)

14 Also known as the *aff* or *AC* (for affirmative constructive); negative is *neg* or *NC*.

Everything was exactly as it should be, except for my opponent, who kept nodding at me. At one point it almost looked like he was giving me the thumbs-up.

What a weirdo. Probably some bizarre intimidation method.

I pressed on. They didn't call me Millicent "Motherfuckin'"[15] Chalmers for nothing.

---

15 Among other things. That's partly why I never tell anyone what it is. Fear keeps them on their toes. Plus, I don't owe anyone knowing more about me than they already think they do.

TAG

Now she was standing at the front of the classroom where we'd been assigned to debate, talking about how the private ownership of handguns ought to be banned, and not only that, it was the moral duty of each and every American civilian to renounce their guns, here and now and forever.

Just a day before, there'd been another high school shooting. It happened up north, but it could have been anywhere, because they were everywhere, over and over again. I'd read about it online—three teenagers had died, plus the gunman, also a teenager—and even if I hadn't, Millicent M. Chalmers was helpfully reminding me of it this very moment.

Our judge, the only other person in the room, was a bearded white guy in a stocking cap. His legs were stretched out under his desk, and his socks said I'M A DELICATE and FUCKING FLOWER on the soles, which I could read because he'd taken off his sneakers, for some reason. He was nodding and smiling and eating up every single one of Millicent's words.

I found myself nodding, too.

"And that, in conclusion, is why every American who is not in the military or law enforcement must relinquish their weapons, and cease to purchase any new ones," she said. "For the present, the past, and the future. It's simply the moral—the right—thing to do." She cleared her throat, smiled at the judge, and sat down.

"Awesome. Neg, your cross-ex," said the judge, eyeing my

name on the ballot in front of him. He wiggled his toes. I wished he wouldn't. "Taggart Strong?"

He and Millicent were both staring at me, waiting.

"You good, man?" asked the judge. I pegged him as a former debater. You could always tell.

I straightened my lucky tie as I stepped to the front of the room. I noticed a door leading to another room, maybe a supply closet or teacher's secret hangout spot, to the left of the chalkboard where Millicent M. Chalmers had drawn diagrams to make her point, a next-level debater move. I wondered what was in that little room, why it was there, who might put things in it, what those things might be. I thought about winning and losing and what really mattered. I thought about how every single one of us contained multitudes, but there was only one way to speak your truth: You had to come out and say it. And then I took a deep breath. Might as well get this over with. It was going to be a bloodbath, no question about that, but it didn't have to go on forever.

MILLIE

After the affirmative presents their initial case, it's time for the negative to ask questions, to try to trip up the affirmative and poke holes in their logic. That's called the cross-ex. Some people are good at it, some are bad, but Taggart Strong was . . . indescribable.

He stood up. Then he sat back down. Then he stood up again and moved to the middle of the room, a few feet away from me, both of us facing the judge. He took a deep breath.

I waited.

"This resolution," he said. "Can you tell me what the resolution is?"

I rattled it off. "Resolved: In the United States, private ownership of handguns ought to be banned."

He made a face. He looked tortured. "Are you aware of the Second Amendment?"

"Sure," I said. "'A well-regulated Militia, being necessary to the security of a free State, the right of the people to keep and bear Arms, shall not be infringed.' But I would argue that (a) *militia* does not necessarily entail civilians, and (b) even if it did, the fact that this was an amendment means that the Constitution—the very document by which we live—is capable of change, and, in fact, it must be a living document in order that people may continue to live, i.e., they don't die of gun violence. I doubt the founding fathers would have been very happy to see the situation we have right now in America, in which an average of thirty-eight thousand people die due to guns per year. That's one hundred a day."

He nodded. I took his silence to mean he wanted me to keep going, so I did.

"The trouble with guns, as I stated in my opening remarks, is that they kill people. And my value proposition is life. For more people to live, guns should not be owned by private citizens. There are currently almost four hundred million guns in circulation in America, and America leads other high-income nations in gun violence. If you take away guns from civilians, you change that. It's inherently true."

He looked pained again. "But . . . what's the expression? Guns don't actually kill people. People kill people. Are we going to outlaw people?"

"People, using guns, kill people," I clarified. "If fewer people had guns at the ready, fewer people would die from guns. If there were no guns, no one would die from guns." I threw out a few more stats, just for fun.

"You didn't answer my question, though. Should we outlaw people?"

"That is a ridiculous question," I said. "No, we aren't going to outlaw people. We should just outlaw guns. Problem solved."

"What is ridiculous?"

"Your question."

"No, I mean, define *ridiculous*."

"Arousing or deserving ridicule; extremely silly or unreasonable; absurd; preposterous. See also: Everything you're saying."

I looked at the judge, who appeared to be holding back a chuckle.

"But if you try to take guns away from people who have guns, what's to stop them from trying to shoot you in the process?"

"I don't see how that . . ."

"Argghghhhhhhhh!" Taggart Strong was letting out some sort of primal groan. "I'm sorry, I just can't do this! I told them I'd try, but I can't!" he said, dropping his legal pad onto the floor. He started to pace back and forth in his corner of the room.

"Who's them?" I asked.

He didn't answer.

"Terrible arguments deserve terrible questions," he said, still walking back and forth, covering a three-foot-long swath of lino-leum floor. "So here you go: Do guns kill bears? Do guns kill rabid, howling wolves? Do guns kill mustachioed enemies of state? Do police need guns to keep order? What if police didn't have guns? Wouldn't that be better? Would dinosaurs have become extinct if they had guns to protect them?"

"Are you trying to Gish gallop[16] me?" I asked.

He ignored me, on some sort of roll only he comprehended. I stood and listened as he tied ridiculous—by definition—knots around himself. Cross-ex is only three minutes, so pretty soon, time was up. The judge was sitting there slack-jawed. "Alrighty, then. Negative, you're up . . ."

I sat down, and Taggart Strong moved to the middle of the room and started talking. "I tried," he said, "I really did. But this resolution is completely effed. How could anyone, in good faith, argue against this? Did you hear about the shooting that hap-

---

16 A *Gish gallop*, named after the creationist Duane Gish, is when an opponent throws a bunch of bizarre, random arguments at you in hopes of confusing you and making refutation impossible. It is rare to win on a Gish gallop. And as Gish gallops go, this one was especially wack-a-doo.

pened three days ago? Thirty people were killed. Two of them were *babies*. What this country needs is massive, widespread gun reform, both civilian and otherwise."

Was this some sort of prank? He was arguing the affirmative. I sneaked a peek at the judge, who was writing rapidly on the ballot in front of him. I could not *wait* to read it.

Taggart Strong stopped talking, which meant it was time for my cross-ex. I'd just gotten up from my desk and was standing next to him, facing the judge, about to speak, when a fire alarm went off. I thought I heard a scream in the distance, and then a thud. People banging on lockers. People running down the hall. Someone yelled what sounded like "Shooter! Help!" and someone else screamed. The three of us looked at one another, a moment of, *Holy shit, is this actually happening to us? At a debate tournament, where we were arguing about this very thing? How utterly on the nose.*

But of course that's where it would happen, my brain said. *Why wouldn't it? It happens everywhere.*

I'm embarrassed to admit this, but I became all the clichés. I couldn't move. I couldn't speak. My feet were frozen to the ground, heavier than the lead that made bullets. The judge, I'll never forget his face. He looked scared, but there was something else, too—determination. He slid his feet into his sneakers, tied them in a flash, and jumped up from his desk. He grabbed his tote bag and jogged to the door of the classroom, which he opened wide enough for us to see people flowing by. "Stay here," he told us. "Hide." And then he flicked off the lights in the room, ran into that hallway, and joined the fray. He was gone.

They say what you do in a crisis defines you. Your character in an emergency is who you are, free from the filters of congenial society.

Taggart Strong looked at me. I looked back at him. He waved at me, ushering me over, trying to get me to move. We had to find a safe place; we had to hide. I opened my mouth, but no words emerged. I tried to lift my feet. Nothing.

I am always so prepared. Always ready to do what needs to be done. Independent. Strong. Smart. But in this moment, I was stuck to the linoleum floor of this high school like an old piece of gum. There was no moving my own legs. I tried. The synapses just weren't working.

Great.

I opened my mouth to say "Help!" but I didn't have to. I felt his arms around me, solid and comforting. He grabbed me and pulled me into a supply closet I hadn't even noticed was there.

TAG

In the dark, everything is different. Especially when you're panicking. It's not so much that your life flashes before you—there's no time for that. You're not thinking or reflecting so much as doing whatever your body tells you to do from some deep place inside.

That's the only explanation I can give for why, after the lights went out, something took over that I didn't know I had. Millicent M. Chalmers needed help, and I was the only person there. So I pulled her into that little supply closet at the front of the classroom, closed the door as quickly and quietly as I could, and locked it, feeling briefly thankful that whoever had designed this closet had put the keyhole on the outside and the lock you could turn on the inside. At least we could control *it*.

I took a deep breath and tried as hard as I could not to think about all the other things we *couldn't* control, but that was kind of like telling yourself not to think about elephants. All of a sudden, elephants are everywhere.[17]

---

17 Francine has this book called *Don't Think of an Elephant: Know Your Values and Frame the Debate*. Kind of wish I'd actually read it.

MILLIE

He grabbed me and pulled me into a closet. This debate misfit. He tried to save me.

I didn't know what to think.

I didn't know what to do.

Actually, I did: We had all those drills at school. They taught us ALICE.[18] It appeared we were on Lockdown, after having gotten the Alert. The rules told us we should stay here, in this safe space, until we got the all clear. Most active shooter events were over in less than fifteen minutes. We just needed to wait.

Someone would eventually find us.

I wasn't a praying kind of person, but I prayed that the someone who found us wouldn't have a gun.

I looked around the supply closet, trying to figure out what I would use if we needed to Counter. It was hard to see anything with the lights off. But a stack of books or dry-erase markers weren't much good against an AR-15 anyway.

I was always so prepared, but no one could prepare for something like this.

---

18 The acronym that means Alert, Lockdown, Inform, Counter, and Evacuate.

TAG

I told myself to breathe. Just breathe. It was the only thing I had to do. Like, literally, to survive, I had to keep breathing. Hiding and breathing. But not too loudly. Quiet breaths.

My chest ached from trying to breathe without breathing. It felt like holding my breath underwater.

Pretend it's a drill, I told myself. Maybe it *was* a drill. They never told us whether it was real or not when we practiced at school. They didn't want us to goof around, so they tried to make the drills scary and as real as could be without being actually real. But just imagining it possibly being real was scary enough.

If this was a drill, it was monstrously screwed up. Who would do that?

But all the time, people did things you never wanted to believe they would do. That's what all our debates were about, in a way. The right thing to do versus the wrong one. It was funny, I suddenly thought, that we spent so much time talking about this stuff when in actuality *doing* was what mattered.

In the dark, I heard Millicent M. Chalmers taking her own shallow breaths.

For a while, we just did that. Inhaling and exhaling as quietly as we could while our own thoughts screamed inside our heads.

I thanked the forces that be—God, or whoever is up there—that it wasn't allergy season.

MILLIE

I could hear my heart beating so loudly. Who else could hear it?

Everything was dark. Literally and metaphorically.

We both breathed. I could hear his shallow inhales, and my own.

Just being alive makes a noise. You can't help it.

Seconds passed. I counted them in my head until they became minutes.

In drills, they also taught Run-Hide-Fight. Run and escape if you could. But we were in a windowless room that we couldn't see out of to check for safety, so we were staying put. Hiding meant getting out of the shooter's view and silencing electronics—*check*—and locking or blocking doors. *Done.* And then just waiting, staying in place until law enforcement or authorities delivered the all clear. If we had to Fight, we'd move on to throwing items or improvising weapons. I hoped we wouldn't have to Fight. There was so little to Fight with.

We stayed quiet.

I thought about the people I cared about.

Mom. Kargle. Carlos. He'd been debating a few rooms away.

I hoped he was okay.

I looked at my watch. Ten minutes had passed. It felt like it had been forever already.

TAG

It was dark in here, too, darker than the room we'd just been in. No windows. Allegedly, that would keep us safer. We stood in silence, frozen like statues for a minute, maybe five minutes, maybe ten, letting our eyes adjust.

Eventually, I had to do *something*.

We needed more light. I felt along the wall for a light switch, but she was putting her hand on top of mine, peeling my fingers off the switch one by one and looking at me, shaking her head. Then she was showing me something—her pen—who cared about pens at a time like this? Except it had a tiny little light on the end of it when you clicked the top.

Click.

Millicent Chalmers, everyone.

The penlight wasn't much, but it was enough. We were surrounded by a bunch of janitorial equipment, a dry-erase board with snippets of ancient conjugation written in red dry-erase marker, a ratty beanbag chair, and a bunch of old yearbooks.

A dry-erase board! We each grabbed the nearest end and started rolling it toward the door as another layer of protection. It was on wheels, but it probably hadn't been moved in months, and it squeaked up a storm. "Shhh!!!!" hissed Millicent, and glared at me, as though it was my fault and not the fault of whoever didn't oil their dry-erase-board wheels regularly, or, you know, the shooter himself, for putting us in this position.

My heart was racing. "Let's just lift it instead," I whispered. Once we got it in place, she pressed her foot onto the locking brakes on one side, and then the other.

Click. Click.

Now that thing wasn't going anywhere, at least not without some pushing.

She pretended to zip her lips.

Yeah, yeah. I get it, Millicent.

Clearly, we'd both been through these sorts of drills. Who hadn't?

She was staring at me.

"What?" I mouthed.

She'd pulled out one of the dry-erase markers and was writing on the board, ever so carefully, hardly making a noise. I watched the words create a sentence in turquoise.

Do you have your phone?

Even in a crisis, she didn't abbreviate.

I patted my pockets, but I already knew the answer. I had set my phone to silent prior to the debate—after an incident freshman year that involved a Cardi B ringtone, I was always careful about that. It was resting inside my backpack, which was sitting on the floor next to the desk I'd been using. I shook my head. She handed me my own marker. Purple.

U?[19]

Same. She drew a swooping arrow to the room we'd just been in.

What else was there to say, or do? We just stared at each other.

---

19 I use shorthand for debate notes—debaters call it *flow*, 'cause, you know, you're writing words across the page and charting all the arguments as they *flow*—so why not here, too?

You know that emoji of the face with the teeth clenched, the pained expression? That was us.

Minutes ticked by.

Waiting. Waiting. Waiting.

But nothing happened.

I thought about my mom and dad. My little sister, Mason. She followed the hashtags of my debate tournaments on social media. She was in eighth grade and couldn't wait to get out of middle school and join the team herself. Mason believed in me, even when hardly anyone else seemed to.

You OK? Millicent wrote.

Thnkn bout lil sis.

Is she here?

Home, I wrote. Thank God. And then, to be polite, How U?

She smiled, kind of. 1,000 drills = never enough.

Tru, I wrote. Or way 2 many, mayb?

She closed her eyes. I did, too. For a few minutes, we sat, trying to listen. Was that a squeak, or a pop, or another thud? Did we still hear screaming? Was that a siren? Was someone coming for us, and would they be good or evil? How would we know until it was too late?

We didn't hear anything but each other's breath for what felt like a long, long time.

I started counting in my head until I got to one hundred, and then I started over. I did that again and again.

And then I heard movement.

She'd gotten up. She was writing on the dry-erase board again, as quietly as she possibly could. I watched as the words emerged, wondering what she was going to say about sheltering in place or best practices in an active shooter drill. Millicent Chalmers might be the ideal person to find yourself in this kind of situation with, not that anyone ever wanted to find themselves in this kind of situation. I figured she had a plan.

Question, she wrote.

I nodded, urging her to go ahead. She was in charge. I would do whatever she said. She sure was writing a lot. It took me a second to process, but when I did, I felt like she'd slapped me.

Why do you debate at all if you're just going to make an ass of yourself?

MILLIE

You could argue that I was making an ass of *myself* by writing that. Being mean to poor Taggart Strong, the guy who pulled me into a supply closet at the sound of gunfire. And maybe I was! Look, I didn't debate to make friends. Winners often have a lot of enemies; that's just how it works. Especially when they're women.

You could also argue that I should have been sitting still, my eyes closed, my heart pounding, in fear of what was to be. Would you really get up and write something snarky on a dry-erase board like that when you're afraid for your life? you might ask.

You really might. I did.

But you know what?

I figured, if I was going to die, here and now, I wanted to know: What made Taggart Strong brave enough to approach a debate like that, to say what he really felt, regardless of the rules? Were private school kids just so entitled now that they didn't even have to care about winning?

Also, I'd been keeping track. We'd been sitting there for twenty-four minutes. According to the drills, most active shooter situations are over in ten or fifteen minutes. After the first series of screams and shouts, after our judge left and Taggart Strong ungummed me from the floor and pulled me into the closet, I hadn't heard a peep beyond my supply-closet mate's quiet breathing and occasional nervous finger taps against his legs. I felt pretty sure that the threat had passed. Not sure enough to walk outside and check. But I thought if I wrote very quietly, we would be okay. No one even knew we were in the supply closet.

Maybe this is infinitely too reasonable for you, or not reasonable at all. I only know what I did. And how I felt after writing what I did, when Taggart Strong looked at me like I'd punched a puppy.

I tried to soften it.

Why the pumpkin tie? I added. I drew a little jack-o'-lantern with a goofy face. It's still 3 weeks until Halloween.

After a long moment, he stood up and picked up his own dry-erase marker.

Gift from lil sis. H'ween's her fave.

Oh, I wrote. But he was still writing.

A day u get to be whatev u want & no 1 can stop u.

Still writing.

Guess that's why I debate. I make an ass of myself—

I shook my head, even though it was true, he did.

It's tru, he wrote. But evry time = anthr chnce to say what I rly blieve

He looked at me for a long time then, pushing his hair away from his glasses. That was when I noticed his eyes. He had nice eyes.

For me, that's the whole point

All of a sudden, the words that were always at my disposal weren't.

If you want to win, you follow the rules.

But what if something else was more important?

What if.

I'm sorry. I like your tie.

He looked down at it and smiled a little half smile.

I wrote, But the point of debate is to win, not to argue what you believe.

Is it? he wrote back.

Yes.

Why?

It just is! I wrote.

No offns, but that's not a v good arg.

I gazed at Taggart Strong. His hair was flopped over one eye again. And that tie, that ridiculous tie. But there was something about him.

Parents don't get it, he wrote, shrugging. Team captn, my frmer BFF, thinks I'm losing just to b a jerk.

You're not?

No! he wrote. Just don't wanna say what i know = wrong. 2 many ppl doing that.

I shook my head, too. What a weirdo. A cute weirdo, but a weirdo nonetheless.

Why'd you pull me into the closet? I wrote. You don't even know me.

He smiled again, this time the whole way. He had dimples when he did that.

It was the right thing to do, he wrote, and shrugged like there had never been another option that occurred to him at all.

Thank you, I wrote. And suddenly, I had an idea, and it was audacious and bold and nothing like playing-by-the-rules Millicent M. Chalmers.

I thought: *What if Taggart Strong did a kritik?*

Hear me out. A kritik[20] was this way to debate that started in policy and made its way onto the national circuit in L-D, too. I'd learned about it at debate camp last summer. It allowed a debater

---

20 Or "K"

to step outside the established framework to "critique" something about the resolution or even the competition itself. There were different kinds of kritiks. You could say the resolution was problematic for what it implied or assumed, and thereby couldn't be effectively argued. You could point out flaws in systems the affirmative endorsed—like you could say the government was inherently corrupt and couldn't be trusted to fairly uphold a civilian gun ban, and therefore the resolution should be nullified.

Another kritik was of presentation or performance—for instance, if your opponent's case used "he" all the time, you could present a gendered-language kritik: Your opponent should lose for using language that is harmful or inequitable. You could offer a kritik of debate itself, like that, in policy, debaters talked too fast, which prevented people from understanding, which should be the very point of debate. You could even say that your opponent behaved in immoral ways outside the debate, and therefore shouldn't be voted for. If you came against a kritik, you could kritik the kritik itself, or double down and hold your own with your debate, or claim the harm they mentioned doesn't exist, and on and on.

It was a controversial tactic, frowned on in more traditional local circuits, including our own, but it was also a way to put forth an opinion that fell outside the established debate structure, which made the method kind of cool, ideologically.

Millicent M. Chalmers would never run a kritik. Not if I wanted to take home any of those scholarships I needed.

But someone like Taggart Strong could.

It did not escape my attention that if I was coaching him, I'd know how to beat him, too. Not that a kritik was ever going to win state. Still, if I taught it to him, I could sit back and watch what happened.

I can show you how to argue the way you want and get everyone off your back, I wrote. And maybe even win. If you want.

He quirked his eyebrows up at my message. "Me?" he mouthed, pointing to his chest. His cheeks got red, and he tried to flip that shock of hair out of his eye, but it landed right back in the same spot, covering the lens of his glasses. I smiled. I couldn't help it.

Was he going to write back?

He turned to the board again, and I let out a tiny, quiet sigh.

We better make it outta here, then.

TAG

Were we flirting? Could a person *flirt* at a time like this? Millicent was smiling, reading what I'd written on the board, when I heard the noise. A door opening and closing. She sucked in, as if she could take back her last breath. Because we both knew that beyond the door of this little supply closet was another door, and no matter how far your mind takes you from the crisis you're in, your body stays ready, never fully relaxing until you're truly safe.

Are you *ever* truly safe?

I clapped my hand over my mouth, and she did the same over her own. We stayed like that for a minute or two, what felt like an eternity, listening. We heard footsteps. We looked at each other.

Someone jiggled the handle and then started pounding on the door.

"You in there?" It was a man's voice. Without thinking, I grabbed Millicent Chalmers and moved her away from the door, pushing her toward the beanbag chair, and then, yanking a mop from the janitorial bucket and brandishing it like a weapon, I stood as tall as I could, ready to Fight whoever was trying to get in.

MILLIE

The voice was muffled, since (a) there was a door and a dry-erase board in between us and this person or persons, and (b) Taggart Strong had pushed me into a beat-up beanbag chair and put himself between me and any attacker who might be out there. Now he'd tried to save me twice.

But it wasn't necessary, because the voice belonged to the same person who, about forty-five minutes ago, had been sitting there judging our debate.

He was knocking and saying, "Come out, y'all, everything's okay!" and there was someone else, too, a woman, and then I heard Coach Kargle, big and loud and twangy, shouting, "Millie! Hey there, Millie! Everything is UNDER CONTROL! MILLIE? YOU OKAY?" (I certainly hoped it was under control, because any person wanting to do harm could hear him shouting from here to kingdom come.) I motioned to Taggart to go ahead and unlock the door, but he didn't.

"Francine, is that you?" he asked. "What happened out there?"

"It's me," said Francine. "I promise, you're totally fine. Open the door and we'll tell you everything."

"How do I know you're not being held hostage by a gunman who's forcing *you* to force *me* to open the door?" he asked.

"Would I do that?"

"You wouldn't," he said. "At least, I don't think you would. But I also didn't think this tournament would involve a lockdown."

"Come out and we'll explain everything."

"Millie," said Coach Kargle again. "Y'all are good. I promise."

Taggart looked at me. He reached for his purple marker and wrote on the dry-erase board one last time.

Ready?

I nodded yes.

He unlocked the door.

TAG

Are you sitting down for this? I wish I'd been sitting down for this. I wish I'd had a beanbag chair to fall into. There was no shooter—that's what they said. It was all a "misunderstanding." A false shooter scare.

These things happened, especially given the "political climate," explained our judge, the guy with the socks, who told us his name was Joe Keller and that he was a nonprofit lawyer from Birmingham—and, yes, a former debater himself—who judged tournaments on weekends and had his own little kids at home and hoped they never had to go through something like this. He and our coaches told us we'd been really, really brave. But it could have been so much worse, they said. Everyone was fine.

Of course, by the time you're in high school, you know: Not every trauma leaves physical marks.

We listened as they recounted what had happened.

Keller had tried to put the gunman off our trail when he left the room and turned out the lights. He was trying to find help, he explained.

Francine had been judging[21] another debate several doors down. She'd made the kids hunker down under their desks, and she'd turned out the classroom lights. Like us, she waited. Unlike us, they had no supply closet, nor any dry-erase board to

---

21 Coaches and assistant coaches often step in to judge at tournaments. The judging pool also consists of debate parents and sometimes paid randos from the area—judges with no debate experience are called *lay judges*—as well as former debaters, like Keller.

communicate on. They hid and tried to breathe as quietly as possible, counting the seconds.

Millicent Chalmers's coach, the bald, muscle-bound guy who introduced himself as "Coach Kargle, rhymes with gargle," hadn't been judging that round. He'd been on his way back from the snack machine, eating a Kind Bar, when a group of teenagers behind him started running and yelling, heading for the emergency exits. Someone pulled the fire alarm, which meant more kids and more screaming and running and banging on lockers. The alarm was going off at eardrum-damaging decibels, but Kargle was not the type to react hastily—nor did he run just because people said run—after all, *he* was the coach—so he finished the last bite of his Kind Bar, popped in some earplugs he kept in his pocket for when he had to sit next to the marching band at football games, and headed back into the fray to see what had happened. As kids swarmed past, he took note of a few things: (1) Everyone was supremely freaked out. (2) The rumor was there was an active shooter in the school (a rumor fed by the debate topic that had ostensibly been put forth to lead to an eradication of such moments). And (3) There was no trail of violence that Kargle could see, which reassured him mightily. He headed toward the main administration office, where he hoped adults might be gathered to deal with the situation. Outside, suddenly, there was a distinct *pop-pop-pop!* noise. He ducked, waited until it stopped, then peeked out the window to see a man doing loops around the parking lot on a backfiring Harley-Davidson. (Coach had had a feeling. He'd once had a motorcycle, too.)

First order of business was to go outside and ask the guy, who had no idea he'd terrified an entire school of debaters and their judges and coaches, to stop driving around "like a goddamn fool"

(Kargle's words, not mine). It took some convincing and arm waving for Kargle to get him to understand, but Kargle wasn't Millicent Chalmers's debate coach for nothing. He had a little bit of the gift himself.

Next, Kargle took it upon himself to make an announcement on the intercom, but the equipment wasn't familiar to him, and what came out was a spray of garble and static, which is why, in the supply closet, we hadn't heard anything—and why those who *did* hear only became more panicked. Then he started going classroom to classroom, finding other teachers and coaches and students and explaining what had happened. He found Joe Keller and Francine, and now they were here, repeating what they'd told a handful of other people already. There were more than 150 of us at this tournament. It took a lot longer to quell the fear than to get it started.

I noticed that Francine had mascara streaks running down her face.

"Were you crying?" I asked.

"Only a little," she said. "Okay, a lot. I was so worried about all of you! But it's fine, it's all fine now." Keller handed her a Kleenex, and she dabbed at her eyes.

"We were all worried," he said. Coach Kargle nodded. "We sure as heck were. But, see, it was a whole lotta nothing!"

Millicent Chalmers spoke. Her face was all business.

"So, are we going to keep debating?" she asked.

MILLIE

The tournament was canceled, they said. It was for the best. They made sad faces and told us we should go home and get some rest and put this strange, upsetting day behind us. Get back to normal.

"What is normal?"[22] I asked. "This was a Nationals qualifier—will there be a makeup tournament? If not, don't we have fewer chances to qualify? Is that fair?"

"That will have to be figured out," said Francine.

I had more questions. "How will this affect our overall tournament record? Will there be a score for the portion of the debate we were able to complete? Are there any notes for us?"

"Well, I do have your ballot," said Keller, peeling off the top for himself and handing the bottom copies to me and Tag. "Millicent, you were in the lead."

I wasn't surprised. I folded up the piece of paper and tucked it in my briefcase to look at later in the privacy of my own home.

I pulled out my phone and saw I had a text from my mom. **SCHOLARSHIP ALERT!**◀»◀»🔳🔳 she'd written. **SUPER EXCITING! I'LL TELL U ABOUT IT TONIGHT! xoxo DEBATE LIKE A BOSS!–MOM.** (She signed her name no matter how many times I told her she didn't need to.)

Clearly, she hadn't heard about the shooter scare.

---

22 According to the Merriam-Webster.com dictionary, "conforming to a type, standard, or regular pattern: characterized by that which is considered usual, typical, or routine." In reality, when it comes to humans, perhaps nothing.

I wrote a quick message back to her. **Kargle's bringing me home. The tournament got canceled. Don't worry. I'll explain when I see you. xo**

I glanced up and caught Taggart Strong looking at me. He smiled.

Without thinking, I smiled back.

And I felt something.

Kritik or no kritik, I wanted to see him again. Him and his ridiculous pumpkin tie.

I needed to get out of there. Now.

I whispered to Coach, "Let's go," and grabbed my briefcase and headed to the door. He politely told everyone goodbye, exchanging business cards with the two other adults, and followed.

I could feel Taggart's eyes on me as I left. I heard him say "Millicent," though he said it so softly, almost like we were still hiding in that supply closet, waiting to see what happened next. Hoping it would all be okay.

It was. And also, it wasn't.

Liking Tag Strong could ruin everything.

We'd made some aimless conversation on the way home, trying to take our minds off what had happened, but when he pulled into my driveway, Kargle got serious. He put his truck in park and looked at me. "How ya feelin', kid? Wanna talk about it?"

"I'm fine," I told him. "It's just . . ."

"I'm not sure *I* am," he said. "That was pretty freakin' scary."

"It was. You were really brave."

He shrugged. "Everyone's different when something like that

happens. You did the right thing, taking shelter. That's exactly what you're supposed to do."

"But I didn't," I told him, and he gave me a confused look. "I couldn't move at all. I panicked and froze."

"How'd you end up in the closet, then?"

"Taggart Strong. He pulled me in with him."

"The kid with the pumpkin tie?" asked Coach. "I knew there was something I liked about him."

Coach is a total sweetheart. He and my mom actually know each other from way back in high school. She still calls him "Kenny." A couple of years ago, I found a homecoming picture of the two of them from senior year: His arms are around her, and she's smiling with her eyes closed, all dreamy, and wearing a sequined dress and dark magenta lipstick.

That's the only time I've seen her with that expression.

I'm not sure why they broke up. My mom never wants to talk about it, and some things are way too personal to ask your debate coach. A few years after that picture was taken, when she was twenty-one and working as a bartender, she met this guy who was driving through the state down to Pensacola for spring break (which, I guess you could say, started early). They had a one-night stand; she never got his last name; he never even knew she was pregnant. Nine months later, there I was. Her parents were ultra-conservative and basically cut her off, which means we've always managed on our own. They died a few years ago and didn't even include my mom (or me) in their will. But Mom says you can't change the past, you can only do your best for the future. Not that she'd change the past when it comes to me—I'm the part of her life she never regrets, she says.

When I was little, I had a parade of rotating babysitters as she put herself through nursing school. My favorite was this older neighbor of ours who let me stay up and watch a show she liked called *Crossfire*, where politicians and journalists debated from different sides of the political spectrum—my very first introduction to debate! Yes, I've been a nerd for years, and I say that with pride.

Mom's one of the most experienced nurses on her team now, and she loves it, even if she does work a lot. As for her personal life, she's gone on a handful of dates that I know of, but it's never been serious. She always just laughs and says she's happier spending her free time with me.

But I think their history is part of why Kargle agreed—even though he had zero debate or public-speaking training—to be my sponsor and coach for forensics. That and he felt sorry for me. Sometimes I wished he'd date Mom again. Then, when I went to college, she'd have someone to keep her company. And even though she's right when she says that men can distract you from your purpose, I can't help wanting to fall in love just the same. I mean, who doesn't?

"Can I ask you a question?" I asked. "What do you know about kritik?"

"Kritik, huh?" he said, rubbing his chin. "I hear some circuits are just overflowin' with those kinds of arguments. They kinda leave me cold, though. Seems like a lot of maneuvering to avoid playing the game. But then, if anyone could do it right, you could. Are you thinking of trying one out?"

"Oh, I don't know," I said. "Just curious. We went over the technique this summer at camp, and I wondered how it might do on our circuit. Do you think a kritik could ever win?"

"I wouldn't say never," he said. "A good debater can convince a person of just about anything. But I can't imagine it being easy, not with our conservative pool of judges."

I nodded. "That's what I thought."

"On the other hand, sometimes I do wonder about some of these resolutions, and whether they're worth arguing on their face at all," he added. "Like this one about guns." He shook his head. "I'm just glad that what happened today wasn't a lot worse."

I nodded, picturing myself back in that closet, alone with Taggart Strong. I'd still made no move to get out of the truck. Coach looked at me curiously.

"You sure you're all right?"

"Yes," I said. "Sorry. Just lost in thought for a minute." I reached for the door handle and turned it. "Have a good game tomorrow. I'll see ya Monday. Thanks for the ride, and everything!"

"See ya Monday, Millie," he said. "Get some rest, okay?"

"I will," I said. But I didn't feel tired at all. From somewhere inside me, I felt this tingly sensation. Something new and exciting might be about to happen, if only I'd let it. That was the problem, right there. I was supposed to be staying focused.

But somehow, in an afternoon, everything had changed.

TAG

The ride home was as weird as you might imagine. My teammates and I sat scattered around the bus the school uses to take us to and from tournaments. There are only twelve of us—a decent-sized debate team, but small for a school bus—so we had plenty of room. Cooper Cunningham was sharing a seat with Callory Chapman (they're either hot and heavy or breaking up, depending on the season; we happened to be in a season of loooovvve), but the rest of us were solo, and after we all told the stories of what we'd thought was going on and what actually *had* happened, most of us popped our headphones in, retreating into our own private worlds as we traveled the hour and change it took to get back to our own high school.

When we pulled into the parking lot of the school, Rajesh stood up and addressed us.

"Everyone. As your captain, I have something I want to say. What happened at Montgomery Hills—well, that was a fluke. It wasn't even a real shooting." He made a face as if to mock the fake shooting, like it hadn't had the balls to be a real one, though I am certain we all vastly preferred it to the alternative. "So take a moment and process everything, but then we need to get over it and get back to doing what we do best," he continued. "Debate. We do not give up. We fight to win. We've all got to work as a team and stick together. That's what teams are about." (I could swear, he was shooting eye daggers at me as he said this.) "United we conquer! Divided we fall!" He raised his arms in the air in a victory salute, and there was sparse clapping around the bus. It sounded good on the surface, but we didn't even debate in teams, and no one had said a word about giving up. Rajesh had watched too many World War II movies, in my opinion. In seventh grade, he'd had a serious obsession with *Saving Private Ryan*.

Francine got up next, standing in the aisle at the front of the bus. "I know we're not all huggers, and there is no pressure to be one, but after what happened today, well, I could use a hug or two. If you do not want to partake for any reason, that is totally one hundred percent A-OK. Just scratch your nose when you reach me, and I will not hug you. I'm gonna check in with each of you tomorrow to see how you're processing. We'll get through this."

I've never thought of myself as much of a hugger, but desperate times can change a person. No one seemed to want to leave. Rose Powell was the last person to get off the bus, and by that point we were all standing there waiting to hug her, too. The whole team formed a circle in the parking lot, our arms connecting us, and Francine said, "You are amazing people, each and every one of you; I'm so glad you're all here." I have to admit, I had to wipe back a tear or two. I caught Rajesh trying not to look at anyone. He always cried at the sad scenes in *Saving Private Ryan*, too, though he'd claim he had something in his eye.

And then it was time to go.

My car, Hector, was waiting for me a few yards away. That morning I'd been listening to "Eye of the Tiger," a song from the '80s by this band Survivor—how meaningful everything felt now—and when I started Hector up it came blasting through my speakers. Hector is a vintage station wagon, the kind people call a *woody*. I'd saved up the money I made working as a dishwasher at a restaurant last summer to outfit it with a decent sound system after my dad finally let me have it. It had been his car way back when, and my grandpa's before that, but it was still in really great condition. I loved driving it.

A couple of my teammates turned around at the noise. I opened the window to wave at them, and Cooper Cunningham pantomimed jogging around his own car, Rocky-style. Ricky Yee gave me a big wave. Nothing from Rajesh, who was already inside his brand-new "Barcelona-red" Toyota Corolla, which had been a gift from his parents when he turned sixteen. Rose Powell was in the passenger seat. She lifted her hand to her forehead, saluting me.

My thoughts turned to Millie as I cruised slowly out of the parking lot with the windows down, letting the music play and the wind blow my hair around. I felt glad to be alive. And I wondered if she'd really meant it when she said she'd help me with debate—and if she'd still mean it now.

I hoped she would.

When I pulled into my driveway, Mason came running out to meet me. She'd heard about what happened at the debate from Twitter, and we'd been texting on my way home. You know how some siblings don't get along or fight all the time or whatever? Sure, we have our moments when we're annoying the shit out of each other. But most of the time, we're really close. We love the same old Pixar movies, the Beastie Boys, watching cooking videos on YouTube and trying to replicate their efforts (we just did a fifteen-layer rainbow cake that was soooooo gooooood), and teasing our parents. She's thirteen, not even in high school yet, but in some things she's way smarter than I'll ever be. I'm her big brother, so she looks up to me for advice on the other stuff.

"Guess what's for dinner?" she asked, poking her head into the opened passenger-side window and not waiting for me to answer. "Mom's making your favorites. She's really happy you didn't die." Sometimes we're kind of sarcastic with each other.

I got out of the car and walked around to her. She put her arms around me and hugged me. "Tag. I . . . don't know what I would have done. We have these drills, but I can't even imagine what it's like when you think it's real . . ."

"On the smallest of plus sides, the timing was good," I told her. "I was losing the debate majorly before we had to hide in a closet!"

"Tell me everything," she said, and grabbed my hand and pulled me inside, where it smelled delicious. Mmm. Steak frites. And was the scent of my favorite chocolate cake in the air, too?

My mom yelled from the kitchen, "Tag, is that you? I'm trying your sous vide[23] method!" and my dad emerged from his office, giving me a huge hug, which is a rare occasion that underscored just how bad everything might have been had it gone another way. I hadn't had so many hugs since my eighth birthday. Then Mom was coming out of the kitchen, wearing an apron with flour streaks all over it—definitely a sign of cake—holding me tight and getting flour all over me, which I didn't mind at all. My mom's been so busy with her job as a Realtor that she hadn't cooked much of anything for us lately, and, as the in-house lawyer at one of Alabama's biggest banks, my dad was usually at the office late, or working in his home

---

23 A way you can prepare food (especially meat and fish) by vacuum-sealing it in a bag, cooking it to exactly the temperature you want in water, and then, in the case of steak, putting it in a pan and searing it to get that awesome crispy salty-peppery edge.

office later, except on weekends, when he spent a lot of time golf-ing at the club. Today was obviously an exception.

"Sit down. Tell us everything," said Mom, so I perched on one of the swiveling stools that pulls up to our big kitchen island and watched her cook. Dad handed her a glass of Chardonnay and poured himself a beer in a chilled mug while Mason grabbed two glasses of the sun tea we always had in the refrigerator and handed me one before taking a seat on the other stool. I took a sip and ran through the day's highs and lows, minus Millicent Chalmers's offer.

"So you were trapped in a closet with a girl the whole time?" asked my dad, smiling. "After trying to save her? Hope she's cute."

"Dad, that's sexist and offensive," said Mason. "And rude."

"Is it?" he asked. "Good thing I have you around to let me know."

Mason rolled her eyes.

"She's really smart," I said. "And definitely not *not* cute."

Dad laughed. "Good on you. How was the debating part this time? Any improvements?"

I made a face. "I didn't get very far before the alarms started going off."

"It shouldn't matter what she looks like," said Mason, who was not going to let Dad change the subject yet, and for that, I silently thanked her. "Millicent Chalmers is a debate legend! She's won the Alabama state championship the past three years in a row. If she wins again, she'll be the first debater in Alabama history to win the entire four years she's competed!"

"Whatever she looks and debates like, I hope you were polite!" said my mom. "And gentlemanly. You all must have been so terri-fied! I cannot believe this happened. When I was a teenager the thing I was most afraid of was failing my driver's test. Or not getting tickets to the Poison concert."

"Mom," said Mason. "Your teenage hair band tastes will never not be an embarrassment."

"Tell us again about your crush on Sebastian Bach, Mom," I said, and Dad groaned.

"I'm serious!" she said. "When did the world get so scary? It's not right."

"Neither is a crush on Sebastian Bach," said Mason, looking at me for laughs. I obliged. It felt good to be silly. My mom shook her head, but smiled, too. "Look, he was really good looking back then! All that flowing blond hair!" She sighed. "I just wanted to run my fingers through it."

We all stared at her. My dad touched his own hair, which was neither flowing nor blond.

"Google it!" she said.

"No thanks," said Mason. "But, Tag, now that we know you're safe, inquiring minds want to know: Are you going to see Millicent Chalmers again?"

I reached over and spun her chair so that she swiveled away from me. "We're on the same debate circuit," I said casually. "It would be pretty weird not to, don't you think?"

Mason swiveled back and sized me up. "Mm-hmm," she said. "Pretty weird." She mouthed "You like her!" at me.

I gulped my sun tea. "So what?" I mouthed back.

"Dinner's almost ready—can you two set the table?" asked my mom.

"I already did," said my dad proudly.

"Aren't you sweet," she said. "I'm so glad I married you and not Sebastian Bach."

MILLIE

After Coach dropped me off, I lugged my stuff to the door, where Beau met me, acting like I'd been gone for years. That's one of the best things about dogs—they're always beyond thrilled when you get home, like you just totally made their year, even though you come home every single day. Beau was a rescue and the snuggliest pit bull you'd ever meet. We adopted him after Mom started working so many night shifts. He'd probably try to cuddle with a burglar, assuming the burglar didn't get scared off beforehand, but that was the point, said Mom: "You don't want a mean dog. You just want a dog that looks like he means business."

I gave Beau a bunch of pets, and then I had some things to attend to. First: sweatpants. I went to my room and tugged on my comfiest pair. Next: pizza. I pulled a few slices out of the freezer and heated them up. Then I got comfortable on the couch with Beau curled up next to me. I found a funny movie I'd been wanting to watch and pressed play.

But I couldn't focus. I could barely even enjoy my pizza.

A text dinged on my phone. It was Carlos.

Carlos and I had met at debate camp three summers ago, and we hit it off immediately. He had sent himself to camp, just like I had. There wasn't a team at his school, about three hours south, in Mobile, Alabama, until he took it upon himself to create one, which he captained. There were now six of them on it. Freshman year, I'd tried to get a few classmates to join my team, but they all thought debate would hurt their social lives, and maybe they were right. But now my social life *was* debate, so who really knows?

That was surreal, Carlos wrote. **I don't kno what 2 do w myself. I'm amped & freaked & wired & tired. Maybe I should go for a nature walk. Too bad I hate nature walks.**

I FaceTimed him. "You're not on a nature walk?"

"Hell no," he said. "I'm eating a bag of Flamin' Hot Cheetos and watching terrible TV and telling myself I deserve it."

"You do deserve it," I said.

"I didn't think we'd make it," he confessed. "I texted my mom and told her if I never see her again, I love her."

"Aw, Carlos. What did she say?"

"Luckily she didn't see the message until after I called her and explained everything," he said. "She might have had a heart attack, and I'd be responsible. I wonder how many ancillary deaths have been caused by false shooter scares . . ."

"My mom isn't home yet. I haven't had a chance to tell her."

"Were you scared at all?" Carlos asked. "Tell me you were terrified so I feel better about myself. I almost peed my pants." He crunched one of his Cheetos.

"I thought, for a minute or two—okay, at least fifteen minutes— that we were going to die," I admitted.

He crunched again, emphatically.

"At one point I was so freaked out I offered to help Taggart Strong learn how to run a kritik."

"Who's Taggart Strong?"

"He's on the team from The Park School. Shaggy hair, pumpkin tie? I was debating him when everything happened. Spoiler alert: He can only argue the side he believes in."

"I debated him at Gatlinburg at the end of last year!" said Carlos. "The resolution was 'The United States ought to guarantee universal childcare,' and he was negative, and he started talking about how lack of childcare disproportionately affects those who need it most, and I was like, exactly!"

"Aw," I said.

"Aw-cute or aw-his-poor-addled-mind?" asked Carlos.

"Maybe a little of both?"

"He *is* cute," said Carlos. "Does he have kind of a Timothée Chalamet thing going on, or is it just me?"

"Who's that again?"

"Millie, you are hopeless when it comes to celebrity comparisons."

"But I can quote off-the-cuff from *The Individual and the Political Order*,"[24] I said.

He groaned.

"Anyway, listen to this: When the alarm went off, he pulled me into a supply closet with him. I literally couldn't move. He *moved me*."

"To protect you? Millie. He's a cute *hero*! Tagathée Chala-hot!"

"Except I didn't actually need protecting," I said.

"But he didn't know that. And neither did you. Is that why you offered to help him?"

"I don't know," I confessed. "It just came out. We were writing messages to each other on this dry-erase board, and I asked why he debated at all if he was just going to make an ass of himself . . ."

"Millie."

"He looked so wounded and wrote this stuff about wanting to

---

24 Subtitled *An Introduction to Social and Political Philosophy*, it's a debate classic by Norman Bowie.

argue what he really believed. It made me feel . . . weird. I told him debate is about arguing both sides, not what you believe."

"The way we do it, in school, as a competition, that's true," said Carlos, who had just turned on his debate captain voice.

I sighed.

"But in the long run," he continued, "it's more about preparing us to argue what we do believe. Teaching us to interrogate both sides, to formulate good arguments that will make a difference, and how to know what a good argument even is. What we *should* believe versus what's not worthy of our belief. So he's kinda right, too."

"But you have to see both sides in order to argue well!" I said.

"Sometimes, though, isn't there a side you *shouldn't* see the merits of?" he asked. "Like when it comes to racism or sexism or homophobia? Or, maybe, with regard to guns? I'm just saying, some things just aren't debatable. Or shouldn't be. Even if we keep debating them."

"What should I do?"

"Teach him to kritik. Why not?"

"He's a competitor! And a dude!" I said. "Two things that mean I *shouldn't* help him even if I wanted to."

"So you do want to," said Carlos. He grinned. "You think he's cute! Tagathée Chala-sexyyy."

"Shhhhhh," I said. "You're not helping."

"Look, Millie, seriously: Something made you tell him that. Maybe you owe it to yourself to find out what. You've been super dedicated to debate for a long time! Don't you deserve a little fun, too?"

"Maybe I do," I said. "And maybe I don't. I could argue both sides."

Another great thing about having a dog is you have the best built-in alarm system of all time, even if it sometimes gives you a panic attack. I was falling asleep on the couch when Beau jumped up and started barking, which jolted me awake, my heart pumping faster. But he was wagging his tail, because it was Mom. I heard her key turning in the lock, and I got up, rubbing my eyes, and met her in the front hallway.

"You're awake!" she said. "I was thinking you'd be fast asleep. What a crazy day we had. A tractor trailer hit a bus on the highway, and twenty-five patients were routed to us with injuries. It was touch-and-go for a while, so I didn't have time to write back. Why was the tournament canceled?"

I told her, and she wrapped me in her arms in a tight hug. Mom dealt with real tragedies in the ER. This had not been that. But it could have been. And it felt really good to have her hold me.

"Want some tea?" she asked.

"Sure."

We went into the kitchen, Beau following us happily. Mom put the kettle on, and pretty soon it was whistling. "I'm so sorry you went through that," she said. "We're all just really lucky it was a false alarm."

"Yeah," I said, and took my warm mug in my hands and held it, letting the soothing heat move through my body. "I heard people screaming, and I thought . . . this is it. It's happening to me now, too."

She came over and put her hand on my shoulder. "I don't know what I'd do."

"This boy," I said. "I was debating him. I couldn't move. He grabbed me and pulled me into a supply closet with him to protect me."

She rubbed my shoulder. "You panicked. That happens. The human response to catastrophe is wild; you never know what you'll do until you actually go through it. Anyway, I'm glad there are some good debaters out there doing the right thing. This boy sounds nice. Does he have a name?"

"Taggart Strong," I told her, and something possessed me to go further. "He's a terrible debater, though. I . . . I offered to teach him this debate method that might help him."

She gave me a weird look then. "Really?"

"Well, he helped me. I figured . . ."

"*You owe him?*" she asked, and I nodded.

I could see the storm clouds coming. I should have known not to say anything.

"Millie, you know I hate that sort of undermining women do to themselves. You don't owe him anything!" she began. "He was just doing the human thing. Basic kindness. How is you coaching him commensurate to that? Your debate career is really important. You could win state and set an Alabama record! Scholarship money is on the line, real money. It's senior year. You have to channel your energies into helping yourself—not some random guy you're not even going to know a year from now."

I nodded again. Sometimes it was easier that way.

"Send him a thank-you note. Buy him a coffee. But don't teach him to do what you do. You know what happens then: Sexism being what it is, if the boy can do what the girl can do, the boy will win."

I took a sip of my tea. "Yeah," I said, knowing that I was never in a million years going to send Taggart Strong a thank-you note.

"Good," she said. "Then let me tell you about this scholarship." She dug in her purse and pulled out a printout, which she handed to me. It said INTRODUCING THE MARTHA LINGER SCHOLARSHIP at the top.

"I read about it online," she explained. "A high school debater named Martha Linger won three out of the four Alabama state championships from 1976 to 1979. She came in second her sophomore year." My mom made a sad face. "She passed away last year, and her family just introduced a scholarship in her honor. It goes to a girl debater in the state of Alabama who can take home all four. You're a shoo-in. In fact, Kenny says you're the only one on the circuit who can win it this year!"

"Wow," I said, reading. "A full ride to the state school of your choice, plus ten thousand dollars a year to use as you see fit."

"It's not Yale," said my mom. "But we wouldn't have to worry about loans, or debt, or anything like that."

"That would be great. Better than great."

"So you'll go for it?"

"Definitely."

"I'll pin it to the Alabama board," she said, and walked to the den to do the honors.

I thought about me going to college, and how she'd be alone. She worked so hard, and it was all about me. "Mom, can I ask you a question?"

"Sure," she said, sitting down next to me.

"You and Coach used to date back in high school, right? What happened? Do you ever think about dating him again? Like maybe once I'm at college?"

She looked at me warily. "What brought this up?"

"I don't know, I just wondered."

"Sweetie, he's your coach, so we have a perfectly amiable relationship, but I've got everything I need right here." She swept her arms around the room. "You and Beau and pizza and Netflix . . ."

I raised my eyebrows at her.

"We did date, for a while," she said.

"What happened?"

"We went in different directions," she said, shrugging. "You'll see, those high school relationships eventually become ancient history. It's the stuff you do like debate that stays with you. The important stuff."

"Right," I said. But I had a feeling she wasn't telling me everything.

"That's settled, then." She patted me on the shoulder. "Now, get some rest, sweetie. You deserve a good night's sleep, and so do I."

TAG

After dinner, my parents ushered me into my dad's office for a "chat." (You know when parents call something a chat it's going to be the most unchatlike thing you can imagine, more like them talking and you listening.) They gave me yet another hug and told me they loved me and were there for me, whatever I needed. After some conversation about trauma and what it could do to the human body and how they wanted me to get a lot of sleep and hydrate and eat well over the next few days, they cut to the chase.

"Tag," said my dad. "I know the tournament wasn't completed, but we wanted to follow up on the conversation we all had with Principal Merwin. We appreciate that The Park School is open to student growth in many directions. Hey, that's why we send you there, even if it has changed a lot since my time, and some of their methods are a little woo-woo—"

My mom broke in. "Your dad and I feel that if you don't start doing better on the team, you should seriously consider a different elective. For college. For your future. For . . . well, is debate really worth it, for all this? Look at what happened today! I'm not sure you wouldn't be safer on a football field!"

"Today was a total fluke," I said, echoing Rajesh. "And what about CTE?[25] You can't be serious . . ."

---

25 Chronic traumatic encephalopathy, a traumatic brain injury often experienced by football players and boxers.

"How were you doing in the debate, really, before you ended up sheltering in place?" my dad asked.

I hung my head. "Same as usual, pretty much."

"You weren't arguing the right side, were you?" he asked. "Tag. We know you. You've always had a stubborn streak."

"Even as a little boy, you insisted on calling chocolate ice cream vanilla because you thought it tasted more like how you imagined vanilla to taste," my mom said, and smiled.

"Vanilla is a better name, and chocolate is a better taste," I said. "In my defense. But I'd argue that I *was* arguing the right side. Which may not have been the side I was assigned to argue . . ."

Dad sighed. Mom looked worried.

All of a sudden, I felt angry. All I wanted to do was say what I really felt, and everyone kept giving me shit for it. Why was this so hard? "The girl I helped out at the tournament, one of the top debaters on the circuit, she offered to work with me," I told them. "So why don't we see what happens before you kick me off the team just because you're embarrassed I don't win?"

Now my dad looked worried, too. "It's not that, son. It's just . . . we want the best for you. Extracurricular success matters. College matters."

"You could seriously undermine your future," said my mom.

"I'm fully aware of your thoughts on the matter," I said. "But you purposely sent me to a school that's all about doing things my own way. If you give someone a philosophical backbone, you can't suddenly just swoop in and take it away."

My mom looked at my dad. "He's right; we did pick that school for exactly that. You didn't want him to come out a carbon copy of your worst fraternity brother, if I remember correctly? And I, for one, agree."

My dad rolled his eyes. "Farrelly Fortner. Don't remind me. That guy never had a single original thought—"

"How come the rules change when *you* decide they should?" I asked.

My dad didn't answer, but he looked at me for a long time then. "If staying on the team is what you really want . . ."

"It is."

"Fine," he said. "But, Tag. Figure out how to say what you want and *win*, okay? Help me out. I have clients. We have friends at the country club. They have sons and daughters excelling on their own teams, and they hear about you, and it may be shallow, I'll admit that, but I'd rather get to brag on you than have to explain whatever it is you're doing and *not* winning."

"Isn't winning a capitalist construct, anyway?" I asked. "And, please, do not even get me started on country clubs."

My mom tried to hide what looked like it might be a grin.

"That may well be," said my dad. "But I work in a bank and that's what feeds you and keeps a roof over our heads, so be careful about how much you want to fight that capitalist construct."

"Roofs, as I recall, are *my* business," said Mom, deftly changing the subject. "Where does this Millicent Chalmers, top debater on the circuit, live? We look forward to meeting her!"

"I'm not sure," I said, fake-yawning and standing up. "But I'll let you know when I do. You know, I'm gonna turn in now. Today was exhausting."

"We can only imagine," said my mom.

They both hugged me again, and my mom kissed the top of my head. "We love you so much! We really do," she said.

"We just want to see you reach your full potential, to have every opportunity—" added my dad.

"Love you, too," I said. "'Night."

I went to my room, but I wasn't actually tired. I was ready to re-search. Or, in this case, the right word was *search*.

I was looking for Millicent Chalmers. Turned out, she shared her name with a famous Australian environmentalist and lawyer. That lady hogged the first page of the Google results, but once I clicked through, I found the Millicent I was looking for. There she was, winning this debate and that one, ranked top seed for a bunch of tournaments. There was a piece done in a local paper about her when she was a freshman, and, after a single tourna-ment, jumped from novice to varsity level. They called her "the girl to beat." There were pictures of her standing in front of rooms of people, gesturing and making her point. There were lists of her wins, the trophies she'd taken home, the final rounds she'd been in. I read everything. But I couldn't find what I was really looking for: her email address, a phone number, or some way to get in touch with her. She didn't have an Insta. Or a TikTok. Not that I could find, anyway.

Then I thought about Twitter. Smart people were often on Twitter. Even I was on Twitter, albeit with less than a hundred followers, and mostly to tweet the cooking videos I liked and the latest memes. But if I was there, maybe she was, too.

I typed "Millicent Chalmers" into the search bar of the site, looking for "People." Nothing. Then I tried "Millicent," and a long list of names popped up. There was a Millicent, not Chalmers but "Calmerzzz," with a tiny picture of the very Millicent Chalmers who had smiled at me from the piece in the local paper. Was this her? She followed a few people, all of whom seemed to be debate types, and had a handful of followers, but the account hadn't been tweeted from once. And why had she spelled her own name wrong? Her profile said, "I'm not here to make friends, I'm here to win." That seemed legit.

Millicent Calmerzzz's DMs were open. I wrote *Hey* and was trying to figure out what to say next when my cat, Orion, walked across my keyboard, writing a very important message:

aflagpie;l

adjOQW

CKA'

"Nooooo," I yelled, trying to grab him, but he jumped down, tail twitching, right after he managed to press send.

I glared at him. He looked at me without a care in the world. Cats.

I'd have to try again.

Hey Millie—Millicent?—is that you? My cat sent that first DM, he was on my computer, cats are kind of the worst as it turns out, but anyway, I just wanted to say thanks for today. Hope you got home OK.

I breathed. I kept going.

Oh yeah, this is Tag. You know, from the closet. Um, at the tournament. I just wanted to say I'm really psyched about you helping me with debate. I think it could be a great thing! Um, for both of us. I hope you still want to. You still want to, right?

Now I sounded totally pathetic. I added: *I get it if you don't. We could just be, you know, friends. Either way. Whatever you want.*

I pressed send and immediately felt like even more of a dope. *"We could just be friends"?*

Orion meowed at me to pet him, which I did begrudgingly. At least cats didn't judge you for what you wrote in a Twitter DM.

I thought about the conversation I'd had with Millie in the closet, about the point of debate. Whether it was to win or to say what you really believed, what really mattered. And then I went back to my Twitter account and started typing. *Hey. I spent almost an hour of my life today hiding in a supply closet, thinking I was about to be killed by a person with a gun,* is how I started it. *I want to tell you how that feels.*

MILLIE

I woke up in the middle of the night, my heart beating fast, remembering the swoop of panic, the darkness of the closet, the minutes ticking by. I sat up in bed and tried to shake it off. I turned on the light and saw my briefcase sitting in the corner, which reminded me of Joe Keller's ballot. I still hadn't looked. I was sure he'd given me a bunch of compliments and told Tag he needed to prepare better, that arguing the negative was, you know, kind of key to actually winning negative. And, yes, there were the usual notes for me: *Amazing poise, great setup, excellent backup.* Under Tag's name was this: *You get points for passion. But, buddy, there's got to be an easier way of doing this. Or not doing it? Have you thought about original oratory?*[26] *Extemp? Or maybe a kritik?*

It felt like a sign.

I texted Carlos, even though it was after midnight. **I'm gonna do it. PS, sorry if I'm waking you up.**

LOL, I knew you would, he wrote back. **No worries. I can't sleep.**

Me either. One question: What do I tell my mom? She's totally against the idea of me helping, and I quote, "some random guy you're not even going to know a year from now."

Why do you have to tell her at all?

Good question.

I started looking for ways to get in touch with Taggart Strong, which is how I found his Twitter account. I'm kinda anti-Twitter—it

---

26 In which participants deliver speeches on a topic of their choosing, incorporating evidence, logic, and emotional appeals.

seems like a place where people just yell at each other, or pat each other on the back for saying something they already agree with—though I do have an account, @DebatRGrl.[27]

I've never actually tweeted myself. But I didn't have to tweet; I could just hang back and read. And when I found Taggart Strong's tweets, I read them over and over.

Taggart Strong
@TaggartStrong
Um. Was it something I said?
🌐 Alabama   🕐 joined June 2018
301 Following   **98** Followers

Tweets

↓ Pinned Tweet
Taggart Strong · @TaggartStrong · 8/13/19
OMG @ParryGripp you are the boss of all things pancake!!! https://www.youtube.com/watch?v=hwuKlpPln_M!
💬 3   ♻ 2   ♡ 11

Taggart Strong · @TaggartStrong · 10 m
Hey. I spent almost an hour of my life today hiding in a supply closet, thinking I was about to be killed by a person with a gun. #montgomeryhills #shooterscare
💬 11   ♻ 7   ♡ 21
ⵏ

Taggart Strong · @TaggartStrong · 8 m
I was in a false shooter situation at a HS debate tournament. We 100% thought it was real. Alarms went off, people were screaming & running. We hid out till we could get the all clear
💬 2   ♻ 6   ♡ 22
ⵏ

---

27 I know, corny, but I created it in eighth grade, when I was trying to find out more about debate. A lot of debaters and tournaments use Twitter.

Taggart Strong · @TaggartStrong · 5 m

Imagine the shock and horror of finding yourself in this situation, even though it happens ALL OVER THE COUNTRY OVER & OVER AGAIN. To people way less lucky than I was

💬 3   🔁 5   ♡ 17

|

Taggart Strong · @TaggartStrong · 4 m

Imagine how your parents would feel. Your brothers, your sisters, the people you love. And imagine it in reverse—how you would feel if THEY were gone bc of something like this

💬 1   🔁 2   ♡ 8

|

Taggart Strong · @TaggartStrong · 3 m

For what? So some people can walk around with guns, acting like big shots? Bc they're too scared of who they'd be without them?

💬 1   🔁 1   ♡ 3

|

Taggart Strong · @TaggartStrong · 1 m

At least my parents and sister got to hug me tonight. I'm one of the lucky ones. And I'll still b thinking about this 4 a v long time

💬 0   🔁 1   ♡ 1

There he was, saying what he felt, putting it all out there. It was its own kind of fearless.

I decided I would do something a little bit fearless in return.

TAG

My phone rang, waking me up from a dream. We'd been in the closet together, but we were talking, not writing on a dry-erase board but really talking, and then she leaned in to whisper something in my ear, which may be why I had this wild idea that she'd figured out my number and was calling me.

"Yeah?" I answered, a little bit breathless.

"Tag, how are you doing?" asked a woman, but it wasn't Millie, it was Francine. "How do you feel today?"

"I'm good, I guess," I told her. "A little tired. I was actually sleeping—" I sat up in bed and tried to shake off the cobwebs that remained. What day was it? What time? And then I remembered why I was home in bed instead of at a debate tournament, deep in the second round of the day by 10:00 A.M.

"Let yourself rest. Give yourself time to process," Francine was saying. "We can talk more about everything on Monday. By the way, Tag, I liked your tweets about the experience. They were very brave. And you captured things so powerfully."

"I don't know about that," I said. "I just said what I felt."

"Saying what you feel *is* brave! Especially in this day and age."

"I guess."

"It sounds like the Speech and Debate League is going to provide a new resolution for you all to work on. Something that's not about guns. We should know more about that soon," Francine told me. "In the meantime, I just wanted to check in and see how you were doing. I was thinking—"

She kept talking, but I'd gotten up and was looking at my computer now.

There were some predictably trolly responses to my anti-gun tweets, people who told me I was a pussy or to go ahead and shoot myself. I did have a handful of likes, and some retweets, and a couple of people who applauded me for saying what people needed to hear.

I'd kind of hoped I'd go viral, I guess, and maybe that would help get Millie's attention. But I wasn't on Twitter to get famous. I'd said what I thought; that was good enough.

Then I saw the little blue dot indicating I had a DM. I clicked. It wasn't from Millicent Calmerzzz. It was from someone called @DebatrGrl. Their Twitter avatar was a yellow legal pad. Their Twitter bio said, *I'll see your point, and I'll defeat it.* Their DM said, *Hey. If you're up for this, I am, too.*

Millicent? I wrote in return. And maybe I spoke it, too.

"Tag?" Oh shit, I was still on the phone with Francine.

"Francine, I better go, my mom's calling me," I said. "See you tomorrow?"

"You got it. Hang in there, Tag," she said.

"Uh-huh," I managed. I put my phone down and waited for @DebatrGrl to write back.

Somewhere deep in my gut, the same way I knew what was right and what wasn't, I just knew it. From here on out, my life would be divided into two sections: Before I hid in the supply closet with Millicent Chalmers, and afterward.

MILLIE

That week, we learned that competitions would be put on hold for the rest of October as the Speech and Debate League hustled to put in place security protocols and come up with a new resolution everyone could agree on. I never would have thought that was a good thing, except now that I'd decided to help Tag, we needed the time.

I, in particular, needed the time. It was the Saturday of our first meeting. I'd told him to be at my library at 2:00 P.M. sharp. And I was late. I was never late.

Even worse, it was for purely superficial reasons. I'd spent the past forty-five minutes trying to figure out what to wear.

He'd only ever seen me in suits and dresses. I didn't want to seem like I was trying too hard—what was I trying for, anyway?—but I also didn't want to look like I'd just rolled out of bed. In the end, I settled for a pair of jeans and my gray DONT HATE, DEBATE! hoodie. I put on a little bit of mascara and a little bit of blush and brushed my hair and that was that. Mom was at work, so I jumped on my bike, thankful that it was a cool fall day and I wouldn't get too sweaty on the way to the library; even more thankful I didn't have to tell her where I was going and why.

I found him at the front door, patiently waiting. That hair was still swept in front of one eye. He had on a hoodie, too, but his said WHAT? across the front.

"Sorry I'm late," I told him.

"No worries," said Tag, smiling at me. He pushed the hair out of his eye and straightened his glasses. "Nice hoodie."

"Thanks," I said. "I like yours, too."

He turned and showed me the back, which said I HEARD YOU.

"Impressive," I said. "A full conversation on your torso."

"So, this is the library where Millicent Chalmers's famous cases are constructed!" he said, bouncing up and down on his toes. "I'm pretty excited, to be honest."

"I'm sure looking forward to this has been the highlight of your week," I told him.

"It has!" He opened the front door of the library and gestured for me to go in.

"Thanks," I said, feeling silly. "You're so polite."

"My dad always said that if there's a woman around, you let her go first," he told me.

"What if she wants you to go first, though?" I asked.

"Like if there's a moat of alligators and she wants to see if they'll attack, in which case she'll take another path and mourn your death but honor your sacrifice?"

"Exactly," I said, laughing.

We walked through the first set of doors, and I opened the next, ushering him in before me.

"Thanks," he said. "I never would have expected Millicent Chalmers to be afraid of alligators."

"Just the invisible ones," I said.

"Let's go at the same time," he said, and put out his elbow for me to loop my arm through as we walked through the interior doors together. Which, for some reason, I did.

"Hi, Millie!" said Mrs. Mendez, my favorite librarian, as we passed the front desk. "I was hoping to see you. We just got in some new philosophy inventory I think you'll want to check out."

"Your last recommendations were perfect," I told her, and glanced at my companion. "This is Taggart Strong. He's a debater, too. From Birmingham."

"Hi," he said. "Call me Tag. Only debate judges and angry parents call me Taggart."

Mrs. Mendez laughed. "Gotcha, Tag. Cool name. Welcome to our little Hopewell Crossing slice of book heaven. Nice hoodies, both of you. They're in dialogue with each other."

Tag grinned at me.

"Total coincidence," I said. "Is the conference room in the back free?"

She nodded. "Go for it—and have fun!"

Would it be fun? I wasn't sure.

I led him through rows of bookshelves and library carrels and filing systems, past the children's section and the comfy chairs to sit in and read and all the way to the quiet room in the back where I liked to work. It had a big table and lots of chairs and was reserved for speakers and workshops, but Mrs. Mendez let me use it when no one else was.

"This is a great library," Tag said. "It smells just the way a library is supposed to. Like books and thoughts and purpose."

I inhaled. "I love that smell."

When I opened the door to the conference room, Tag gasped. One wall had a huge dry-erase board attached to it. "Is this like immersion therapy?" he said, pulling out a chair and sitting.

"We owe that other dry-erase board a lot," I told him. "We couldn't have communicated without it."

"True," he said. "You know, I was really happy to get your DM.

I'm glad you're still down to help me. You don't have to. But it's really cool that you are." He looked me right in the eyes and smiled. His were hazel, with gold flecks. I felt this warmth surge through my body. Was I blushing?

He was still talking. "I had reached out to this person I thought was you on DM, actually—well, my cat did, and then I did, but I never heard back from them, which is good, because they're not you at all."

"Your cat *tweets*?" I shook my head, trying to focus.

"I mean, no, he kind of walked across the keyboard and let lose a garbled string of letters before he managed to press send. But then I actually wrote something to @Millicent Calmerzzz—'calmer' with 3 z's . . . It had your picture. Maybe it's a bot. You know how bots just steal things off the internet; it's probably nothing at all." He frowned, clearly wondering if he should have told me any of this information, which did not in actuality seem like "probably nothing at all."

"But it's my name, too. Or almost my name. And my face." I picked up my phone to check out the account. "Found it," I said. "They haven't tweeted anything yet. But that doesn't mean they won't. I'll tell Coach Kargle about it. Maybe we can get it blocked. For now I'll report it." I pressed a few buttons and then set down my phone. I breathed. "That's kind of all I can do at the moment. Should we get started?"

He nodded. "You're the boss! I don't even see myself as your competitor. I'm just a guy who's making an ass of himself at debates."

"I'm sorry I said that," I said. "It was mean."

"Technically, you wrote it," he said. "But it was true!"

"Well, I've been thinking about what you said about debate,"

I told him. "About winning versus saying what you believe. Like I mentioned in the closet, maybe there's a way to do both. But first, I think we need to go through some Debate 101. Then we'll move on to kritiks."

"Kri-what?"

"You have to know the rules before you can start messing with them," I said. "I hope you have something to take notes with?"

He pulled a pen and paper out of his backpack. "Ready, Coach!"

"Rule number one: Never call me Coach."

TAG

Millicent Chalmers looked different in her civilian clothes. It was disconcerting, like when you see your FedEx guy at the grocery store, or a teacher at the gym. It seemed wrong, even though she looked good in her casual clothes. She was pretty. She was pretty when she debated, too, but it was like she had on a uniform. This felt like the real her.

She erased the board and wrote a string of numbers across it: 6–3–7–3–4–6–3. Those were the components of a debate.[28] She added two little upside-down Vs above her number string, putting a 4 on top of each V.[29]

Then she jotted down the resolution about guns and looked at it for a minute. She shook her head with a frown. "I really hated that one," she said, erasing it. "Let's try this, instead."

RESOLVED: JUSTICE REQUIRES THE RECOGNITION OF ANIMAL RIGHTS.

"How would you approach that, as the affirmative?" she asked. "Come up and write down your best ideas. Just off the cuff, as you think them."

Usually, compiling a log of initial ideas took me hours rather

---

28 That's 6 minutes for the affirmative constructive, 3 minutes for the negative cross-ex, 7 minutes for the negative constructive and first rebuttal, 3 minutes for the affirmative cross-ex, 4 minutes for the first affirmative rebuttal, 6 minutes for the negative rebuttal, and 3 minutes for the affirmative conclusion. Whew!

29 That was prep time: 4 minutes for each of us, to be used throughout the debate, or, if you were Millicent Chalmers, to be skipped like a badass.

than minutes, in between looking at my phone and watching You-Tube cooking videos that piqued my interest (do *you* know how to poach a perfect egg?) and breaking to make snacks inspired by what I saw. But she was staring at me, so I got up and wrote as quickly as I could: Animls shld have rts bc they're alive. Humans value life above all else.

She circled the word *justice* and drew arrows pointing to it.

Right. Somehow I had to connect it to that. Not giving rts to animls = unjust! I added.

She shook her head and erased everything I'd written.

"That's overly simplistic. You need some real logic to play into your argument, to connect to your value. Think backward about what matters, and why what matters matters."

This is hard, I wrote.

She crossed out my complaint with a big X. "Do you want me to help you or not?"

OK OK. (1) Humns *r* animls. We were. And we all shared this world together. Even though humans were the ones who did bad things, usually, and the other animals had to deal with it. That seemed unfair. Maybe there was something to that.

She nodded, encouraging.

(2) Humns r animls who blieve life shld not be taken unjustly from other humns . . . aka animls! Hmm! I thought about how in building this case I'd want to define *animals*, *humans*, and *justice*. I needed to define what human rights are, and what they've been considered to be, and show how animals were due similar rights and that acknowledging them would be better for everyone. Who was that guy who talked about the social contract? Jean-Jacques Rousseau? This = social contract!, I wrote on the

board. Did that include animals, and if not, why not? I'd have to look it up.

(3) Humns r animls + can suffer + kno animls can suffer. Suffering = bad/unjust/immoral. And then I had a real brain wave. Humns hate ppl who hurt animls! I thought about how an early sign of being a serial killer is torturing cats. I thought about how testing makeup on rabbits hurts and sometimes kills those baby bunnies, and about how people throw paint on fur coats, or go vegan and stop eating meat and any animal products completely. No animl rts = suffering!/immoral/unjust.

I glanced at her. She was smiling.

(4) 2 Make humn suffer = unjust = 2 make animl suffer = unjust. I was writing fast and furious now, channeling my inner Millicent Chalmers, and even pulled out a full sentence of my own. Justice requires that we apply it to <u>all</u> animals. I underlined all, and then I stopped to think. If we were really good people, we must not only try not to hurt others, including animals, we must also help them! 2 b moral = 2 b just = 2 b happy = animl rts!

She drew a big check mark on the board, and then, as I watched, waiting for praise, she wiped the whole thing clean. "Not bad," she said. "For a first try. Now, what about the negative?"

Oh jeez. This was the sort of thing that hung me up. It just felt wrong to argue the other side. But then, genius struck (even if I was mostly kidding). I went up to the board and wrote.

Burgers r dlicious?

She shook her head, but she laughed. I felt like I'd won a prize.

"Are you hungry?" I asked her. "'Cause I brought sandwiches."

"Are you just buying time?" she asked, but I had grabbed my backpack and was already pulling out my haul.

"Turkey, brie, and apple with drizzled honey mustard, or goat cheese, sun-dried tomatoes, and arugula with balsamic glaze? Both on sourdough. I wasn't sure if you were vegetarian."

"You brought me a sandwich?"

"Made 'em, too." I shrugged. "I like to cook. Not that sandwiches count as cooking, exactly. It's more like assembling."

"They count! And I'm not vegetarian." She took a seat at the table across from me. "Even if I *have* argued that people should be."

I nodded. "We can each have half of each, then. More variety." I'd already split the sandwiches in halves before I left home, and now I pulled out one of each and put them onto a paper plate for her. She reached for the plate, but I pulled it back. "You have to have a pickle on the side. It's a rule." I reached into my bag again and took out a jar of pickles, putting a spear on her plate next to her sandwich halves, and another on my own.

"Wow," she said. "You carry a jar of pickles around? That's . . . something."

"I made them, too."

She took her first bite of turkey, followed by a nibble of pickle. "Okay, Tag, I take back my pickle snark. This is incredible."

"It's not bad. I really like how my honey mustard came out this time. The balsamic could use some more tang, though."

She stared at me like I was someone she'd never seen before. "So, you're this secret master chef. What else are you going to surprise me with?"

"I almost forgot the iced tea." I reached into my bag again and pulled out a thermos and two paper cups, pouring some into each and passing her one.

She sipped. "How did you get into cooking?"

"I always liked it. I would watch my mom cook, and I started to do it with her, and then I started making up my own recipes. I love how if you just follow a recipe, you get something cool, you know? And then, when you know enough about how things work, you can break the rules and throw in your own twist," I explained. "Plus, cooking frees me up to think about stuff I never would have imagined otherwise."

"Maybe you need to start cooking in your debate rounds, then," Millie said. "Figuratively or literally. I'm sure the judges would like these sandwiches."

She smiled, and I felt it in my stomach. A zing.

"What else do I need to know about you?" she asked. "By the way, I think your balsamic glaze—is that what you called it?—is excellent."

I tried not to beam like an asshole.

"So, I was wondering. Where did your need to always argue for the side you believe come from? Have you always done that?"

"Is this part of my training?"

She shrugged. "It might help if I know more about you . . . why you do what you do."

"It wasn't always a thing for me," I explained. "Especially at the beginning. But by the end of last year, it started to feel really hypocritical, standing up there and saying 'vote for my side' even though I didn't think my side should win. I didn't *want* that side to win. You know? So why was I arguing for it?"

"Because you're on a debate team?" She was giving me the same sort of look that Rajesh had.

"Well, it's not like there's a cooking club," I said. "I had to do something."

"You could have started your own, like I did with debate."

"You started your own team?"

"There wasn't one. So, yeah," she said.

"That's badass," I told her. "But I cook plenty at home. And I like debate. I want to be doing it. I don't even really mind losing. It's just that everyone else gets mad at me when I do."

"Do you really not care if you win or lose?"

"I have to admit," I said, taking another bite of pickle and crunching, "it would be great to do it my way *and* win."

"Well, you should be able to argue both sides, to fully interrogate the question, before you decide which side you're on. You know about the burdens in a debate round, right?"

"Um . . ."

"I'll remind you," she said, giving me a slight eye roll. "No question of values can ever be determined one hundred percent true or one hundred percent false. So neither debater is required to prove the *absolute validity* of their side. You're just trying to win by showing how your side is *more* valid. That's your burden in a debate. But also there's a burden of clash—you have to go against the opponent. You can't just agree with them or argue nonsense that isn't related. And you have to debate the resolution."

"But what if the resolution sucks?" I asked. I looked back at the dry-erase board and thought about the one she'd erased. "What if a question of values *is* one hundred percent true or one hundred percent false?"

"There's a way to get around that. It's called a kritik, spelled with a *k*. I learned about it at camp last year. You critique the resolution, or the other debater, or their case, or their language, or whatever it is that you can critique, and you try to start a new conversation entirely. The only thing is, it's not really done that much in L-D. I don't know many Alabama judges who would go for it. So you might still lose. But you'll at least be playing the game."

"So I get to argue what I believe, whether I get the affirmative or the negative?" I was intrigued. "And Rajesh and my parents and Merwin might let up?"

"Ideally, yes."

"I'm interested."

TAG'S SIMPLE REFRIGERATOR PICKLES

- Cut up some cucumbers (any kind works), either the round way or the spear way, depending on your preference and the size of mason jar you have on hand. Keep the peels on. No one needs peel-less pickles.

- Chop up a small onion, and a handful of fresh dill, if you have it. (Try to get some! Dill is kinda what makes pickles.) Put all that in your mason jar, leaving an inch of space at the top, for your liquid to completely cover the pickles. Keep the lid off because you're going to add that liquid next.

- If you've got a pint-sized mason jar,[30] put a half cup of vinegar (I like apple cider vinegar, but you can try other kinds), a half cup of water, and your spices (try pinches of peppercorns, mustard seeds, red pepper flakes, and even cumin or cayenne) plus a couple of garlic cloves and a teaspoon or so of salt and sugar or honey (to your taste![31]) in a small pot, and heat up the mix until it's simmering, aka letting little bubbles rise to the

---

30 If you use a mason jar larger than a pint, or make more than one jar's worth, you'll want to increase your vinegar/water/spices.

31 This is a really flexible recipe. You can play with the measurements, depending on if you like things more or less vinegary, sweet, salty, garlicky, peppery, etc. Experiment and see what tastes best to you.

surface, until the salt and sugar dissolve. Taste it (careful, it's hot!), see if you like it, add more spices or sugar to your liking. Cool your brine for a few minutes, then pour it into your mason jar, over your cukes.

- Pop a lid on your jar, and put in the fridge. Your pickles will be ready to eat in 24 hours.

- You can also do this with other veggies, like green beans and carrots and peppers and even cherry tomatoes!

MILLIE

Just before 6:00 P.M., Mrs. Mendez poked her head into the conference room. "We're closing shortly," she announced. "Millie, I've got the books I mentioned at the checkout counter. One of them is by an early feminist—I think you'll really enjoy it. Or maybe *enjoy* is the wrong word. You'll find it edifying."

"Thanks," I said, wiping the dry-erase board clean. "We'll be right out."

"What feminist?" asked Tag, who was picking up our trash and putting it in the garbage. He seemed genuinely interested.

"Her name is Mary Wollstonecraft," said Mrs. Mendez. "She was the mother of Mary Shelley, who wrote *Frankenstein*, though Wollstonecraft died very soon after childbirth. So many women did in those days." She shook her head. "She had a brilliant mind, groundbreaking for her time. For any time, really."

"Mrs. Mendez is a debate research queen," I explained to Tag. "That Hegel stuff was . . . chef's kiss." I put my fingers to my mouth and puckered.

They both watched me, amused.

"I've never heard *Hegel* and *chef's kiss* used in the same sentence," said Tag.

Mrs. Mendez laughed. "See you at checkout." She left, and we gathered our stuff. I glanced up to find Tag looking at me.

"Hey, do you want to go do something?" he asked. "Maybe get some food that's not a sandwich? All that theorizing made me hungry again. And I don't have to go home right away."

"I can't," I said automatically. But it was Saturday night. And I was having fun. A weird kind of unexpected fun, but fun. "Well, maybe. But just for a little bit. I have some plans." (My plans involved scouring the internet for more scholarship and financial aid options, but he didn't need to know that.) "I'll leave my bike here, and you can drop me off when we're done?"

"Sweet," he said. I checked out my books, and we went outside, where I found myself walking with him to his car. I'd kind of taken him for a Land Rover type, but instead he was unlocking the doors of a pristine retro station wagon with wood panels.

"This is Hector," he said.

"Hello, Hector," I said, inhaling as I got in. "You smell good, Hector."

"It's the car tree," Tag said, pointing to the air freshener that hung from his rearview mirror. "Black Ice. I've never smelled real black ice, so I have to imagine they've taken liberties, but I can't prove it. Anyway, smells good, which is the main thing."

"Why'd you name your car Hector?" I asked.

"Greek mythology," he answered. "I had this idea that when I wanted another car, I'd name it Achilles, and Achilles would be, like, Hector's heel, but then I found out Hector means 'to bully,' and it's not wrong, really; this car definitely owns me sometimes. And it's definitely doomed. Just look at all the miles on this baby." He patted the steering wheel lovingly.

"Did you know that Hector didn't even approve of the war between the Trojans and the Greeks?" I asked. "He was a lover of peace. But he got stuck fighting it anyway. And he very nearly won—until he was murdered by Achilles."

"Killed because Achilles found a loophole in Hector's armor," said Tag, starting the car. "A tiny gap in the neck area."

I looked at him, impressed.

"We studied *The Iliad*," he said. "And I have a good memory."

"It's like debate," I told him. "You look for the weaknesses in your opponent's armor, and then you take your best shot."

"But Hector was the moral hero of *The Iliad*!" said Tag. "He wanted to keep the community together. Achilles strove for glory; Hector was simply trying to preserve his world. Should he really have been the one to lose?" He looked behind us, carefully pulling out of the parking spot.

"And yet, everyone knows Achilles, not Hector."

"True, but he does has the dubious honor of reminding everyone of heels . . ."

"Ha!" I said.

"Not to interrupt this important Homeric discourse," asked Tag. "But where should we go?"

"A surprise. I'll direct you," I told him. "Pull out of the parking lot, then take a left."

We cruised down the road, and I tried to see everything through his eyes. "There's my high school," I said, pointing. "Note the giant football field, the pride and joy of the community. Not that I make many games."

"You're too busy shooting into your opponent's weaknesses." He looked at me and smiled. My body tingled.

"That's our post office," I said, gesturing toward a small white building, "and the town courts, or shall I say court. Our Chinese restaurant; the sesame noodles are incredible. And there's the bar where my mom used to work ages ago." We drove by, and I waved at it. "It hasn't changed much since then. Another left at the light here."

"Where's your dad now? Or is that too personal? I've only heard you mention your mom."

"I never knew him at all," I told him, and when he frowned in sympathy I shook my head. "It's no big deal. Really."

"That must be . . . ," he began, but he was about to miss an important turn.

"Make a right!" I yelled, and he did. "Drive down this way," I instructed, indicating the way. "Park. Okay, get ready for the very best pizza in the whole town. It's also the only pizza, but don't let that sway your opinion."

"I can't wait," he said.

Everybody knows everybody in my little town, so when I walked in with a random teenage stranger no one had ever seen before, the eyes were sort of on me. Luckily, the only eyes in the place belonged to the owner, Nick Pinino, who had been making pies for me and my mom pretty much every Friday night for the past decade.

"Hey there, Millie," he said, giving me a wave. "Who you got with you?"

Tag waved back. "I'm Tag," he said. "A debater friend of Millie's."

Then the door opened. One of Kargle's football players walked in with a girl and looked over at me. I grabbed Tag's hand and pulled him to the first empty booth I saw. "We'll just sit here," I told Nick. "Send over one of the usuals. Please. And two iced teas."

"Sure thing," said Nick. "Comin' right up."

"So, how'd you get into debate in the first place?" asked Tag. "I can't believe you're the only one on your team. That's dedication."

"Do you really want to know?" I asked.

He nodded.

"Hillary Clinton," I said. "Remember the 2016 election? Like, a thousand years ago at this point?"

He nodded again.

"Mom and I watched the debates together. We were so excited that a woman had been nominated. There's this one in particular, Hillary and Trump, you can see it on YouTube. His debate style was so wrong. He lurked behind her and interrupted and made faces. She stayed calm. He got belligerent. But somehow, more people in the end sided with him than they did with her—or they didn't, in terms of the popular vote, but that's another story. The whole thing still floors me."

He hadn't laughed or busted out the anti-Hillary slurs yet. So I kept going.

"That's when I decided that when I got to high school, I'd start a team, even if I was the only one on it. I thought, if I'm ever in that situation, I want to be as cool and calm and smart as she is. But also: I want to *win*."

I studied his reaction, wondering if he'd make fun of me. But he just sat there, quietly listening.

"I was good, and that created its own momentum," I continued. "I got better, and there were some bad things that came with that. That Millicent Calmerzzz Twitter account is not a surprise, exactly. There's this group of guys on the circuit who've been harassing me ever since I started taking home trophies freshman year." I frowned. "They want me to quit. But if I win state this year, I set an Alabama debate record, and that means I'll almost definitely get a full scholarship to college. There's one called the Martha Linger that pays for literally everything. Which I need."

"And you should get it," he said. "Though it sucks that you have to get a scholarship to go to college. Education should be free! We're supposed to live in a society that supports equality, so why do some kids get the best educations money can buy and others—"

"Don't even have debate teams at their schools?"

He nodded. "Exactly. It's such hypocrisy." He pushed his glasses up his nose. "Don't you think?"

Carlos was right: He was cute.

"Well, given that they're not about to make college free and the whole debt forgiveness thing has yet to happen, I have to figure out *some* way to go."

"Why?" he asked. "Not judging, just curious. Everyone is so focused on college as the requisite thing to do post–high school, but have they really thought about *why*? Just because something is what's been done doesn't mean it has to stay that way forever."

"I've just always wanted to," I admitted. "I love the idea of ivy-covered buildings and strolling through quads and studying in the library and even taking exams . . ." I shrugged. "It's so romantic, somehow. But also, on the practical side, you need a degree to do a lot of things. Sometimes just so people believe you *can* do those things."

"But there are a ton of things you can do without a degree," he said. "Don't get me wrong: I'm not anticollege, but I am against it as a one-size-fits-all solution. "

"Maybe because you *can* be," I told him.

"Maybe," he said. "Personally, I want to do some other things first. But we're talking about you. You should go to college. You absolutely shouldn't quit debate. Who are these guys who are harassing you?"

"I don't want to talk about them," I said, shaking my head.

"I'm sorry, I didn't mean to bring up bad stuff." He put his hand on mine on the table. My heart was beating fast all of a sudden.

The football player who'd come in suddenly appeared at our table. He eyed me and Tag. "Hey," he said. "You seen Kargle?"

I slipped my hand out from under Tag's. "Not recently," I told him.

"Well, if you do, tell him I'm looking for him," he said. "The team has some plays to run through before the game tonight. If he's not busy, you know, with y'all's debate stuff or whatever."

"Okay," I said, and the guy went back to his booth. The girl he was with looked over at us, probably wondering who Tag was, too. Like I said, small town.

"Hey, y'all!" Nick was back. "Total brain fart. Did you say you wanted sweetened ice tea or unsweetened?"

"Unsweetened for me, please," I said.

"Same!" said Tag.

"Sure thing," said Nick, and went to get our drinks.

"I was thinking," I said. "I don't think we should tell Kargle and Francine about us working together. It's not against the rules, exactly. But, you know, it might be better just to avoid any questions—"

Tag was nodding. "My team captain, Rajesh, doesn't need to know, that's for sure."

"Good," I said. "Then we are officially keeping this on the DL."

He sat back and considered me. "You know, I had the idea that Millicent Chalmers was all about winning, no matter what," he said. "You *are* about winning. But it's different. The real you is different."

"It's better to debate someone who's good at debate," I told him. "It makes us all better," I added. "I mean, how am I supposed to argue against you if you argue *my* side?"

"I guess you're right," he said. "But in the real world, that's not how arguments work. Instead there's this massive sea of people shouting as loudly as they can for attention, or using rhetoric to convince people of stuff that isn't good or true at all. People who don't pick a side, or who argue both, are assumed to be weaker. Meanwhile, we're told that our voices can change the world! But how do you speak louder than the sea to a crowd that doesn't want to listen? How do you make it so everyone who deserves to be heard actually is? That's what I want to figure out." He looked at me seriously. "Still working on it, obviously."

I shook my head. "I'm good in the debate world," I admitted. "I don't know how to make the actual world act any better."

"You want to know what I think is the most important thing about debate?" he asked.

"What?"

"You can tell when someone else is full of shit, and call them out on it."

I laughed. "Can I ask you another question? What's the story with your car?"

"You don't like Hector?" He drew a wiggly invisible line down his face, imitating a tear.

"I love Hector. Hector is the bomb. But why Hector? I picture you driving a brand-new Lexus. Or maybe a Tesla."

"My parents do have a Tesla," he admitted.

"See."

"But I liked the idea of having a classic car. Hector was my dad's, and his dad's before that. It's more meaningful."

"Ha," I said. "Like generational wealth. Keep passing it down, right?"

He frowned. "Well . . ."

"Don't get me wrong, Hector *is* kinda cute," I said

Tag smiled at me. "Just wait till you hear the stereo system I put in him!"

Nick appeared again, setting a wire rack on our table and placing a steaming pie on top of it. He pulled a pizza cutter out of his apron pocket to do the honors. "Extra cheese and a few scattered jalapeños, as per usual."

"My mom and I always get this," I told Tag. "It makes your mouth feel truly *alive*."

"I'm psyched," Tag said.

"It's the best pizza I've ever had," I said, and Nick beamed.

"And it's on me," he said. "Millie, your mom told me you won that big debate competition in Anniston in September. The entire thing! Congratulations! It's good to have a smart girl like you in our town. You class the place up a few notches."

"Thanks," I said. "That means a lot."

Nick turned and walked back to the counter.

"There's a guy who values the important stuff," said Tag.

I stuck my tongue out at him and picked up a slice, blowing on it for a second before taking a bite. He did the same, grinning at me.

"My mouth is on fire!" he said. "But I'm into it."

I didn't let him drive me home, even though he offered. Instead, he dropped me off at the library and I rode my bike back in the dark, which I'd done a million times before, passing the lit-up football stadium where most of my school, including Coach Kargle, was watching the game. I hoped the football player from earlier had found him, but I didn't need to be his secretary. In another world, maybe football games and cheerleading and hanging with that crowd would be my life. But I'd chosen differently: Debate was my world. I checked my watch: We'd stayed out past nine o'clock, talking and laughing and eating an entire pizza. Next weekend, we were meeting at the library again.

Mom's Honda was under the carport. Unlike Hector, it didn't have a name and it hadn't been handed down from generation to generation in perfect condition. It was just what we could afford. It had come cheap because the previous owner had an ex who'd keyed FUCK YOU on it after they broke up. My mom had painted it over herself. You could barely see it, and only if you really knew what you were looking for.

She was standing in the doorway, still wearing her scrubs from the hospital. "Hey!" she said as I came in. "I literally just walked in the door."

"Hi!" I gave her a kiss on the cheek.

"I feel like I haven't seen you for more than a minute in ages," she said, hugging me. "Doing a double after three days in a row, woof, I am exhausted. Where were you?"

Beau was whining at my feet, wanting pets. I kneeled next to him and put my face in his fur, which gave me the chance to avoid eye contact with my mom as I didn't so much as lie, but didn't tell the whole truth, either.

"The usual," I said. "Library, working on debate stuff." We

walked into the kitchen with Beau following. I put the books Mrs. Mendez had given me on the table and sat down.

"I'm so proud of you, all the hard work you keep putting in," Mom said, sitting across from me and pulling another chair close so she could prop her feet on it. "Ah, that feels better . . . I am *positive* your debate success is going to pay off. Four years of state wins in a row! That's Alabama history in the making."

"I hope so," I said.

"Hey, did you eat yet?"

"Yeah, I got pizza after the library."

"By yourself?"

I nodded, hoping the lie wouldn't come back to bite me. "I hung out and talked to Nick."

"Well, sit and talk to me while I heat up some dinner." She got up and walked over to the fridge, opening the freezer and staring at it for a while. "Are these little chicken potpie things any good?"

They didn't compare to Tag's sandwiches, but I couldn't say that. "Pretty decent," I told her.

She popped one in the microwave and sat back down. "How's Mrs. Mendez?"

"She's great," I said, gesturing to my book pile. I handed her the Wollstonecraft. "This one is by the mother of the woman who wrote *Frankenstein*. She was an early feminist."

"Neat!" My mom opened the book to a random page and cleared her throat: "This is from a chapter called Observations on the State of Degradation to which Woman Is Reduced by Various Causes," she said. "'I lament that women are systematically degraded by receiving the trivial attentions, which men think it manly to pay to the sex, when, in fact, they are insultingly supporting their own superiority.' Wow." She read some more: "'So ludicrous, in fact, do these ceremonies appear to me, that I scarcely am able to govern my muscles, when I see a man start with eager, and serious solicitude to lift a handkerchief, or shut a door, when the LADY could have done it herself, had she only moved a pace or two.'" She put the book down. "I always think that, too. I can open my own damn door. Pay me fairly, why don't you?"

I thought about Tag's dad telling him to open doors for women, and how much better it would be if sexism just didn't exist. And yet, it was nice to have doors opened for you by someone you liked. It felt good. Was that bad?

The microwave dinged. Mom got her chicken potpie and a fork and sat back down, tasting it. "You're right: Pretty decent," she said. "Want to watch a show or something?"

I looked at the Wollstonecraft book—it was called *A Vindication of the Rights of Woman*. "I might keep working, instead," I told her. "I'm kind of in a zone, you know?"

"Don't work too hard," she said, scooping more potpie into her mouth. "Only my daughter would study all day and all night on a Saturday."

She wasn't completely wrong. I did go to my room and start reading Wollstonecraft.

But I also thought about Tag.

PART TWO

November

Resolved: The "right to be forgotten" from internet searches ought to be a civil right.

TAG

"Have you ever done something you're not proud of?" Rajesh asked. It was the first week in November, and we were debating the new resolution, which Millie and I had been working on regularly. On Saturdays, we'd meet at her library and run through different arguments and cross-ex questions and thinking on the fly. Mrs. Mendez would give us a heads-up ten minutes before the library closed. We'd head over to Nick's and eat pizza and talk about everything else, like whether we were still having nightmares about the shooter scare (sometimes), how Hector was handling the recent spate of cold (he seemed a little tired, tbh), my latest recipe in the making (I was working on a chocolate lava cake with the perfect melt-to-cake ratio), and the latest wacky scholarship opportunity Millie had stumbled upon (there was one for champion duck callers, she informed me).

I'd gotten lucky with this resolution, or, more likely, it was her help. Francine had taken me aside to tell me whatever I was doing was working. Merwin kept giving me the thumbs-up whenever he saw me in the halls. My parents were thrilled with my debate improvement, though they were still bugging me about college. Meanwhile, Rajesh kept shooting me daggers. You couldn't win with him.

"Something that might embarrass or humiliate you . . . something you wouldn't want a good friend to know about—much less everyone in the internet-accessible world?" He was standing about three feet away from me, his legs positioned in a wide upside-down V. He'd explained it was the "Tory power stance," which conservative members of the British Parliament used to convey their confidence.[32]

"Sure," I said. I was standing in a regular stance, but I did have on my favorite T-shirt, which has an illustration of Jesus riding a dinosaur on it. "I wouldn't be human if I hadn't done something I regret," I added.

"Like what?" He stared straight ahead. "An example, please."

"Um . . ."

"Anything. What first comes to your head?"

I thought about Millie. Was it wrong if I had a full-blown crush on her? Also: Should I actually *do* something about that? Or did that risk our friendship, which was now one of my favorite things about debate?

"Tag?"

"What was the question again?"

"Have. You. Ever. Done. Anything. You're. Not. Proud. Of." Oops, I was pissing him off.

"Um, one time I was riding my bike to your house back when we were in fifth grade and I looked down at the spokes and I thought, *I wonder what would happen if I stuck my foot in the spokes*, so I did, and I completely flipped over on the bike and busted my butt, and Juliette Hershey drove down the street at that same moment in her dad's Miata—remember that car? We were obsessed! Anyway, she saw me picking myself up, covered in dirt, my knees all bloody, and I could tell she was about to die laughing. That was pretty regrettable." I smiled at Francine, who was timing the debate while our teammates watched.

---

32 Also called *the Beyoncé*, but *she* makes it work.

Rajesh exhaled audibly. "Fine. What if the whole world knew about that? What if Juliette Hershey had videotaped you, and posted it online, and it had gone viral?"

"That would be pretty mean," I said. "Also illegal, since she was driving. Ultimately, that would be more regrettable for her than me, given the way that the internet hordes tend to punish people who behave like assholes. Have you ever read the AmItheAsshole subreddit? Now, that's full of folks who should really regret their behavior! But it also seems to indicate a desire on the part of society for lessons about what's right and wrong to exist online as an ethical reminder . . ."

"Tag." He rolled his eyes. "The point is, no one wants their 'regrettable'"—he did air quotes to punctuate—"'behaviors'"—another set of air quotes—"all over the internet, for anyone to see and spread. Do they?"

"It depends what you define as regrettable," I said. "Some people put that sort of stuff up like it's their job. Have you heard of TikTok? I know you have—I've seen some of your music videos." That got a chuckle out of the crowd.

I looked around. Cooper Cunningham was passing a note to Callory Chapman; Emmett Khoo was doodling in his notebook as he listened—it helps him think, he says; Rose Powell was taking notes on her iPhone; and our two freshmen, Davis Rudge and Morgan Watkins, were staring up at Rajesh and me, enthralled. Francine was writing on her legal pad, which I could see was marked "Tag" on one side and "Rajesh" on the other. On the opposite side of the room, Fentress Jackson was debating Celia Carrera, with Tori Griffith timing them and offering critiques. Those were my teammates, minus Ricky Yee, who had a dentist appointment. We each had our own talents and our own flaws on the debate circuit. Little did anyone know that my new talents were directly linked to Millicent Chalmers.

"But more importantly: What you *want* is different from what you have a right to. Isn't it?" I paused for effect, and then gestured around the room, proud of myself: "What we want, any of us, is inherently different from what we have a *right* to."

"Time's up," said Francine. There was a smattering of claps around the room. "Tag, I love how you finished that! And Rajesh, excellent pacing and tone. Great job, both of you."

Rajesh sat down, fuming, and scribbled across his legal pad. We had two weeks till Birmingham Public. We had a resolution. And, thanks to Millicent Chalmers, there was no need for a kritik. I could actually see both sides when it came to this issue.

Francine's Notes

<u>RAJESH/AC</u>

- Let's talk about that power stance, not sure it's working.

- I <u>love</u> your opening speech. Esp. the Prof. Viktor Mayer-Schönberger quote: "We essentially have undone forgetting. The past has begun to follow us." <u>Wow!</u>

- Tone & energy great in constructive. Keep that up entire debate.

- CX: Don't let us see you get mad! Tag is getting away from you and wasting your time. You want him in your control, but do it calmly.

<u>TAG/NC</u>

- Major improvements in confidence and your ability to tackle both sides! Parents and Merwin = :). Now, you just gotta get in those college apps!

- Not sure about the bike story, or the use of "butt" in a debate, but if you want to kill time in a CX, you did it. Next time, tell us more about how we need subreddits, i.e., internet history, to teach us what not to do!

- What people want and what they have a right to (or need?) is indeed v diff.! More on this, pls!

Hey there, Speech & Debate Friends!

WE HOPE YOU'RE READY FOR one of the most competitive events of the fall season, the **BIRMINGHAM PUBLIC TOURNAMENT.**

The fiercest teams in the South will participate in seven Nationals-qualifying rounds in policy, public forum, and L-D. Make sure to bring your D-game[33]!

We'll also have events in extemporaneous speaking, original oratory, dramatic and humorous interpretation, and more.

Please check the tournament website for more information, and be aware of the additional security procedures following the incident in October. Arrive early for metal detector checks, and note the list of banned items.

Safety first. Debate second.

Jay Nelson
Executive Director, Birmingham Public Debate Tournament
"Always Making a Statement"

---

33 You know, for *debate*.

TAG

The weekend before Thanksgiving, we were back. Hundreds of high school students filled the enormous cafeteria of an even more enormous high school, gossiping among themselves and shooting looks at the teams to beat. Birmingham Public was always a big tournament, but because debate had been on hold since the shooter scare, suddenly it was a welcome-back party with a dose of extra-agro energy. I was nervous, for all kinds of reasons.

This is cheesy, maybe, but it's true. I could just *feel* when Millie walked into the room. Her dress was one of those fitted-but-not-too-fitted things my mom calls a sheath in this dark green color, and she had a black blazer over it. She looked great. Her hair was down instead of up in a bun. As I watched, she reached up and tied it in a knot on top of her head, sticking a pen through it to keep it in place. When do girls learn that trick?

She was with Carlos, who was wearing a sports coat and a floral-patterned tie. They were deep in conversation as they found a table and sat down. She pulled out a manila folder and showed him something, and he laughed. They bent over the folder, heads together, working.

Rajesh elbowed me. "Creepin' on Chalmers?"

"What are you talking about?"

"You're staring. It's a little . . . obvious." He glared at me.

"Dude, why are you so mad at me? I don't get it. I'm doing better—shouldn't that make you happy?"

"We'll see. You haven't actually competed yet." He sighed, looking a little bit more like the Rajesh I used to know. "Anyway, I'm not mad. I just don't like how you're fraternizing with the enemy. It doesn't make us look good. It might even be an ethics issue."

"*Fraternizing?*" I asked. *Did he know?* I tried to play it off. "We were stuck in a closet together while everyone thought there was a gunman loose in the hallways. If there's an ethics issue, I don't think it has to do with me."

"Look, you're eventually going to have to debate her again," he said. "You clearly have a thing for her." We both glanced over. Now she was standing up and talking, holding papers in her hand but not looking at them. She didn't need to; she had both cases memorized. Carlos was timing her. I felt wildly jealous for a second.

"So what?" I said. "Even if I did have a thing for her, it's not like we're dating. But if we were, there's no rule against that! Lots of people from different teams hang out and even work together. That's the whole point of"—I gestured at the room, full of different groups of teenagers talking and prepping—"this. It's not just about winning."

"So you *do* like her," Rajesh said quietly. "Tag. You're eventually going to have to debate her again. What do you think is going to happen when you have to compete against someone you've got a crush on?"

"This is such a nonissue, I'm embarrassed for you for asking it," I said, pulling the three-ring binder that contained my notes out of my backpack. "Can you leave me alone so I can do what I'm here to do, please? Go work on your Harvard application or something."

He got up, letting his chair squeak loudly against the linoleum floor, only second to fingernails on a chalkboard in terms of getting the tiny hairs to stand up on the back of your neck, but he couldn't resist trying for the last word, too.[34] "Fine," he said. "But if you don't start *actually* winning soon, you can consider yourself off the team."

"You can't kick me off the team," I told him. "That's Francine's call. And Principal Merwin's. And, for the record, they're cool with how I'm doing."

"Don't test me, Tag. If your team doesn't want you here, neither will they," he said, putting his face close to mine. "By the way, everyone knows what *really* happened in that closet. If the debate administrators find out, you're toast." I didn't have a chance to challenge his use of *toast* [35] before he turned and walked away.

"Whoa," I whispered.

Rose Powell had been sitting across from us the whole time, pretending to stare at her phone. Now she looked over at me. "You know why he's being like this, right?"

"Not really," I admitted. I straightened my pumpkin tie.

"He's jealous. You're doing better, for one."

"He wanted me to!"

"That's true, but reason takes a second place when it comes to emotion. And jealousy is a bitch. Last year at Nationals, Millicent Chalmers ripped Rajesh a new one in the very first round. He then had to stick around for two days, waiting, until she won the whole thing. You didn't know?"

I shook my head. "I didn't go to Nationals last year. I didn't win enough to qualify . . ."

"Are you secretly dating her?"

---

34 If you hadn't noticed, debaters *love* the last word.
35 A very good food that doesn't deserve that treatment.

"No!" I said. It wasn't a lie.

"People say y'all had sex in the closet." She gazed at me appraisingly.

"Is *that* what he meant by fraternizing?" I was dumbfounded.

"Did you?"

"No!" I said. "Definitely not! People say that? What people?"

"I heard it from some Chatham's Laker," she said. "It seemed far-fetched that anyone would want to take off their clothes in the middle of a shooter scare. But people like to believe lies more than they want to believe the truth, sometimes."

I put my head in my hands. "What if Millie thinks *I* spread those rumors?"

"If you hadn't heard it, maybe neither has she," said Rose.

"Maybe you're right." I thought for a second. "Hey, how do *you* know all this? About everything."

She shrugged again and smiled. "I listen, and people tell me things. It's my secret power. We all have one. So you call her Millie now?" She looked at me intently.

I was saved by a flutter of movement at the front of the room. The tournament director was pinning the list of today's debate assignments to a bulletin board. There was a crowd circling the board, but he held them off, a microphone to his mouth.

"The first round will begin in thirty minutes!" he said. "Debaters! Printouts of the schedule, today's assignments, and room numbers are here and have been sent to you digitally as well. Judges, please pick up ballots in the tab room.[36] New assignments will be released tomorrow morning at seven A.M. sharp. Good luck, everyone!"

---

36 The room at every tournament where scores are tabulated and winners are verified.

Breathless, Rose showed me the first-round assignments on her phone. "Tag. You're up against Millicent Chalmers again!"

I felt like I might puke. But I also felt excited.

Rajesh was looking at me as if I'd done this on purpose.

Across the room, there was Millie. She raised her hand, waved, and smiled. Her real smile, not the smug one.

"Are you going to talk to her?" asked Rose.

"I guess I have to," I said. "We're debating each other."

MILLIE

As Tag approached, Carlos backed away with a huge grin on his face. "Break a leg," he whispered. "Or whatever's lucky in this instance. Actually, don't break anything. That's probably the luckiest."

"Shhhh," I told him, taking a deep breath. *Never let 'em see you sweat; never let 'em see you lose your cool*, I told myself, and turned to Tag, who was staring at Carlos's tie. "Man, is that a cheeseburger and a slice of pizza?" he asked, pointing. "A hot dog? And a taco! I thought it was just a boring old tie from across the room."

Carlos stepped back toward us, still grinning. "I order my ties online. They're all a little bit cheeky. Cool pumpkins, by the way."

"Thanks, man. It's my lucky charm." Tag looked down at his own tie lovingly.

"Well, I gotta prep," said Carlos. "I'm going against a Chatham's Laker; they can get kinda squirrelly. Catch y'all later."

"So," Tag said as Carlos headed for the cafeteria doors. "Am I allowed to hide in a supply closet for this whole debate? 'Cause I have to admit, I'm a *tiny* bit intimidated! Okay, a lot intimidated."

"You've spent more time alone with me than pretty much any other debater on this circuit, minus Carlos," I said. "What's there to be afraid of?"

That's when I actually looked down at the schematic Carlos had handed me earlier with a gleeful crow that I was going against "Tagathée Hottie-met" and saw who our judge was. "Oh, dammit."

"What's wrong?" Tag asked.

What's wrong was Edmund Culhane. He'd been one of the biggest debate bros on the circuit before he graduated a year ago and, because this is exactly how these things happen for rich boys at prep schools, was given the job of assistant coach of the Chatham's Lake debate team, a gig he did while attending college at the nearby university attended by all the Chatham's Lakers who didn't get into better schools. He'd had a halfway decent record, but he got ahead by spreading rumors about girl debaters, bullying them during cross-ex, and, sometimes, getting them to leave the circuit altogether. He was personally responsible for the departure of my friend Ana Clark, a Georgia debater I'd met at camp sophomore year. After she beat him, he'd retaliated by telling everyone she was a man who wrapped her penis around her leg so she could pretend to win as a girl. It just wasn't worth it, she'd told me—walking into rooms and hearing guys cough the word *penis* into their hands.

And then there was what he'd done to me. But getting into it would upset me too much right before a debate.

Tag took the paper out of my hand. "Why does this name look familiar? Is this that kid from Cheater's Lake—he's a *judge* now?"

"Cheater's Lake? Is that what you call it?"

"Yeah, because of how many SAT scandals they have."

"Yet they still promise the best Ivy acceptance rate in Alabama for their boys," I said. "Kinda makes you think." I frowned.

"Does this have something to do with those guys on the circuit who've been harassing you?" he asked. "You don't have to say yes or no. Just, um, blink if I'm close."

I blinked. "But, you know, a person *has* to blink. Or your eyes will dry out."

"That whole team is super shady," said Tag. "I can't believe this guy is a judge now."

"He's actually their assistant coach. So he judges *regularly*."

"That's even worse." Tag shook his head. "Total example of failing upward. None of them are even that good at debate, and yet, they win anyway."

"It's the whole prep school network. Judges vote for them because they were prep school boys, too. And no one sees them for who they really are. Or, they do, but they don't care. They help each other, and it repeats, over and over again."

"What are you going to do?"

I stopped and looked at him. "What I always do. Try my best to win. What are *you* gonna do?"

"I guess I have to do the same."

"Good."

We passed a big clock hanging on the wall. "Is that the real time?" I asked. "Crap, we're going to be late."

We scanned the halls, looking for our room number.

"It should be right around here," I said.

"There's 213-B. Aren't we 213-A?" asked Tag, and I double-checked the schematic. Yes, we were, but all the rooms we were seeing were *B*s, which meant we must be on the B level. "I hate this school's layout!" I said. "This happens to me every year."

"It's worse than the Birmingham airport," said Tag. "I was once lost in that place for longer than my actual flight . . ."

"*Where is the stairwell?*" I asked. I was *never* late to a debate. We now had just three minutes before we were supposed to start. *Why did Edmund Culhane have to be the judge?*

"There are stairs up there," Tag said, pointing, and we jogged to them, breathless. Our room was right at the top. As we entered, I tried to wipe away the sweat dripping down my nose. Culhane was seated in the middle of the room wearing khakis and a blue blazer, the same outfit he used to debate in. He'd added a backward baseball cap. His lip curled, doing what his face seemed to consider a smile.

He nodded at Tag, doing that man-recognize-man thing, before turning to me.

"Well, hello there," he said condescendingly. "Who do we have? Millicent M. Chalmers? Bonus points if you tell me what the *M* is for." He leered in the direction of my chest, and I clutched my blazer together. He cackled.

"You're cutting it close," he said, glancing at his watch. "You have fifteen seconds. Unless you want to use some of your prep before the round begins? I'll only deduct a little if you do." He grinned again. "Less than I'll deduct for the color of your dress, anyway. Bold choice, green."

"I'm ready now." I put my briefcase down at my desk and moved to stand in the front of the room. I could have used a minute, but I wouldn't give him the satisfaction.

Tag gave me a tiny thumbs-up, and Culhane smirked and started his timer.

"What are you waiting for?" he asked.

TAG

Edmund Culhane was one of those guys who waves at a girl to go ahead of him in the cafeteria line, chivalrous and kind, except it's all an act, and he's using the moment to look at her butt. "Nice ass," he'll tell her, to get her to blush, to show he has power over her. Worse, he'll take a picture and share it on the internet with a rating. I hated the way he was talking to Millie: so condescending, and at the same time, flirtatious. And instead of telling him off the way he deserved, she had to be polite for the sake of debate, to get his vote.

"Nice," said our judge, looking at Millie's legs as she concluded the affirmative. "And I mean it."

Barf.

"Your turn, Strong," he said, nodding me up to the front. "Go ahead, cross her Xs." *What did that even mean?* He chuckled into his hand. Dear God, I hated him.

I grabbed my legal pad and joined Millie, looking at our judge. He winked at her.

I couldn't believe what I was seeing. He was doing all this out in the open, right in front of me. I'm sure a lot of male debaters wouldn't even notice, or would play along—after all, they wanted to win the points he had to give. And he was careful. He could deny he'd done anything, or say that it had all been a big joke, that Millie was too sensitive. But it was a level of constant harassment that would have you wanting to leave debate entirely if you had to deal with it.

"So, according to your case, treating everyone fairly would mean giving them another opportunity in life, free to move forward without the hindrance of a public internet record depicting their very worst moments," I said. "And this upholds your value premise of social fairness?"

Culhane pursed his lips and nodded.

"Yes," she said. "Essentially."

Edmund Culhane squinted and scribbled on his ballot.

Millie continued. "When those mistakes have not resulted in loss of life or freedom for another, and when the person who has made the mistakes has learned from them, as I explained in my constructive. This is not a license to forgive all crimes or expunge all records, particularly when it comes to acts that have brought irreparable harm to others. Civil rights may be limited, as we see with the criminal justice system."

Culhane leaned back in his chair and let out a yawn. "Can we pick up the pace a little? This is a snooze fest. And Millie, can you stop talking in such a *high pitch*? It's hurting my head." He muttered. "Girl debaters."

Suddenly, I couldn't stop myself.

"So, if someone hasn't learned from a mistake, or is just a jerk through and through, whatever's said about him online can just stay there forever?" I asked.

"Again, essentially," said Millie. "If a person is intent on causing continued harm, I consider that an exception from the resolution."

Culhane was now staring at his phone.

"Got it," I said. "So in the case of this doofus in front of us, Edmund Cul-de-sac-of-a-brain, it's fine to keep his shady-ass history on the internet for everyone to see, because they might need it in order to protect themselves, and anyway, he probably shouldn't be let out of the house by his parents?"

"I . . . ," said Millie, and trailed off.

"What did you say?" asked Culhane, putting his phone down. "*What did you say?* I heard what you said."

"Then you don't need me to repeat it," I told him.

"Seriously?" he asked me. "Wow." He smiled, and I felt sorry for his teeth, having to wallow around in that smile. He stood and grabbed his ballot, and then looked at me with a sadistic expression. "Too bad, you were going to get my vote." Then he got even crueler. "I heard about what happened in the supply closet. That's just *nasty*. You lie down with dogs, you wake up with fleas."

"I *like* dogs," I said. "Dogs are good people."

He left the room, slamming the door behind him.

"That was dramatic," I said, trying to make light of it, even though I'd get a zero for the round and I'd probably be reported to debate administration for hassling a judge. Neither my parents nor Merwin would like that. Still, it was worth it, picturing the look on Culhane's face when the words I'd been saying registered in the part of his brain that understood language.

Millie looked confused, but more than that, she looked angry. "What was he talking about?" she asked. "The supply closet?"

I'd better just come out with it. "Apparently some people spread a rumor that we slept together when we were hiding at Montgomery Hills."

"We slept together?" She shook her head. "As if."

I know it's shallow and beside the point, but *that* did not make me feel good.

"Wait, and I'm supposed to be the *dog* in that scenario? A dog with *fleas*? And you told him you *like* dogs? What the hell, Tag."

"I didn't mean it like . . ."

"Who spread that rumor?" She crossed her arms in front of her chest. "Did *you* spread that rumor? I will *destroy* you if you spread that rumor."

She got *very emphatic* when she was angry.

"I didn't, I promise! I don't know who did or when, but Rose told me about it today. She heard it from someone at Cheater's Lake."

"And you didn't tell me? Tag."

"I didn't want to tell you right before a debate! I was figuring out what to say!"

She shook her head and frowned.

"Are you okay?"

"No, I'm not okay," she said. "Did you do *anything*? Or did you just smile to yourself and think, 'Cool, cool, that'll blow over and no one will really think it's true so it can't hurt anyone and maybe it will help my pathetic little reputation a little bit, if anything'?" She wasn't mad; she was furious. "Were you ever going to tell me?"

"I was," I said. "I just was figuring out . . ."

"Don't bother," she said. "Isn't this what you're always talking about, saying versus doing? You can say you're sorry, but until you do something about it, it doesn't prove much. A rumor like that might not hurt you, but it does hurt me. People believe it. People think differently about me."

I nodded. "I'm sorry." I noticed the poster hanging on the wall at the front of the room. It said, KEEP CALM AND DEBATE ON.[37]

"And what you just did up there in front of Culhane, all that macho posturing, I don't need it, either. No one asked you to fight

---

37 Thanks, poster. Very helpful.

my battles for me. Stop trying to save me and just be a friend. This isn't about who gets to be the hero." She started putting her stuff in her briefcase, getting ready to leave.

"What was I supposed to do? I was trying to help you!" I said. "I helped you before. I just wanted to help you again."

She stopped and looked at me. "That was different. Tag, let me lay it out for you: If there is a presumed shooter and I cannot move, yes, you are allowed to grab me and pull me to safety. If we are debating in front of a judge I absolutely despise, you are not allowed to call him out in front of me just because you decided that was the cool and manly thing to do. That was for you, not me."

"But . . ."

"If you'd done it for me, you would have thought about whether I wanted it first. You would have let me do my best and not undermined the entire debate. Ugh!" She picked up her briefcase, but she didn't leave. Which meant I had another chance.

"You're right," I said slowly. "I didn't think about any of that."

"You said what you said because you wanted to. It wasn't about me; it was about you."

"I know you said sorry doesn't count, but I really am sorry," I said. "It just made me so mad, looking at his face! That stuff he said to you, the way he was looking at you . . . I let out what I felt in that moment. I promise I wasn't trying to hurt you." I needed to make her understand, I wasn't one of those jerks, I wasn't. "I'm really, really sorry."

She put her briefcase back down. "I know," she said, calmer now. "He is honestly the worst. All those guys are huge misogynists. Even their coach is. But you just have to ignore it. You can't admit they have any power over you. And you definitely can't admit they have any power over me. That's not your place. We don't know how they'll retaliate, but you can be pretty sure they will, and it's going to involve me."

"I have an idea," I said. I pulled out my phone and logged onto my Twitter account. I hadn't tweeted since Montgomery Hills was canceled. I'd been waiting for something I needed to say, and here it was. I typed.

"Wait—what are you doing?" she asked. She sounded panicked.

"I'm going to set the record straight," I told her, typing some more. "But not without your approval. How's this?" I showed her my phone. *I HAVE SOMETHING I NEED TO SAY, AND THIS IS IMPORTANT*, I'd typed. *There is a rumor that I had sex with another debater when we were hiding during the shooter scare at Montgomery Hills. That is 100% not true, and people spreading that rumor need to get freakin' lives.*

"Aren't you supposed to not feed the trolls?" she asked.

"We're past that now. Not feeding the trolls never works in reality. You have to pick your battles and, when it matters, say what's right."

"Okay," she said. "But don't use my name."

"Obviously not." I pressed send, and then I decided to make it a thread.

Yes, she is very cool and very smart and really pretty and pretty awesome, but it did not happen. Furthermore: Women are not objects to have sex with, and they are definitely not dogs, and they don't have fleas. They are people. I showed her my phone.

She nodded. "Maybe cut the dogs and fleas part. I don't think we need to go there."

I did, then pressed send. But that wasn't all.

Also, we both thought we were going to die, which is not exactly the time you think about getting it on.

Now she was reading over my shoulder. Her hair smelled like lemons. I wanted to breathe in that lemon smell for as long as I could. "Okay?" I asked.

"Okay," she said.

Send. Last one.

If you spread this rumor, you need to think deeply about why you're saying something like that. What's wrong with you, anyway? Get your own life and stop slut-shaming people!

"I guess that counts as doing something," she said. "At least, it's a start. Thanks."

"You're welcome."

She grinned. "It was kind of awesome to see Culhane melt down, I have to say. That's gonna sustain me through the next bout of being called 'a pretty little lady with a good head on her shoulders.' Guys like that, they dish it out, but they can never take it."

I made a face. "Sorry, again."

"I have an idea. If you're disqualified from this tournament, which I have a sneaking suspicion is happening right now, you should ask to shadow me. You can if you're not an active participant, then it doesn't count as scouting. Not that I'm the best debater out there . . ."

"You actually are, though," I said.

"I was being facetious. I *have* won state three years in a row," she continued, sticking her tongue out at me. "What do you think? This could be part of your training program!"

"Let's talk to Francine. And Kargle—the two of them can talk to administration."

"Tag?"

"Yeah?"

"Do you really think I'm 'very cool and very smart and really pretty and pretty awesome'?" she asked.

"Not only that, I think you have perfect word recall," I said.

She smiled. "The start of your debate was pretty good. I'm impressed. And that cross-ex!"

I smiled back at her. "I have a good teacher."

"Shall we?" This time she put her arm out first, and I linked mine through it.

I was hooked.

We found Francine in the cafeteria huddled with Coach Kargle and the guy in the suit who'd passed out the debate assignments. Across the room, over in the corner, was Edmund Culhane. He glared at me. I remembered how Millie had said they'd retaliate, and I felt a little sick to my stomach. It was a reminder that words were powerful. You had to be careful with them and not just spew them out wherever and whenever you felt like it.

"Tag, Millie, you're here," said Francine. "Join us, please. This is Jay Nelson, director of the tournament."

"Hi, Mr. Nelson," Millie and I said, taking a seat at the table.

"Mr. Nelson says the two of you had some words with a judge," Kargle explained. "I said that doesn't sound like Millie. Want to tell us what happened?"

"It was my fault!" I blurted before Millie had a chance to answer. Then I remembered what she'd said, about me fighting her battles for her. I stopped talking and looked over at her.

"Tag is right," said Millie. "It was all him," and Kargle nodded. And then she stopped and sighed. "That's not right. It wasn't all him! It was Culhane who kept being creepy."

Our coaches looked at each other, and Francine raised an eyebrow. Jay Nelson looked concerned.

"What does that mean?" asked Coach Kargle. "What did he do?"

Millie took a deep breath. "He was very flirty. But also kept, like, negging me. He kept looking at my legs and . . . my chest."

"Are you sure?" asked Jay Nelson. "These are serious accusations. Is it possible you misinterpreted?"

Francine groaned. "Jay. Are you kidding me? You're going to question the top debater in the state for misinterpreting harassment? Would you do that if she were a guy?"

Kargle grunted.

Nelson said nothing, and Francine gave him an "I didn't think so" look.

"He told her she shouldn't talk in such a high voice," I said. "He basically said girl debaters suck. He told me to 'cross her Xs' when it was time for cross-ex. He said he was going to take off points for the color of her dress, too."

"Still," said Francine, shaking her head. "It's still happening. I remember when male debaters on the circuit would tell me because I'm Asian I'm supposed to be subservient and let them win."

Millie looked at her. "What would you say back?"

"Nothing," said Francine. "I'd just beat them. But I kind of wish I *had* said something, you know?"

Millie nodded. "Tag wouldn't have said what he did if Culhane hadn't started it."

Jay Nelson leaned across the table, looking at us seriously. "What did you say, Taggart?"

"I used him as an example of the exception in the affirmative," I said.

"Go on, please," said Francine.

"I said that in the case of Culhane, it would be okay to keep his internet history alive on the internet forever so that others would know what a creep he was, essentially," I said. "There would be a value to society in that."

Francine put her hand over her mouth, where the edges were tweaking up. Kargle looked at me, nodding slowly.

"I said that his parents shouldn't let him out of the house," I added. Might as well get it all out. I glanced over at the corner of the room where Culhane had been sitting with his cronies, but now they were gone. "I said he had a cul-de-sac for a brain."

"Hmm," said Jay Nelson. "I'm not sure this constitutes a disqualification for the girl, in any case."

"'The girl' is right here," said Francine. "And she has a name."

Kargle now looked at Francine, and he definitely smiled. "That's right. There is no reason to cut Millie out of the conversation, or the competition. She was just doing her job in that room, and that boy was harassing her! If anyone should be disqualified, it's him."

"Not Tag," said Millie, putting her arm on Kargle's shoulder. "He was trying to help."

"No, no, Tag is fine. He should compete," said Kargle. "I mean that Culhane creep. Get him outta here! I've dealt with enough of that 'locker room talk,' however you try to hide it, with the football team. This is debate! We don't need that here, too." He stood up, waving his arm at the air in a way that would kill a swarm of flies— truly, the coach was an intimidating size and shape—and I saw Jay Nelson flinch a little.

"Millie can continue in the tournament," Nelson said, and Kargle sat down. "The problem with Taggart is that he behaved in a way that violates the tournament's code of conduct. He directly insulted his judge."

"What if those judges are harassing the debaters?" asked Francine. "Seems a little unfair to me. Is Culhane going to be disqualified as a judge as well? Or, for that matter, as an assistant coach?"

"I'll have to look into that," said Jay Nelson. "I don't believe we have a rule about that."

"Why not?" said Kargle.

"We've never . . . needed one?" offered Nelson.

"You mean you've never been called out on needing one," said Kargle.

Nelson appeared to be shrinking into his chair.

"Also unfair is the fact that they've both been given zeros for this round, which they weren't able to complete because the judge left the room," pointed out Francine. "Millie was likely to win before this, and Tag has been doing so well in practice. And where, exactly, is the ballot that shows a record of these zeros? I'd like to see them. This is a qualifying tournament! Scholarships are at stake here!"

I wanted to give Francine another hug.

"Culhane said he didn't bother to fill out the ballot because of the automatic disqualify, which would render their points as zeros," said Nelson.

"And you just believed him?" asked Francine.

"I saw writing on his ballot," said Millie. "He definitely had a ballot."

"Go get the ballot," said Kargle.

"I'll track down the ballot," Nelson said, and went in search of Culhane.

Francine turned to me. "What in the world, Tag?" she asked. "And Millie, I am so, so sorry this happened."

"He was a real douchebag," I told her, and Millie nodded. "It's true."

Kargle leaned in. "What do you two want out of this? An apology? Get him booted from judging forever?" He gave Millie a sly grin. "Should I slash his tires?"

"Kargle!" said Millie, laughing. "You wouldn't!"

"Wouldn't I?" asked Kargle, who was quickly becoming one of my favorite people at this tournament.

"I just want to keep debating," said Millie. "Even if they do give me a zero for this round. I can make up the points. I know I can."

"What if they give you a bye?" asked Francine. "That way you don't have any negative impact on your record; it's just a free pass to the next round."

"You can only get a bye if there are an uneven number of competitors, though," said Kargle.

"Why should those rules matter when someone already broke the far more important rules?" Francine asked. "It says right on the ballot not to comment on the appearance of debaters. Or to make comments of a personal nature. Not that it should *have* to even say that."

"Let them disqualify me and give Millie a bye," I said. "If they let me shadow her for the rest of the tournament, I'll learn more than if I debated on my own. Plus, I *am* the one who started things."

"Is that what you want?" asked Francine. "We can fight this disqualification. It doesn't seem fair to me."

"It is," I said. "What I want."

"What about what Millie wants?" asked Kargle.

We all looked at her.

"Sure," she said. "Tag can shadow me, and, yeah, it wouldn't be the worst thing if they pulled Culhane for the tournament. Or forever." She smiled. "That would make me feel a lot better."

"We'll see what we can do," said Francine.

"Nelson's coming back," noted Kargle.

"Millie and Tag, thank you for your candidness." Francine was excusing us. "And, Tag," she said. "Nice cross-ex move. I'm looking forward to more of that. Minus the disqualification part."

Millie and I headed across the cafeteria, where we found a quiet space to pretend to study our cases while keeping watch on our coaches and sneaking looks at each other. Nelson had a quick talk with Francine and Kargle, gesturing and shrugging his shoulders. They beckoned us over again. Culhane was gone, and so was his ballot. His teammates claimed he'd had an emergency. (Kargle shook his head. "An emergency of his own making," he muttered.) The good news was, if I wanted to shadow Millie, that was fine.

I did. And she won every round.

After the last debate ended that day, we said good night. "See you back here bright and early tomorrow," she told me, getting into Coach's truck. I boarded the bus that would take my team to the hotel we were staying at for the night. We'd often stay up late in our shared rooms, shooting the shit and goofing around. Except since Rajesh didn't want to bunk with me, I had a room with Cooper Cunningham, who'd absconded to Callory's room. So it was just me, alone, with my phone. That's when I finally looked at my Twitter again.

My tweets about Millie had a few likes, a few retweets, a few trolls responding because I said "sex" and "slut-shaming," but mostly a lot of nothing. Who outside our small world even cared? I didn't have enough followers to make an impact. Even so, I was happy I'd said something that had made a difference to her. I wondered: Could you have a voice if only a very few people actually listened? Was that the start of having a voice? And what did it mean to have a voice, anyway? Who got one, and who didn't?

I texted Millie. **U awake?**

Yeah, she wrote back. **Just got home.**

You're home? Why?

Kargle drove me here.

R U not competing tomorrow? R U OK?

I'm fine! I never stay at the hotels, she texted. **I like being home. I don't have to worry about bedbugs.**

There R no bedbugs! I wrote, looking down at the mattress I was sitting on. **I hope there R no bedbugs. OMG, what if there R bedbugs? What do bedbugs look like? I feel itchy.**

Google it. I'll be back tomorrow.

I couldn't believe she would go all the way back and forth each time. **What time do U have to get up tomorrow?**

My alarm is set for 5:00 A.M., she wrote.

Hey, if UR not too tired, wanna FaceTime? I crossed my fingers on both hands and waited.

The bubble appeared.

OK.

She picked up on the first ring, and I grinned.

She smiled back.

"I like your poster," I said. She had one on her wall behind her that said DEBATERS: WE'LL TAKE THE WORDS RIGHT OUT OF YOUR MOUTH.

"People are always giving me debate stuff," she said. "Once you say you're into something, it's like they never forget it."

"Well, you can't see my actual room since I'm at the hotel. So you'll just have to believe it's full of pizza," I told her.

"I could maybe get down with that, if people wanted to give me free pizza for the rest of my life," she said.

My fear of bedbugs gone, I leaned back against the pillows I'd propped myself up with. "What are you doing?"

"Reading my cases through again. And thinking about what you said to Culhane."

"Ugh, I'm sorry, again."

She paused. "I might as well tell you why I was so upset earlier. Remember when I mentioned those guys who had it out for me?"

"Culhane is one of them?"

She nodded. "My first debate I ever did, freshman year, as a novice, was against him. Before we got in the room together he came over to introduce himself. Out of earshot of the judge, he told me that if I sent him nude pictures, he'd let me win. Later, I found out he'd done this to a bunch of freshman debaters over the years."

"Oh my God," I said. I sat up straighter.

"That's not all. I did *not* send him nude pictures, but he managed to circulate pictures that he claimed were of me. And when I won, he told everyone it was because of those pictures; that I'd sent them so he'd let me win, and that he felt bad for me so he did.

That night, they taped a bunch of those photos to the door of the hotel room where my mom and I were staying. She'd come with me for my first debate. She found them when she went to get ice."

"Jesus."

"You couldn't see the person's face, but whoever it was had my hair color and body shape. Mom freaked out, telling me I was going to ruin my chances at winning debate and possibly my whole future, too. When I finally got through to her that it wasn't me, she wanted to sue the whole team. To file a report with the Speech and Debate League. To leave. And to key their cars."

"Your mom?!"

Millie shrugged. "I don't know, she'd just bought her own car, which had been keyed; maybe that was inspiration."

"Why did your mom buy a car that had been keyed . . . Oh, never mind, that's not important."

"I convinced her to let us stay, and I went on to win the tournament. For a long time after, she wrestled with whether I should keep debating. She was worried that way worse would happen, that it wasn't a good place for me. And she wasn't wrong. But in the end, the chance for me to win college money was too great. I shouldn't have to give that up because of a bunch of assholes. Our compromise was that I'd stop staying in hotel rooms at all whenever I could help it. It's true, it helps with money, too, but that's the real reason." She paused, her mouth set in a hard line. "Now you know."

I vaguely remembered the nudes story. It had been a rumor freshman year. I hadn't remembered it had been Millicent, just some girl, and I had felt at the time like it was just as much her fault as anybody's. For taking the photos, for letting them get out. Now I was starting to see things differently. It made me feel sick. Even if she *had* sent him the pictures, that wouldn't have been her fault, either. She hadn't shared them with the world. He had.

"I'm really sorry," I said.

"Yeah. So there's been, like, this *thing* hanging over all my debates ever since. I won that whole tournament, but there are still people who think I got it through other reasons. Kargle addressed it with their coach back then, and you know what he said? 'If girls can't handle playing the game, they shouldn't compete.'"

"Isn't that illegal? And doesn't distributing pictures like that count as child porn? Why didn't y'all report it?"

"We tried. Plenty of minors saw the pictures, including me. But Chatham's Lake has a ton of rich lawyer dads on their board and in their alumni association. You can't win against them, even if you're right. They donate a huge amount to the cops every year, and they have a bunch of judges on their side, too. They always get away with it. The best thing to do was forget about it and move on. The more you fight, the harder they come back. So Culhane still has it out for me. There's no amount of punishing me that's enough."

I just listened, nodding.

"They bullied a bunch of girls into leaving. Some of them were friends of mine. But every time I got close to wanting to quit, I said no. I refused to let them win. And I worked harder and harder and harder." A tear ran down her face. "I refuse to cry!" she said, wiping it away.

"This is awful," I said. "What can I do to help? Can I murder him?"

"As much as I love the idea of ridding the world of sexism and misogyny completely, I don't think murder is the answer," she said.

"Where do you think he went? Where did the ballot go?" I asked.

"Guys like that have a lot of hiding places. They're all about making things look good on the surface and doing shitty things in the background," she said. "And sometimes they're powerful enough to do them right in the open. We haven't seen the last of him. When guys like that are challenged, they go HAM."

"Ooh, not to change the subject, but ... you know what would be good right now?"

"You're going to say ham, aren't you? That's a way better subject, to be honest." She laughed. I loved that sound.

"I mean, am I wrong? Hey, have you ever had a croque monsieur? It's this French panini with ham and cheese, and it is soooo good. I had the best one of my life in Paris last year, and ever since, I've been trying to re-create it."

"Wow, Paris," she said. "What were you doing there? French club or something?"

"Oh, no, it's my mom's favorite city. We go every year. She shops, and we eat all kinds of great food, and last year I got to do a cooking class . . ."

"I'm jealous," she said. "I've only been to Athens."

"Athens is amazing! The Parthenon, it totally gave me chills, just thinking about ancient civilizations and . . ."

"Athens, Alabama, Tag. Alabama."

"Oh."

"There *is* some pretty good barbecue there, though," she said.

"We should go sometime."

"Maybe," she said, and gave me this heart-melting smile.

We talked for a while longer, until I saw her yawn. "It's late!" I said, looking at the little hotel clock. "We should get some sleep. Especially you. You're gonna win this whole thing tomorrow. Right?"

"That's the plan," she said. "Thanks, Tag."

"For what?"

"Making me feel better."

"Anytime," I said. "'Night, Millie."

Tag's Souple[38]
Croque Monsieur[39] Recipe[40]

- **Preheat your oven to 425 degrees.**

- **Make your béchamel, an easy white sauce that sounds fancy because it's French. Here's what you do:**

  1. Melt a half stick of butter in a small pot on medium heat.

  2. Add a quarter cup of flour, whisking in to mix.

  3. Keep stirring.

  4. After a few minutes, gradually add a cup and a half of milk.

  5. Keep stirring and keep on low to medium heat until the sauce is combined and thick. Watch it! It can boil over, and you don't want to clean up that mess.

  6. When it's thick enough, add salt, pepper, a sprinkle of nutmeg, and a dab of dijon mustard, to taste. Mix in and take off the heat. It's okay if this sits for a while.

- **Cut a few slices of ham (about 4 per sandwich) and shred a cup of cheese per sandwich (ideally gruyère, because it melts really well, but you can use parmesan, fontina, Emmentaler, Jarlsberg, etc.: or a combination!).**

---

38 "Flexible" in French. Don't stress! Use the ingredients you have; it will still taste great.
39 Can be translated as "Mr. Crunch"—don't you want to make it now?
40 Top with a fried or poached egg and it's a Madame. (Mme. Crunch to you.)

- Get your bread ready. For a classic sandwich, use sliced white bread, but again, your choice! You can toast the bread first if you like it crispier, or leave it soft. If you're making 2 sandwiches, lay out 4 slices on a baking sheet lined with foil or parchment. Spread all 4 with your béchamel sauce. Top 2 of them with ham slices and shredded cheese. Put the other 2 slices of bread sauce-side down on top. Put some more béchamel on top of them, and more shredded cheese!

- Bake until the cheese is melted, a few minutes, and then broil for a couple more minutes (keep watch so as not to burn) so the top gets all crispy and delicious, like the topping of French onion soup. Mmm.

MILLIE

The next morning, I put on my black pencil skirt and this crisp white button-down shirt Ms. Cheney found me at Goodwill, perfectly pressed and tucked in and buttoned all the way to the top. I threw my trusty suit jacket over it to complete the power ensemble, and slipped on my debate shoes, which have the tiniest bit of a heel that doesn't kill my feet.

"You look awesome," Mom said when I came out of my room. "Strong. Smart. Gorgeous." She was wearing her nurse scrubs and making us both to-go coffee in thermoses.

I sat down at the table.

"Ready for day two?" she asked.

I nodded. I felt better than fine. I felt great.

Coach honked his horn.

"Knock 'em dead, honey," my mom told me, giving me a kiss on the cheek and handing me a coffee thermos. "I know you will."

I grabbed the coffee. "I will."

I walked into the Birmingham Public cafeteria, and there he was, tie around his neck, foil-wrapped sandwich in his hand.

"Hi," he said, handing it to me. "Taste."

I took a bite. Cheesy, salty, oozy goodness. Perfection, really. "Is this . . . ?"

Tag grinned. "A croque monsieur. I convinced one of the

cafeteria ladies to let me into the kitchen at 5:00 A.M. Used all the debate skills I could muster, and it actually worked. She made me wear a hairnet, but it was worth it. Granted, some of the ingredients back there are not exactly what I'd use in ideal circumstances, but on my fourth try, I think I got pretty close to the real thing."

"It tastes like the real thing to me, not that I know what the real thing tastes like." I handed it back to him, but he waved me off.

"No, I made it for you. You need fuel. You're gonna win, I know it. Not just this one. The whole thing. By the way, I really like your outfit. You look like you're about to kick ass and take names. So many names."

I shook my head. "You're too much, Tag."

"That's good, though, right?"

It was.

TAG

Here's what I learned from watching Millie debate:

1. Some judges were fine, even great—supportive and decent the way you'd expect. So were some competitors.

2. Some competitors and judges were completely average, neither good nor bad. They were just . . . competitors and judges.

3. Then there were the guys Millie went up against who tried to flirt, winking at her during rounds, or winking at their male judges as if they were on a team together and she was the entertainment. She got comments on her outfit when none of the guys did. One judge told her she was proof girls *could* debate, and I'm pretty sure he thought it was a compliment. Another judge gave her the win, but noted she should be careful "lest her overly assertive tactics undermine her likability." I heard male competitors making jokes about her, and I'm sure she heard them, too. But she stayed calm, smiling that smug smile (which I was starting to see was the mask she used to keep people from getting to her, getting too close, or getting a reaction), and arguing her points clearly and effectively.

After six or seven preliminary rounds, the typical debate tournament goes into finals. This tournament was big enough for an octofinal round,[41] and Millie was one of them. So was Rajesh, and also Rose Powell—it was her first time to break, and when she heard Jay Nelson call her name as a finalist, she jumped up and down and screamed, and our entire team joined in. Carlos made it, too. So did a couple of the guys from Cheater's Lake we'd seen commiserating with Edmund Culhane before he left the tournament. They all kind of looked the same in that overwhelmingly white prep school way, arrogant in matching ties and crew cuts, sneering at everyone they saw as beneath them, which was *everyone*.

Most tournaments have rules against *scouting*.[42] But in the final rounds, everyone who's no longer competing can watch and take notes, so our team split up. Half of us went to watch Rajesh debate Carlos, and the others got to see Millie vs. Rose. I was in it with Millie for the long haul.

Final rounds also have three judges instead of just one, which means it's a lot harder to pull the crap that Culhane tried. There's usually an audience, ranging from a handful to hundreds, depending on the size of the tournament. As a debater, it's a lot more intimidating to have so many people in the room. I was nervous for Millie, but she seemed fine. She'd done this a million times already.

Just before her debate with Rose, though, she pulled me aside. "I want you to see something," she said. She set her briefcase on the floor and showed me her hands, palms down. There were

---

41 Sixteen debaters. After that come quarters (8), semis (4), and finals (2).
42 If you're competing, you can't share notes on another debater or their case with your teammates or anyone else, and you can't go watch other debaters in preliminary rounds, either.

these tiny pen marks in between the knuckles, fine little etchings like a miniature prisoner might make on the miniature walls of a miniature cell, counting the days in captivity.

"Yikes," I said. "What kind of pens are you using that get all over you like that?"

"I did it on purpose," she said, but I wasn't following. "It's ballpoint—it doesn't hurt," she added. "Don't look so upset. I'm not engaging in self-harm. It's more like self-help."

"What do you mean?"

"When I'm sitting there in rounds and one of the guys I'm up against says something rude or sexist, or when a judge does, or when I feel like I'm being discriminated against because I'm a girl, I make a tiny mark," Millie explained. "By the end of most tournaments, I've got ink all over me. But it calms me down. I don't react in the moment. I can get ahead of it and win. And then, at the end of the tournament, I wash my hands and all that ink goes down the drain. Somehow, it makes me feel better." She smiled. "I just wanted to show you. Since you've been with me the whole time."

I couldn't think of what to say after that.

"Wish me luck," she said, and turned and walked into the room.

"Good luck," I whispered. I found a seat in the audience, which was already full of people. "Let's begin," said one of the judges, this twentysomething in a Samford hoodie. The other judges, two middle-aged debate parents, nodded, putting their pens to their ballots.

Rose stood up, cleared her throat, and began. "What's the one thing we all want in life?" she asked. "Happiness!" There was a little quake in her voice at first, and for the first thirty seconds she looked straight down, but as she kept going she got more comfortable, making eye contact with the audience.

I'd heard her case in practice, and it was pretty good. Making the "right to be forgotten" a civil right would enhance the happiness of every single member of society, she argued, because it would eradicate the bad things on the internet that could and did hurt people—not just those who were mentioned in the headlines, but also those who read those bad things and were affected by them. She used data from researchers who'd studied the effect of online negativity on members of society, and she quoted this philosopher Jeremy Bentham, the founder of utilitarianism, a doctrine that essentially declared actions right if they promoted happiness for the majority of the people involved. Who didn't want to be happy?

Then Millie got up for the cross-ex. "So, happiness is your main value?" she asked.

"Yes," said Rose. "Happiness as defined by what causes the most pleasure for the most people, after you subtract suffering."

"I see," said Millie. "And what if the happiness of some was directly related to the suffering of others?"

"What do you mean?" asked Rose. "Like in the case of someone who enjoys torturing others?"

"That's one example," said Millie.

"I'd argue that's not true happiness."

"Do you consider happiness an objective state?" asked Millie. "Is there one thing that makes people happy or unhappy?"

"There are general things that lead to the happiness of people that we can pretty much agree on . . ."

"What about justice?" said Millie. "Is justice objective? Is it more important to have a just society, or a happy society? And can a society truly be happy without justice?"

"I'm not sure," said Rose.

"Let me put it this way: Can members of an unjust society be happy? Truly happy?"

"Well . . . ," said Rose.

In the end, Millie won by declaring happiness a subjective state that could never be achieved constantly or equally throughout a society (there would always be those who weren't happy, for any number of reasons, both uncontrollable and controllable), but justice could be upheld in a way that was fair to all—that was the whole point of justice! In order to be truly just, she said, those who had done wrong must be accountable for their actions. The deeds they'd committed couldn't be erased; the people they'd hurt had to feel them forever, so they should have to, too. Further, the websites or pages that shared the stories of what they'd done should not be erased from a free society's internet; it was a valuable demonstration of right and wrong that kept us understanding and upholding justice.

Kinda like a Reddit AmItheAsshole, I thought.

In the end, the judges stood and clapped.

"Now, that's how it should be," said the guy in the hoodie. "None of that wobbly-voice stuff!" Rose and Millie exchanged a glance before Millie grabbed a pen and made a mark on her hand.

Millie and Rajesh advanced to quarters, where Rajesh was up against one of the guys from Cheater's Lake, and Millie was against a homeschooled debater who argued that we needed public examples of wrongdoing to shame people into good behavior—and even if some were harmed, the ends justified the means. Millie got the judges to vote affirmative instead. Rajesh won, too, which led the Cheater's Lake bro to make some rude comment about Pakistanis going back where they belonged. Rajesh informed him that (1) he was not Pakistani, and (2) no one in America "belonged" here if we were to abide by the definition that you had to have originated here—unless, of course, you were Indigenous, which none of the debaters at Cheater's Lake were. The Cheater's Lake bro walked away at that, shaking his head.

I went up to Rajesh after that. "You okay, man? You're killing it. Both in and out of the debate. Don't listen to those crap morsels spew their racist bullshit. Do your thing."

He looked at me but didn't smile. "That's exactly what I'm trying to do."

In semis, Rajesh and Millie were up against each other. It was a good fight, but Millie won, again, and you could see that even Rajesh expected it.

In the very last round, which was held in Birmingham Public's auditorium so everyone could watch, Millie was up against the last Cheater's Lake kid standing, a guy named Blanton Bodie.

Millie grabbed my hand before we walked in that room. Her fingers were ice cold. But it wasn't about her opponent. "Angela Tennant!" she'd whispered, and I'd peered into the auditorium to see who she was pointing to.

Angela Tennant was talking to Jay Nelson, using a lot of hand gestures. She was a tall Black woman in a red dress and bright red lipstick.

"Her lipstick matches her dress perfectly," whispered Millie. "I am in awe."

"Who is she? A judge?" I asked.

"She's not just any judge," whispered Millie. "She runs the Winners' Tournament!"[43]

"Have you gone?" I asked, assuming the answer would be "of course," but Millie shook her head. "It's expensive. My mom and I have to fund all the travel and lodgings and stuff ourselves. Unless I can get a scholarship, like I did to Nationals the past few years, it's not an option. And the WT doesn't do scholarships. It's school-fundraising or you pay out of pocket."

"What if you did a GoFundMe or something?"

She made a face. "Then everyone would know I didn't have enough money to do it on my own, and they could add 'poor' or 'charity case' to my list of sins? Or, worse, demand something in return? Great idea!"

"Come on, Millie. Everyone gets help from someone."

"Yeah, but not everyone's as lucky as you, where the strings don't show," she told me. "Or they're the socially acceptable kind of strings, so no one even cares; in fact, they're a benefit rather than a detriment. Anyway, Angela Tennant is amazing. She debated in the nineties and won Nationals twice. She's the first woman of color to do that."

"And she's headed our way," I said. "Do you always use her first and last name when talking about her?"

"Yes," said Millie. "She gets more than one name. She deserves them both."

"When do I get to know your third name, or really, the second name, but the one, you know, in the middle . . . ," I asked.

"Shhhhh," said Millie, because Angela Tennant was right there,

---

43 The Winners' Tournament was one of the most famous invitationals, held at a different host college at the end of every school year. I'd never done well enough to be invited.

and she was talking to us. "Hello," she said. "Millicent Chalmers! I can't wait to see what you have in store for us."

Then there was a shadow over us, and Angela Tennant glanced at her schematic. "And Blanton Bodie, from Chatham's Lake. Nice to meet you," she said.

Blanton Bodie grunted. "Hey," he said. I couldn't tell if he was looking at Millie's legs, but my hands found their way into tight fists anyway.

"Follow me, you two," Angela Tennant told them, ushering the finalists to the front of the auditorium, where they took their places behind podiums. I slipped into an empty seat.

"Allow me to introduce myself," she said, holding up a microphone to address the crowd. "I'm Angela Tennant, director of the prestigious Winners' Tournament, now a decade running." Everyone applauded. "I'm proud to be here to judge the final L-D round at Birmingham Public, which many of you know is my alma mater and where I first debated—and won." A bunch of Birmingham Public students stood and cheered. Angela Tennant waited until they were done, and then swept her hand toward a woman seated in the front row of the auditorium, who wore a visor and a tennis skirt, and the man on her right, who had on a suit and tie. "Our two other judges for this round are Naomi Johnson, a debate parent from Vestavia Hills; thank you for taking some time out in the midst of your own tennis tournament to be here"—Naomi smiled graciously and sipped from an eco-friendly canister of water—"and Lofton Fields the Third, from the Birmingham legal institution Lofton Fields Handy and Waverly."

Lofton Fields raised his hand and waved. He was exactly what Chatham's Lakers grow up to look like.

"And you all know Jay Nelson, tournament head," added Angela Tennant.

"I'll be timing the debate," said Nelson, holding up his timer.

"Competitors, ready yourselves," said Angela Tennant. "Audience members, please find a seat. Immediately." Yellow legal pads and laptops filled the room, pens and fingertips at the ready. "Millicent, please call heads or tails."

Jay Nelson flipped a coin.

"Heads!" said Millie.

"It's tails," said Jay Nelson.

"Affirmative," said Blanton Bodie.

"We have Blanton Bodie on the affirmative, and Millicent Chalmers on the negative, discussing the resolution: That the 'right to be forgotten' from internet searches ought to be a civil right," said Angela Tennant. "Please proceed."

Blanton Bodie gazed out at us, blinking. I almost felt bad for him. I wondered if he was any good, and if he wasn't, how he'd gotten this far. But then, I guess you didn't have to wonder. I looked over at Millie. She was the picture of calm.

Angela Tennant coughed.

"The clock is running," said Nelson

"Yes, sir," he said. And he began.

I have to admit, Blanton Bodie's affirmative was not terrible. He argued that because so many good men's lives had been destroyed, in numerous ways—jobs lost, inability to get new ones, harassment, death threats, reputations ruined, and so forth—by what was written about them online, the right to be forgotten, or to have that negative stuff about them removed from internet searches of their names, was just and fair. It was akin to a civil right in that it allowed humans to have a better chance at that which we were all granted by the Constitution: life, liberty, and the pursuit of happiness. Oh, and the EU and Argentina were already doing this. Didn't the United States, which considered itself an "exceptional" country based in justice, need to deliver the same to its citizens? His delivery was smooth, and his presence was solid. He even managed a few casual hand gestures, and he looked the judges in the eye a bunch of times. But he wasn't Millie level, or even Rajesh level.

I could almost see her brain chugging as she flowed his speech, logging counterarguments on her legal pad. She wasn't marking anything on her hands now. She was just doing what she was meant to do.

She stood up for cross-ex and started by asking him a very simple question. "You said that good *men's* lives have been destroyed, right?" she asked.

He nodded. "Indeed, and in a way that degrades their lives, liberties, and pursuit of happiness."

"And your case is based on equality?"

He nodded again. "Yes."

"Thank you. Nothing else."

Blanton rolled his eyes, thinking he'd gotten off scot-free. Until Millie started with her negative constructive and rebuttal.

"Esteemed judges," she said. "I'd like to note that my opponent cannot with any sense of true fairness posit a case in which only men deserve life, liberty, or the pursuit of happiness in society," she began. "Further, his criterion of equality makes what could be an honest mistake into something nearly farcical. Who is due equality? By his words, 'good men.' So let's talk about some of these good men, and what they've done, and who has suffered the most because of them . . ."

Blanton turned bright red. Two out of three judges nodded and started writing furiously on their ballots.

I decided to live-tweet the whole thing, for a record of how awesome she was. I hoped she wouldn't be mad.

Taggart Strong · @TaggartStrong · 40 m
If @BodieBlants can't establish that resolution would be upheld fairly for all, which is the definition of his value prop, judges must vote neg, says @DebatrGrl #BirminghamPublicTourney
💬 10 ↻ 4 ♡ 22

Taggart Strong · @TaggartStrong · 35 m
Why good men? What about women and nonbinary ppl? What about the victims of these so-called good men? @BodieBlants case is inherently anti-equality and also deeply harmful, says @DebatrGrl #BirminghamPublicTourney
💬 7 ↻ 3 ♡ 19

Taggart Strong · @TaggartStrong · 32 m
Who has option of seeking the right to be forgotten? Can this be distributed equally thru soc or does it rely on privilege? asks @DebatrGrl.
💬 4 ↻ 3 ♡ 15

Taggart Strong · @TaggartStrong · 32 m
Privilege shld b given to those who do the work, says @BodieBlants. Once work is done, harm should b removed. @DebatrGrl asks "what work? who gets to do it? how is that fair? And isn't fairness req for equality?" #BirminghamPublicTourney
💬 3 ↻ 6 ♡ 11

Taggart Strong · @TaggartStrong · 22 m
How is losing your job or security or home or reputation fair? asks @BodieBlants. Says "the means cannot justify this ends." #BirminghamPublicTourney
💬 9 ↻ 3 ♡ 5

In the end, the judges declared Millie the winner. Blanton Bodie
stomped off the stage. He passed me, mumbling something that
sounded a lot like "supply closet slut," though maybe he was saying "my eye is so shut." Millie stood there a little dazed, almost like
she was looking for someone—*me?*—but Angela Tennant rushed
over first. I followed. "I want to see you at Winners'," she was telling Millie. "You deserve to be there. Stay in touch—we'll make
it work. Here's my card." And then she looked over at me. "Hey,
weren't you the kid who had that great Twitter thread about gun
control?" she asked me.

I couldn't believe she'd read it, or even knew who I was. "You
saw that?"

"I follow all the debate tournament hashtags," she said. "Bring
some of that to your next tournament."

"The resolution isn't about gun control, though?" I was confused.

"The passion. The rhetoric. That's how you do it." She waved at
the room. "Tell us what matters to you, and why it needs to matter
to us, too."

"I'm trying to do that more," I said. "I just tweeted Millie's
debate."

Millie looked at me sharply, and for a second, my stomach sank. But Angela Tennant nodded.

"I like that," she said. "The voices we amplify can be even more important than our own."

Millie smiled at me, and Angela Tennant waved us out. "Go ahead, the awards ceremony will be starting soon," she said. "I need to get myself a cup of coffee. Millicent . . . I'll see you again. In the meantime, stay strong."

Millie grinned. "I will."

Taggart Strong · @TaggartStrong · 3 m
Woot! @DebatrGrl wins against @BodieBlants 🔥 🔥 🔥 😈😈😈 at
#BirminghamPublicTourney!
💬 3   🔁 5   ♡ 23

MILLIE

Coach Kargle opened the passenger door to his pickup and helped me in, no easy feat considering the giant silver Alabama-shaped trophy I'd just been awarded.

"Nice going, Millie!" he said.

You know what else was nice? Taggart Strong. He'd made me a croque monsieur for breakfast that morning. Who did that? Also, it was *good*.

Coach Kargle shut the passenger door and made his way around the truck to the driver's side, getting in and fastening his seat belt before he put the keys in the ignition. "Got everything?" he asked.

I felt my briefcase pocket for my phone, and it vibrated.

"Yep," I said, pulling it out.

There was a text from Tag.

Hey, it said, with a bubble indicating more on the way. I felt my mouth form a smile. And I waited.

The bubble disappeared, then started up again. Then disappeared. Then started again.

Sorry, he wrote. **Rajesh keeps looking over the bus seat to see what I'm doing. I swear, the guy has some sort of radar.**

Ha ha, I wrote, and then felt totally stupid for writing *ha ha*.

I know, right? he wrote. **Anyway. Thank you for letting me follow you around all tournament. Now I'm more scared to debate you than ever.**

Ha ha, I wrote again, cursing myself as I did it.

Seriously. You're pretty amazing.

I put a bunch of blushing emojis in a row and felt a little better. Pictures were easier than words sometimes.

The bubble started and stopped again.

Coach looked over at me curiously. "Your mom sure is texting a lot," he said.

"It's not my mom," I said.

"Carlos?"

"Tag Strong."

"Huh," said Coach, and stroked his chin. I couldn't read his reaction.

The text came through.

Wanna hang again soon? Pizza + library???

"So what's going on there?" asked Coach, his eyes on the road, trying to prove he hadn't been snooping. "Anything I need to know?"

"Well," I said.

"You two were pretty inseparable all tournament," he noted.

"That's because he was shadowing me."

We stopped at a stoplight, and he looked over at me, shaking his head. "There's more," he said. "I'm not a total old fogy. But you seem happy. I like that."

"Me too," I told him.

"Now, I do feel like I have to say this, as your coach: You've put a lot of yourself into debate these past few years. And you're lining up all the right stuff to come in as winner for state. Fourth year in a row! That's incredible. You've even got the Martha Linger Scholarship on the table! So, whatever's happening . . . just be careful."

"I know," I said. "Don't tell my mom, okay? Tag and I, we're just working together. Bouncing some ideas off each other, you know? Like I do with Carlos . . . but she wouldn't get it. Her mantra is 'No boys! They'll destroy your focus and lead you to ruin.'"

"I won't say anything," he said, smiling at me. "But I suspect it's not like with Carlos."

"Okay, it's not *exactly* the same." I smiled back. I couldn't help it.

"*Heartache* will destroy your focus," he said. "That I know. And sometimes it just happens, when you least expect it, and there was nothing anyone could do about it."

Now I wondered if he was talking about himself.

"When it comes down to it, the heart wants what it wants—or else it does not care,"[44] he said.

"Emily Dickinson!" I said.

"It's the one quote I remember from high school English," he said. "Not to mention a Selena Gomez song."

"You're kind of destroying your old fogy cred," I told him.

He smiled again and looked at me. "Millie, it's easy enough to make good decisions when you know exactly what you want. Where it gets confusing is when the things you care about seem to take you in different directions. And that's pretty much inevitable. It's part of growing up."

I nodded. "My heart wants to win. But it wants other things, too."

The light turned green.

He turned back to the road. "And you should have all those things. Trust yourself. You're on the right path. I know it."

---

44 From a letter Emily Dickinson wrote to her friend Mary Bowles, consoling her after her husband's departure to Europe. She went on to say, "We won't break. We look very small—but the Reed can carry the weight."

Mom came outside when she saw us walking up the driveway. She grabbed my trophy from Coach Kargle, who'd kindly offered to carry it inside, and gave a big "Wahoo!" announcing my victory to everyone in the neighborhood. "My daughter, champion of the worldddd!" she sang, dancing along to her own rhythm. Beau, trapped behind the screen door, whined to be let out.

"Hey, Kenny," said Mom.

"Hey, Molly," he said, and smiled. "Your girl did mighty fine, as always."

"Thanks, as usual, for all your help," said Mom, smiling back at him.

Beau whined again.

"Okay, okay, y'all," I said, pushing my way in. "I'm starving. And poor baby dog wants attention!" I crouched on the floor to hug him, and he leaned into me, whining with happiness.

Mom followed me in. "'Bye, Kenny," she yelled.

"'Bye, Molly," he said. "See you Monday, Millie!"

"Later, Coach!"

"Let's celebrate!" said my mom, pouring each of us a sparkling apple cider, our celebration beverage of choice. "It's my night off, and it's another win for you! What movie do you want to watch? Or we can just gaze at this beauty." She put the trophy next to the box of pizza on the coffee table.

"You're hilarious," I said.

"Do you want to do the honors and add it to the trophy room?" she asked.

We may only have a two-bedroom house with a yard the size of a postage stamp (it's fenced in for Beau, which makes it seem even smaller, not that he complains), but we do have a trophy room.

It's actually a modified closet. Freshman year, I started having a problem with trophies. They were all huge, and I was winning so many of them, and I know this seems like I'm playing the world's smallest violin here, but there wasn't enough space in my room or in the living room, and who wants to look at debate trophies all the time, even if your name is on them? The school didn't want them. The storage cases are for the "big things" that are "important to the school, and school spirit," aka the guys' sports teams. I called a few places to see if anyone would accept donations, and I found this pawnshop that would take them off my hands and resell them to strangers (who in the world wants someone else's old debate trophy?), but then I felt kind of sad giving them away. They were proof of this thing I worked really hard at.

Mom had the brilliant idea of turning our hallway closet into a trophy room. We painted the room purple, "the color of royalty," and outfitted it with rows of shelves on all sides, and now I line the trophies up, one after the other, the ones that are goblets and the ones shaped like states and the ones that are silver platters and the ones that are keys and the ones that are medals and the ones that look like tiny Oscars. The latest I always display front and center, a reminder to go for the next one.

After doing the honors, I returned to the couch and grabbed a slice. Beau gazed at me, hopeful.

"What should we watch?" I asked. "Something romantic and funny this time?" My mom was way into thrillers. I was not.

She grabbed her own pizza and took a bite. "Nick's never disappoints. I guess I can compromise and do light romance for one night. Hey, what about this: A group of teen girls vow to defeat a male bully, but the tables are turned when he confesses he's in love with one of them?"

"No bullies!" I said. For a second, I thought of Culhane, but as quick as I could, I pictured Tag instead.

"I got it!" said my mom. "Two fiercely competitive high school debaters have to cocaptain a team and start to fall for each other. Hmmm? But don't get any ideas. We need to keep our eyes focused on that prize: The Martha Linger Scholarship!"

"Yep," I said. "Eyes on the prize."

TAG

The morning after Millie won at Birmingham Public was a Sunday. I woke up with Orion kneading dough on my chest and purring. I glanced at my clock: Slept till almost noon again—how had that happened? He meowed at me and kept working on my chest. "Okay, okay, I'll get up," I told him, and he batted my face. He followed me downstairs. "Has anyone fed you yet?" I asked him, and he twined in and out of my legs, purring some more. I poured him some cat food and myself some coffee, and sat down at the kitchen table.

I'd only had a sip before Mason came barreling in, carrying a laptop. "Have you seen it?" she yelled.

I almost spilled my coffee down my T-shirt. "What?" I asked.

"Someone posted a YouTube video of Millie's final round," she said, putting the computer in front of me. "But they dubbed over it. It's . . . pretty gross." She pressed play. There was this high-pitched voice, like a guy pretending to talk like a girl, saying the most obscene stuff and . . .

"Stop it!" I said, closing the laptop. "No more."

"Yeah," said Mason. "It's awful."

"Also, not even true. I live-tweeted that debate! She said no such things, and I have proof!"

"I don't think whoever posted this cares," she said, opening up the laptop again and stopping the video. "It's already got a bunch of thumbs-ups. And the comments, they're awful."

"Where are Mom and Dad?" I asked her.

"They went to that hospital fundraiser," Mason said. "They'll be there all day."

I grabbed my phone and called Millie.

She answered right away. "Hey, Tag."

Mason watched me.

"Have you been online today?" I asked.

"Not really," Millie said. "I was reading. Should I be?"

"No," I said. "What you should do . . . if you want to . . . is drive to my house. I need to show you something important."

"Your house? What are you talking about?"

"I'll send you my address. Actually, I can't believe you've never been here. We need to fix that."

"Tag, I don't have a car. My mom has ours, and she's at work."

"Oh. Then . . . what if I come to you? Hector's been aching to take to the road."

"What's going on? You're making me nervous."

"Just stay offline until I can get there, okay? It has to do with Edmund Culhane and the Cheater's Lake assholes."

"Oh God," said Millie. "Please just tell me what it is. I can't sit here and wonder—it will drive me insane. Is it the Millicent Calmerzzz account?"

"It's not Twitter. It's a YouTube video." I glanced down at the computer again. "Someone filmed you in the final debate, but they dubbed over your voice saying a bunch of things you didn't say. About blow jobs and . . . well, you can imagine."

When she spoke, it was brusque. "Text me the link, and I'll send it to Coach Kargle and get it taken down," she said. "He's dealt with things like this before."

"Promise me you won't actually watch it," I said.

"I promise," she said, but I didn't believe her.

"I can still come over," I offered. "If you want company."

"I'm not really up for a coaching session, to be honest." She sounded mad. Sad and mad.

"It might be good for you to have company?"

"Really, you want to make a forty-five-minute drive to come hold my hand during my moment of harassment from a bunch of prep-school bullies who will probably go on to become Supreme Court justices? Why bother, Tag? This keeps happening; it's always going to happen. Just do your own life—don't worry about mine." She was definitely mad. But not at me, I didn't think.

"I like driving," I said.

"You want to come hang out with me because . . . you like driving?" She sounded incredulous. "I don't know if I should be offended or not."

"I actually do like driving!" I said. "And I have nothing else to do today. And *Licensed to Ill* is forty-four minutes exactly, and I can listen to that on the way . . ."

"What a compliment," she said.

"Allow me to rephrase that. I would really like to see you and offer whatever support I can, or just help take your mind off things." I was rapidly googling as we spoke, trying to find something that might entice her. "We could go to a movie! Or hit up a rock-climbing facility. Or, um, go to the Sonic Drive-In in Cullman. They have slushies made with Red Bull now!"

She laughed. "That sounds horrible!"

"What about fried pickles? Please tell me you like fried pickles."

"Tag."

"No?" My heart sank.

"I don't like fried pickles. I love them."

And it lifted right back up. "Good. I'll see you in an hour. Text me your address."

"Ugh! Fine." At least she was laughing again.

I hung up. "You're going to see Millicent Chalmers? Can I come?" Mason asked.

"Not this time," I told her.

She looked disappointed, but she nodded. "I get it. Are y'all dating?"

"No," I said.

"Are you sure? The Sonic Drive-In sounds like a date!"

"Stop snooping on my phone calls!" I said. But she looked so disappointed, I felt bad. "We're just friends hanging out. She needs a friend. After that video . . ."

Mason sighed. "Why are some boys so awful? Am I going to have to deal with those kinds of boys when I'm a debater, too?"

"Jesus," I said. "I hate thinking about that."

"What should I do if it happens?" she asked me.

"You should scream and yell and never let anyone make you feel like you're not as good as they are," I said. "You should know that you're better than people like that from the start. That's why you should do debate. So you know exactly what to say, and you can say it loud enough for everyone to hear you, and listen."

"On it," said Mason. "I'm already looking at debate camps. Just have to convince Mom and Dad to send me. They think I might be too young."

"You're, like, more mature than I am sometimes," I told her.

She gazed at me. "Girls mature faster. We just don't get credit for it."

"Damn," I said.

She smiled at me. "You like her, don't you?"

"Yes," I said.

"You have to tell me everything when you get home!"

Within ten minutes, I had fresh-brushed teeth and a clean T-shirt on and was on my way to Millicent Chalmers's house.

She lived in a neighborhood of unassuming one-story houses. Hers was painted a really pretty blue. When she opened the door and met me on her front porch, her face was so stricken I wanted to give her a hug. Instead, I just stood there awkwardly, my arms at my sides, because uninvited hugs are sort of the worst, and she was already dealing with a bunch of uninvited stuff.

She was wearing this sweatshirt with cats all over it.

"For some reason, I thought you were a dog person, not a cat person," I said.

She looked down at her shirt. "I think you can be both. I also like hamsters. It's so cute how they hold things in their cheeks. But cats have such *attitude*."

"You have to meet Orion," I said. "He's the sassiest cat there is. If you read his tweets, you'd know."

She gave me a half smile.

"You watched the video, didn't you?" I asked.

"It was worse than I thought," she admitted, nodding.

"I told you not to," I said.

"I know, but information is power!" she said. "Now at least I know. And they could really hurt my reputation. There are codes of conduct with debate, and it seems like girls are always getting called out for stuff when boys aren't. Another completely unfair reality." She sighed.

"Did you talk to Kargle?"

She nodded. "He's on it."

Something started barking furiously, and I jumped.

"That's just Beau," she said. "You were right. I *am* a dog person. And he just woke up from a nap. Want to come in and meet him? His bark is much bigger than his actual bite."

"Actual bite?" I asked, and she laughed. "Don't worry, he's a total sweetheart."

She opened the door, and I followed her inside, hoping she was right.

MILLIE

On the Sunday that Tag offered to come over, I'd been reading the Mary Wollstonecraft book that Mrs. Mendez recommended. Wollstonecraft was British and lived in the mid-to-late 1700s, a time when women couldn't vote and getting married meant you were basically the property of your husband (if you got divorced, he'd get custody of your kids, no questions asked). She'd had a couple of love affairs with men who appeared to be Victorian England's version of fuckbois, and two illegitimate[45] children. Society tried to shame her for not being the sort of woman she was "supposed" to be. The world claimed that women were too fragile and emotional to think clearly, but she kept arguing that women could reason just as well as men could, and deserved the same rights and education.

I was papering the book with Post-its. (I love Post-its.) Wollstonecraft was still old-school in some ways—after all, she was of her time—but there were a ton of amazing quotes, like: "I do not wish [women] to have power over men; but over themselves" and "It is far better to be often deceived than never to trust; to be disappointed in love, than never to love."

Then Tag called.

Honestly, I wasn't all that surprised that the Chatham's Lake guys had launched a gross counterattack. When women do stuff guys in power don't like, when girls step out of their "acceptable"

---

45 Why do we call kids whose parents aren't married *illegitimate* when they're as legitimately children as anyone?

role, they get slammed for it. That's how misogyny works. It happened to Mary Wollstonecraft, and it was happening to me.

Sexism had been going on for so long, you'd think we'd be used to it by now. But I never got used to how much it hurt. Part of me always thought, if I won enough, maybe the hurt would go away. That hadn't happened yet, though.

☺

I was nervous about him seeing where I lived, in our little house in a nothing neighborhood best known for being close to a Qwik Mart, but when I opened the door, I immediately felt better. I let him inside and introduced him to Beau, who stopped barking and tried to lick his entire face, and then Tag rolled around on the floor with him wrestling and Beau was totally in love, and I think Tag was, too. At one point, he looked up at me breathlessly while Beau slobbered and head-butted him for more pets. "Is this okay?" Tag asked. "I came to see you, not him. But I really do love dogs. And cats. And maybe even hamsters. But, um, I love humans, too. Not, obviously, in the same way."

My heart melted like a croque monsieur.

Tag didn't act weird about the size of my house, but he did freak out a little when he saw my trophy room.

"Holy crap," he said. "You've won all of these? I mean, of course you have."

We were in there together, this tiny closet, with our shoulders touching. I thought about grabbing him and kissing him then—I could picture it, almost, and wouldn't *that* take my mind off everything else?—but I held back. I thought about what my mom would say, about the agreement we'd made: *No boys. Don't get involved with something, or someone, that's going to derail you now. Stay focused. Eyes on the prize.*

And who knew if Tag even wanted that. If he wanted *me*. Maybe he really did just want to figure out his way to win, to get his parents and principal and Rajesh off his back, and to be nice to someone who was having a bad day.

But also: What did *I* want?

Tag picked up a trophy featuring a lady in a dress, her hand gesturing in the air. "Great likeness," he said.

"That was from the Alabama Women's Tournament last year," I said. "Most of the time, if a trophy has a person on it, it's a dude." I pointed to a few.

"I've been wondering, how'd Kargle get to be your coach?" asked Tag. "He looks like he'd be more at home with the men's wrestling team."

I laughed. "He's actually the assistant football coach. I had to get a sponsor for tournaments. I asked the history teacher, the AP government teacher, even the vice principal of the school, and they all said they were too busy. My mom and Kargle are friends, or at least, they used to be, and she suggested I ask him." I shrugged. "He's the only one who said yes. He always gets to his football games late now, but he says he doesn't mind."

"Wow," said Tag, but I didn't know if he was responding to my story or the trophy he was now inspecting, a glitter-laden star concoction from a tournament hosted at Dollywood.

"This is . . ."

"Basically, beautiful," I finished for him.

"I was going to say genuinely gorgeous," he said. "Or fantastically fab. Enigmatically elegant."

"Questionably quirky," I said. "It's all of that and more."

"That's cool about Kargle, though."

"He's actually a pretty great coach," I said. "He may not know every single obscure philosopher out there, but that's easy for me to figure out, especially with Mrs. Mendez's help. I've caught him watching debate videos online, thinking about techniques and arguments I could use. He even talked to the school about putting some of my trophies on display, but apparently there's no room for stuff like that, even though they keep lining the halls with more display cases for the sports teams."

"He has your back," said Tag. "I like that. Francine is like that, too."

"She seems awesome."

"She was a debate star, too, way back when. She's tough but fair, and she just wants us all to figure out what we really want. I don't think she even cares so much if we win; it's about what we learn, and how we get better at conveying ourselves to other people. Rajesh, on the other hand, just wants us to win."

"He seems . . . intense. He's a good debater, though."

Tag sighed. "He used to be my best friend. Now I think he hates me, because of how I started debating last year. And my friendship—can we call this a friendship, officially?" He pointed at me and then back at himself, and I nodded.

"You're at my house and I'm showing you my trophies and my dog hasn't bitten you yet, so sure."

"Yet?!" He opened his eyes wide.

I giggled. "Beau would rather bite a sandwich."

"Next time I'll bring one for him," Tag said. "As for Rajesh, I don't think our friendship—thank you—is helping matters. I think he's jealous."

"Of how we were temporarily stuck in a closet together, scared out of our minds?" I cocked my head, thinking of the possible options. "Or of how you get to be friends with a girl who gets you disqualified from a tournament when you try to stand up for her?"

"You don't feel bad about that, do you?"

"Only a little bit. Because I think you were gonna do really well at that tournament!"

"Well, apparently what I did set in motion other things, too. Which you wouldn't have to be dealing with now if I hadn't. Do you want to talk about . . ." He gestured to the living room, where my computer waited.

I didn't. "Tell me more about Rajesh."

Tag picked up another trophy, looking at it thoughtfully. "He's always been smart and great at school. But he used to be fun, too. Now it feels like his only goal is winning debate and getting into Harvard."

"Maybe he thinks you were arguing badly on purpose, to be funny, or that you think you don't have to follow the rules everyone else does?" I asked. "That can piss people off."

"Is that what you thought?"

"Kinda," I said. "At first."

"But not now?"

"Now I know you." Again, we were so close. All I had to do was lean in. But I stopped myself. "Not that I really know you. But I know you more."

"You know me a lot," he said, and he put down the trophy and took my hand. "Is this okay?"

"Yeah," I said, though I could barely get a word out. I forced myself to think past the hand that was holding mine, and how it made me feel. *Focus, Millie! What were we talking about? Rajesh.* "There's so much pressure. To get into a good school so you can meet the right people and get a good job and have a good life. It all piles up, and it can feel like you don't have that many chances, that you only have one shot. It's not all Rajesh's fault. Parents can be really intense, too."

"Like your mom?" Tag asked.

I nodded. "She really just wants what's best for me." I thought about the Martha Linger Scholarship, and about Mary Wollstone-craft. Education. Opportunities. My future.

But there was also my present, right here and now.

Tag put my hand down gently and picked up a trophy shaped like a football. I let out my breath as quietly as I could.

"Did the quarterback go home with a gavel?" he asked.

I shrugged. "Things get weird in trophy world. Anyway, if you're spending this much time thinking about Rajesh, maybe you should talk to him. We've only got so much high school left. It seems like you should have a best friend around for that."

Tag looked skeptical. "He's being such a dickhead, though."

My phone pinged. I looked to see if it was Coach Kargle updating me, but instead it was Carlos, who I'd texted after Tag called earlier. He'd sent me a series of heart emojis, along with a GIF of a kitten dangling from a tree that said HANG IN THERE. And then an all-caps message: **HOW IS IT GOING W TAGATHEE CHALA-CUTE?!**😘

Tag watched as I texted back a string of prayer hand emojis, indicating *I'm trying*, and then a **CALM DOWN WE'RE JUST FRIENDS.** "It's not Kargle, it's just Carlos," I told him.

"How did y'all get to be so tight?"

"We met at debate camp ages ago," I said. "I liked him from the start. He's all the way down in Mobile, so we really only see each other at tournaments and camp, but we talk all the time."

"I know he's not your boyfriend, but did you ever have, like . . .

a thing?" Tag was staring intently at the medal attached to a ribbon he was now holding. I'd won it freshman year.

"No. Carlos and I are not right for each other romantically for any number of reasons, one of which is that he likes boys, not girls. And I am a girl. If you hadn't noticed."

"Ohhhhhhhhh," said Tag. He slapped himself on the forehead. "Oh. God, I'm an idiot."

"Carlos does think one of the guys on your team is hot," I said. "Ricky? I'm not just gossiping—he told me to tell you that when I said you were coming over. Is Ricky single? he wanted to know."

"You told him I was coming over?" Tag's lips turned up at the corners. I tried to stop staring at them. "What did he say to that?"

"What I just told you."

"Ricky is single," said Tag, and we both grinned at each other.

"No offense to your trophy room, but want to do something else?" he asked, carefully putting the medal back down in its proper place. "Show me what Millicent Chalmers does when she's not debating, or talking about debate or people who debate. That might take your mind off things."

"Want to see my college room?" I asked, laughing.

"You mean the room we walked through that looks like the *Law & Order* detectives are investigating a cold case about Yale?"

"It's a lot," I said. "I admit it."

"How about something outside the house?" he suggested.

"You've seen about all there is around here. It's not like Birmingham."

"Yeah, yeah, the big city," he said. "Woo-hoo. You should see our airport."

"We have the library. Nick's. A couple of bars, some takeout places, three restaurants, a diner, a Laundromat . . ."

"Show me again!" he said. He was so enthusiastic I couldn't help smiling.

"I do really like the library," I told him. "It's where I coached this guy, once . . ."

"All roads lead to debate," he said.

"You don't get good unless you practice. But you know what's really amazing? If you do practice, there's a pretty decent chance you get good."

"I see that," he said. "Now, shall we?" He put out his elbow the way he had before, inviting me to crook my arm through it, and I did. My stomach growled. I hadn't had lunch yet. "Are you hungry?"

"I could eat," he said.

TAG

After we drove around for a while talking and then stopped for pizza at Nick's, we really did go to the library. But we weren't working on debate this time. She took me by the hand and gave me a proper tour.

"There's lots of stuff you've never seen in here," she said. "Like, right here is my favorite carrel." She pointed to an area of the library that had sectioned-off desks with high walls, for privacy. "Last year the librarians started joking that they'd inscribe my name in it if I won state again, and look, they went ahead and did it!" She pointed to a little plaque that bore her name.

"So, seriously: What's the *M* for?" I asked. "What if I guess? Marvelous. Magnificent. Monounsaturated."

"Yes, the last one."

"No, but really. Molly? It would be embarrassing if your name was Millie Molly Chalmers. I could see how you might not want to share that."

"No, but Molly *is* my mom's name."

"Martha? Like the scholarship lady?"

"Why is everyone so obsessed with my middle name?" she asked, exasperated.

"Well, partly it's because you have that initial hanging out there. It's like a tease."

She frowned. "Don't even go there."

"I'm not calling *you* a tease. It's just tantalizing. A single initial.

A mystery. It leads to questions. People can't help it! Oooh, is it Mystery?"

"No!" She laughed. "What's *your* middle name?"

"It's Cornell, which is actually my mom's maiden name. No relation to the college. See, easy. Now tell me yours."

She shook her head. "No matter how much I might like you, I'm not telling. I have to have some things that I get to keep for just me, you know."

"You like me?"

"Shhh," she said, and pulled me over to the philosophy section. We were standing between Kant, who, I remembered from Francine, argued that philosophy aims at answering three questions: "What can I know? What should I do? What may I hope?", and Kierkegaard, the father of existentialism, a theory that posited that people are free agents who have control over their choices, when things got serious.

"Tag. I have to tell you something."

"Is it about how much you like me?" I asked.

"Well. Sort of."

"I'm listening." Suddenly I got a bad feeling. "Did something else happen with those guys? With Culhane? The Cheater's Lake jerks?"

"No," she said. "This is something else."

"Do you want to sit down?" I asked. I took her hand and led her to a couple of chairs in a quiet corner. We sat, looking at each other. "What is it?" I asked. She didn't seem to want to let go of my hand.

"My mom and I have an agreement," she whispered. "Senior year, no boys, no romance; I need to focus on debate and college and scholarships. No distractions. I can't risk it. I could lose everything I've worked so hard for. My mom doesn't even want me helping you, honestly. So while I really do like you . . ."

"Ah," I said. "But . . ."

"But," she said. "That's the thing." She leaned toward me. "Maybe, when it comes down to it, I don't care about my mom's rule. I want what I want."

"Did you know that when people are in a traumatic event together, there's something called trauma bonding? It makes them feel closer right away," I said.

She looked at me. "Do you think that happened to us? The shooter scare?"

"I do. But I think it's more than that, too."

I don't know who kissed who. Maybe it happened simultaneously, both of us close enough together that our lips were just meant to touch, each of us moving infinitesimally so they would. I do know that it lasted for longer than I thought it might, but still not as long as I'd hoped. I'd kissed girls before, but this time was different. I could feel a rushing in my ears, like a wave cresting on the ocean, like a rocket taking off, like the hot, hot heat of my blood pumping inside my human body. I wanted it to keep going as long as possible. Then someone walked near us and coughed. We jumped at the noise, looking at each other. Millie was blushing.

"Mrs. Mendez," she said.

"Hey," I added.

"Whoops," said the librarian, who was also blushing. "I seem to have taken a wrong turn." She slipped out of the stacks and was gone.

Millie turned back to me, her face still red. "Oh God. That wasn't embarrassing or anything."

"Before we invoke religion, can we go back to something for a minute?" I asked her. I leaned forward, and I kissed her again.

She pulled away again. "I like you a lot," she said. "Too much."

"Me too! I like you, I mean. Not that I like me. I mean, I do like me, when I'm with you." *Words, don't fail me now*, I told myself. "And it's not too much. How could it be too much? I think it's exactly the right amount."

She looked down at her hands. "I just don't know if we should do this."

"Why not?" I asked, a knot in my stomach starting to form. "You mean, because of debate, and what your mom said?"

"Because of debate and . . . everything. Because my reputation is more at stake than yours will ever be. I'm a girl. I need to win a scholarship, and for that, I need to win debate. You go to a private school, and your parents have money, and you've never even thought about not being able to afford college, if you even decide you want to go."

"I have thought a lot about the rising costs of student debt and . . ."

"Theoretically, you have. Like you could debate about it. You're not truly worried for yourself. There will always be money for you to do what you want to do."

"That's true, I guess," I admitted. "But it's true for you, too. With how hard you work, you know you'll be rewarded . . ."

She shook her head. "It's not the same."

"I don't understand," I said. "We're all humans. We have choices. It's like Kierkegaard said, we can make decisions. We have free will."

"Sure, I have free will. But my options are different from yours. You're like a triple threat in privilege: boy, white, has money. So whatever they try to throw at you, you can fight, and, honestly, they're not gonna try to throw that much at you anyway, *because* you're white and a boy and you have money. Don't you see how it's different? If they spread a rumor about how you had sex with another debater in a supply closet, your reputation goes up! But mine plummets. It's a total double standard. Look at all the women who say 'MeToo' and what happens to them next. They have to go through hell just to support themselves in a fight that wasn't anything they wanted to be doing in the first place, and even when a guy does get reprimanded, there's never any real payback for what *the women* lost. Mary Wollstonecraft was right. It's all bullshit. It's been bullshit for *centuries*. Remember Blanton Bodie's argument from the last debate? You're destroying those poor men's lives by keeping up an internet history that shows they destroyed other lives! How is that fair when they were the life-ruiners of someone else in the first place?"

I nodded. While she was right, I'm ashamed to say that part of me just wanted to get back to kissing. "But listen, you're Millicent M. Chalmers. You have a plaque in this library with your name on it! Looks at how much you've done already. You're a role model. And a really great debater."

"And what does that give me in the end?" she asked. "Tag, I don't know. Unless I win state and get that scholarship, is any of it worth it? Even after that: I can never let up. I can never stop working so hard, because what if I lose everything?"

"You won't; I won't let you," I said. I pulled her closer.

She shook her head. Was she telling me no? The knot in my stomach grew spiky and painful. But as much as it hurt, I had to listen. I had to be ready to walk away, to give her what she needed. That was important.

"But in the end, what Emily Dickinson said is true, too," she said.

"Emily Dickinson?"

I didn't have a chance to ask what she meant because she was kissing me again.

Later that night, when I pulled up into my driveway, I knew one thing for sure. I didn't just like Millicent Chalmers, I *really liked* Millicent Chalmers. I thought about what I would tell Mason, and what I would keep to myself. There was a lot I wanted to keep to myself, to just sit with in my room where no one could see my goofy grin and think about for a while.

But there was a surprise waiting for me: Rajesh's Corolla was parked in my spot. I pulled in behind him and walked into the house to find my former friend at the kitchen table with my family, just like it was the old days and we were alternating between our houses for dinner. Except no one was eating. He had a handful of Nationals pamphlets in his hand, and a clipboard that said DONATIONS at the top sat on the table in front of him.

The nerve of him coming to my house like everything was normal! But then I thought about what Millie had said. I could try.

"Hey," I said. "It's been a while."

"Hi, Tag," he answered flatly. This wasn't going to be easy.

"Hi, honey," said my mom.

My dad nodded his hello, and Mason tried to signal me without my parents noticing.

"Long day waiting at the car repair shop, huh?" asked Dad. "Mason told us. Did they have the part you needed?"

I gave Mason the teeniest wink. "They had to get it from a specialty store in Huntsville, since it's a discontinued item, but they finally fixed it," I said. "Hours after they told me it would be ready."

"We can see that," said my mom, glancing at her watch. "We waited for you for dinner. Rajesh, would you like to join us? It's country-fried steak night!"

"Oh, no, ma'am," said Rajesh, pointing at his pamphlets. "My parents expect me home soon. I just wanted to come and talk about fundraising for Nationals. It looks like a few of us on the team have a chance. If you and Mr. Strong would like to make a donation, we'd be so grateful."

"Yes, of course," said my mom, digging through her purse for her checkbook. "How's five hundred dollars?"

Rajesh smiled. "That's awesome!"

"Maybe it will also be the incentive Tag needs to get there himself," said my dad, clapping me on the back.

"I'm doing a lot better," I muttered.

"Oh, Tag's got plenty of incentive already," murmured Rajesh.

"What's that?" asked my mom.

"Can I have one of these brochures?" Mason interrupted. "I want to put it in my debate scrapbook."

"Mason," said my mom. "Those are for parents and donators."

"You have a debate scrapbook?" Rajesh asked. "You're not even on the team."

She looked at us, disgusted. "I want to be the next Millicent Chalmers."

Rajesh started laughing. "No, you don't."

"Yes, I do," she insisted. "Why wouldn't I? She's awesome." Mason stood tall with her hands on her hips, and for a second she reminded me of Millie.

Rajesh leaned toward her as if he was making a confession. "Mason, you're too young to understand all this, but let's just say that Millicent Chalmers is not a very nice girl. And there's plenty of proof of that online, if you want to go there."

I stood up. Rajesh didn't want or need my friendship, and Millie did. I thought about how I had the privilege and resources to protect me while she was out there fighting for herself all the time. "That is absolutely not true," I said. "That video is a lie; she never said that stuff, and you know it! You were there! Why would you believe that crap about her?"

"I saw the video," said Mason. "I wasn't there, but I don't believe it, either. The quality is pretty bad, for one. You can tell it's all dubbed. And it isn't even what she said. Tag has a record of that on his Twitter. When he live-tweeted the final with Blanton Bodie . . ."

My parents watched us, confused. "What are y'all talking about?" asked my mom. "Some video?"

"Must be one of their memes," said my dad.

"Rajesh," I hissed as soon as he had my mom's check in hand. "Let me walk you to your car. Now."

He was already getting his stuff together. "I have to leave anyway," he said. "Thank you again, Mr. and Mrs. Strong. The team"—he glared at me—"very much appreciates your generosity."

Outside, we stood and stared at each other at the top of the driveway. He had taken his power stance.

"You're going to have to move Hector for me to get out," he finally said.

"I'm aware of that," I told him. "But first I want to know, Are you the person behind that video of Millie?"

There was this look in his eye, and I'm not sure I recognized my old friend. "Do you really think I'd do something like that?"

"I actually kind of do," I said. "You've always been ambitious, but you've never been like this."

"Like *what*?" he asked. "Tell me, please." It was a challenge.

"So pathetically focused on success that you forget about the people you've known your whole life. So obsessed with getting into Harvard that you'd destroy someone else's reputation for it. It's not going to work, Rajesh. All you've managed is to bring yourself to a new low. Harvard's not going to want someone who'd do this! Good luck getting into a crap university." I spat my words out.

"You think you're so goddamn smart," said Rajesh, stomping his foot on the ground. "You think you can break the rules . . . actually, you think the rules don't apply to you in the first place. You mess around, pulling down our team ranking, and you use debate as an opportunity to consort with the enemy! What the hell were you doing letting them disqualify you so you could follow Millicent Chalmers around all day and 'learn' from her? What did you 'learn'? If anyone's an embarrassing loser, it's you. You might as well wear a T-shirt that says EMBARRASSING LOSER. You probably have one of those already, don't you?"

I shook my head. "I have a shirt that says THIS IS AN EMBARRASSING MOMENT, but that's an entirely different matter. Rajesh. I just don't get it."

"You don't get what?"

"Why do you hate me so much? It's not like I'm actively hurting you."

"Are you sure about that? If I don't get into Harvard, some of that is on you."

I shook my head. "I don't think that's how it works—"

"Move your car." He'd taken out his keys. "I'm late for dinner."

"Fine." I got into Hector and pulled him out of the driveway and waited for Rajesh to get in his own car and leave. For someone who was late, he sure took his sweet time. I could see Mason in the doorway, watching.

"Do you really think he did it?" she asked when I got inside. "That just doesn't seem like him. I mean, yeah, he'd hustle to get to Nationals, and he really might lie, cheat, and steal to go to Harvard, but he's not an evil misogynist."

"I don't know," I said. "I don't think I know him at all anymore. I'm not sure I ever did."

"What's so great about Harvard, anyway?" Mason asked. "It's too far away, for one. And cold."

"Yeah, not my scene, that's for sure," I said. "A bunch of stuffy Ivy Leaguers."

"They probably all wear cardigans," Mason said, laughing.

"And pocket protectors."

"There are some cute ones now," she said. "I saw them on Etsy."

"Rajesh better not have ruined my appetite," I said.

"Nooooooo. We only get country-fried steak night twice a year!" she said.

"Let's go get some, then," I said. "Also, great thinking about the car repair shop! I appreciate that."

"How was Millicent?" she asked.

"Good," I said, smiling.

"Yay!" she said. "I have something I want you to do for me now."

"What's that?"

"I have a presentation to give to Mom and Dad."

"A presentation?"

"You have my back, right?" she asked.

"Always."

"Go tell them to sit on the couch and wait, and I'll be right there," she instructed me. "Get them drinks. Make conversation."

We were all waiting on the couch as instructed when Mason came down. She'd put one of Mom's blazers over her sweatshirt and had the kids' chalkboard we used to play with under her arm. She set it up next to her and grabbed a piece of chalk.

"What's all this?" asked my mom.

"Shhh," I said. "Watch and listen."

"Good evening," said Mason, making eye contact with each of us and smiling. "My name is Mason Annabel Strong. I'd like to talk to you today about why I should go to debate camp this summer."

"Mason," said Dad. "Dinner's getting cold. Can't we do this later—"

"Shhh!" interrupted Mom. "I want to hear what my daughter has to say." She leaned forward, watching.

Mason was writing on the chalkboard as she talked. "First," she said, drawing a #1 followed by the word COMMITMENT. "I have already shown a deep commitment to debate. For instance: (a) I have a debate scrapbook, as noted earlier this evening, even though I'm not on the team yet; (b) I read and listen to Tag's cases, and I talk to him about arguments; (c) I follow a bunch of debaters on Twitter; and (d) I've been taking an online class called 'How to Get Your Point Across Better.' Debate camp is the logical next step. It will prepare me for joining the team next year as a freshman."

I was impressed.

"Second," she said, drawing a #2 followed by the word VALUE. "Debate has proven to be extremely valuable to teens, especially girls, who are not usually encouraged by society to argue the same way boys are. Debate teaches reasoning and decision-making skills, promotes rigorous thinking, and helps build confidence. It helps kids get out there and start to do what they really want. I might want to be a lawyer, like Dad, someday, or maybe start my own organization to help others, or both. Debate will give me the skills to speak to people so they hear, and to argue any and every point that comes up. That is VALUE." She underlined the word on her chalkboard. "Why not start building that value as soon as I can, at camp this summer?"

Mom and Dad were nodding along.

"And third," she said, "I am super tired of horseback-riding camp." She wrote the word HORSES on the board and drew a big X across it. "I am not a horse girl. No offense to horses or horse girls. But I want to be me."

My mom and dad gave each other a look.

"In conclusion," said Mason. "Because I have shown the commitment to something that will deliver real value and is not related to horses, I should be allowed to go to debate camp this summer. Thank you for listening."

My mom clapped. "Sweetie. That was so good! I had no idea you were sick of horses, though."

Mason shrugged. "I'm just kind of over them. A horse can only get you so far."

I held back a laugh and glanced at my dad.

"Wait, I forgot the best part!" she said. "*Resolved: You will send me to debate camp and not horseback-riding camp this summer.*"

I started clapping, and Mom and Dad joined in.

Orion took that moment to strut through the room. He stared at us and meowed, turned around in a circle a few times, and then curled up by my mom's feet for a nap.

"Okay, Mason, you've made your point," Dad said. "Very well, I might add. We'll look into debate camp. Now, can we eat?"

Later that night, Millie texted. **Are you up?**

I called her right away. She told me that Coach Kargle had gotten the offensive video removed, as it violated the guidelines of YouTube and was a form of slander and character defamation as well. It only had a few hundred views at that point, but she was worried. "Those guys don't stop," she said. "When you fight back, they fight even dirtier. I don't know what they'll do, but it will be something."

"This is my fault," I said. "What I said, what I tweeted—"

"No, it's *their* fault," she said. "And I'm so tired of it. I keep thinking about all the other women who worked their hardest, and thought they could make things different, and were just shoved back down again. If I don't fight back, I'm doing what they want."

I thought about Mason, how proud I was of her. And how I wanted to support Millie, too. "So what should we do?"

"We beat them," she said. "We knock them out of final rounds like they don't deserve to be there, because they don't. We don't just win, we annihilate them—we make them go home empty-handed, and we make them realize there's nothing they can do about it. We make them feel the way they keep trying to make me feel."

"Commitment. Value. And no Horses," I said, thinking about Mason.

"Huh?"

"I'll tell you later. I'm with you on everything, but . . . how do we do it?"

"Practice," she said. "More practice. Which means I'll see you soon—right?"

"Definitely."

MILLIE

November turned into December. We kept practicing. And we kept kissing. I had this new focus: I'd keep winning, and Tag wouldn't just be better at debate— he'd win, too. That way, we could stand together on the stage with the satisfaction of having beaten Chatham's Lake in the process. They'd have to look at us and realize they'd failed.

Sometimes I was sure everything would end in disaster. I'd wake up in the middle of the night, gasping, having dreamed that a shooter was creeping outside my bedroom door, trying to get in. Or I'd wake up worrying my mom was right, that I needed to stop everything I was doing and go back to being Millicent M. Chalmers, the girl from before. In coaching Tag, I was potentially creating the Frankenstein's monster that could beat *me*. What would happen if—when—we debated each other again?

But then there was Tag to talk to in the morning. He always made me feel better.

People on the circuit knew we were together. It had become impossible to hide. But I still hadn't told my mom about him.

He kept saying that it would be better if it was in the open, that she would find out anyway; everything came out eventually. But I just couldn't figure out how to do it. I was so good at speaking. Why did this have me stuck?

I guess I knew why.

I was even starting to like his pumpkin tie.

First kisses are overrated, I decided. It's the kisses that end up being so many you lose count that really matter.

Maybe I didn't know what I was doing, and maybe it *would* end in disaster, but it felt too good to stop.

TAG

December went by in a blur. There were two big tournaments before the holidays: the Cullman County Classic and the Rocket City Championship in Huntsville. They were both Nationals qualifiers, and to no one's surprise, Millie won both. More surprising: I broke to octos at the first (I got knocked out by Carlos, who was wearing a truly incredible tie covered in purple T. rexes), and semis at the second (Millie beat me in that one, and then went on to destroy Carlos).

"It's happening!" Millie whispered as we were awarded our trophies onstage at Cullman. We held hands and looked out at the crowd, and the boys of Chatham's Lake, none of whom had made finals, shot back the mother of all stares that could kill.

Francine gave me a huge hug afterward. "I knew you could do it!" she said. "Look out, Nationals!"

Rajesh was still glaring at me, but with a kind of respect in his eyes. We hadn't talked since the night in my driveway. I saw him in school and at debate practice, but he always looked away when I tried to make eye contact. I felt bad about what I'd said, but he'd been a jerk, too, and it wasn't like he was apologizing.

On the weekends we didn't have debate tournaments, I'd drive to Millie's library and we'd meet and practice for hours, and later we'd get pizza at Nick's.

My parents and Merwin were thrilled about my successes. Mom and Dad wanted to know all about Millie, the debate champ who was now my girlfriend. "When can we meet her?" my mom asked. "I know she lives over in Hopewell Crossing, but you spend so much time there. What are her parents like? What do they do? We need to know these things!"

"Soon," I promised them.

"Where's she going to college? And what's your status on that? Have you sent in your applications yet?" asked my dad.

"She doesn't know! And I will," I said. "I still have time!" I'd compromised and told them I'd at the very least apply to the University of Alabama. It helped that Millie was applying there, too.

"Invite her over for dinner," my mom instructed. But I never got around to telling Millie that. We had so many other things to talk about.

There were a few introductions and crossovers, though. Mason kept begging to meet Millie, so I brought her to have pizza at Nick's with us over winter break. My little sister proudly wore her AOC FOR PRESIDENT T-shirt, and the two of them bonded immediately. And one weekend Carlos was looking at colleges and he drove up to join us; we all tried to brainstorm a Ricky setup that wouldn't seem like a setup, but in the end Carlos told us to drop it; if it happened, it happened.

The week of Christmas, Millie and I went to Nick's, and I gave her her present: a new briefcase, with MMC monogrammed on the side.

"This is beautiful," Millie said, holding it up to her cheek. "So soft! I love it. But, nice try: I'm still not telling you what the *M* stands for."

I pretended to be sad while pulling another gift out of my backpack. "I also made dog treats for Beau."

She took the container and grinned. "These will be a huge hit. Now, for you . . ." She handed me a flat box, wrapped in orange paper and tied with a black bow. "An homage to Halloween," she said. "Regardless of the season."

I looked at it, pretending to ponder. "I'm going to guess this is a . . . puppy?"

"Tag."

I unwrapped it to find a shirt with tiny, beautiful pizza slices dancing across it. I spied something green: "Are those jalapeños?"

"I designed it," said Millie.

"This is completely the best," I told her. "And so are you."

Our pizza came, and we dug in.

TAG'S BEAU-LICIOUS PEANUT BUTTER AND PUMPKIN TREATS

- Preheat your oven to 350 degrees.

- Mix together a cup of flour, a quarter cup of peanut butter (chunky or creamy, whatever you've got on hand will work, so long as you don't have a tiny dog and huge peanut butter chunks, which could be a choking hazard), and an egg. If you have pumpkin puree, add a couple of tablespoons of that, too. Pumpkin is good for dogs' digestion.

- Add in a little bit of water, like a teaspoon or so, and mix again. If the dough isn't flexible and combined enough to roll out, add more water, a little bit at a time, until it is.

- Roll out the dough. You can use cookie cutters to make shapes, but if you want to keep it really simple, just make little balls, about an inch in size. Dogs love balls! Catch!

- Put some parchment paper on a cookie sheet and put the dough balls or cutouts onto it, about 2 inches apart.

- Bake for 15–20 minutes. (Check at 10, and then every 5 minutes after that, to make sure they're not burning!) They should be golden brown at the edges.

- Cool and serve. Bask in the love of your furry friend, who will never complain, even if the treats don't come out perfectly.

MILLIE

We're always changing, on levels that range from the most microscopic cellular developments to what we wear and where we live and who we hang out with to our opinions and sometimes even our deeply held beliefs. It's hard to pinpoint exactly where it happened, but somewhere along the way, I was different. I started thinking less like MILLICENT M. CHALMERS and more like someone who wanted to win, sure, but who also wanted a lot of other things in life. Like friends, and fun, and even a boyfriend.

I felt like me.

Was I allowed to have all these things I wanted, and more? I didn't know. But I decided to stop letting it scare me, as much as I could.

I still hadn't told my mom about Tag, but everything else felt incredible.

Also incredible: the homemade pizza Tag brought us for lunch at the library.

PART THREE

January

———

*Resolved: A government has the
obligation to reduce the economic gap
between its rich and poor citizens.*

MILLIE

In late December, Tag came down and we spent the day at the library together. He worked on his cases and his single college application—to the University of Alabama—and I worked on my many college applications, most of which were due in January. "I still don't want to go," he said, "but this will get Merwin and my parents off my back." I took a picture of him putting the application in the mailbox outside the library so he could prove he'd done it.

"I have a question," Tag announced when we took a break. We were in the conference room eating grilled cheese sandwiches he'd made us, with tomato soup on the side. "The trick is simmering your tomatoes with a parmesan rind," he told me when he pulled it all out of one of those insulated bags that keep everything hot.

"Me first," I said. "Can you be my personal chef?"

"I think I already am," he said.

"Someday I might need to get you to teach me to cook, so if you're not around I can feed myself," I told him.

"Where am I going?" he asked.

"Well, hopefully nowhere," I said, dipping my sandwich in my soup and taking a bite.

"In that case, want to come over for dinner next week? My parents really want to meet you. They've been asking about it for forever. And I'm pretty sure they're not gonna stop."

"To your *house*?"

"My mom says that if we didn't have so many weekend debate tournaments she would have demanded this a long time ago, and, in fact, she's shocked with herself that she didn't and she blames work and the frenetic pace of modern life. It's okay if you don't want to go—I get it. You can say no!" He looked at me and smiled. "But please say yes. And maybe, once you meet my parents, I can meet your mom?"

"Maybe," I said. But something else was worrying me. "Tag, why would I not want to meet your parents? Are you ashamed of me or something?"

"Oh my God, no," he said. "I just didn't know if you'd want to—"

"I do," I said quietly.

"Okay, then," he said. "Save the date. Next Saturday night. We can hit the library for our usual debate session and drive back there instead of having Nick's. I'll plan a menu. I can prep some stuff in advance, and my mom's a really good cook; she and You-Tube taught me everything. Though I'll kinda miss the pizza . . ." He smiled at me.

"Nick's will be there the next weekend," I said.

Tag got serious then. "You know, I've been thinking . . ."

"Yeah?"

"I'm not entirely sure I can argue the negative this time."

"Not that again," I said. "You've proved you can."

"But what if I don't want to?" he asked. "What if it's time for that *k*-thing you told me about?"

"You want to do a kritik?"

"Yeah," he said. "And this resolution seems like exactly the right place to start."

TAG

The next tournament was just a few weeks away, and Rajesh and I were at the front of our debate classroom again, with Francine and the whole team watching. As affirmative, he was listing the overall harm to both individuals and societies that income inequality breeds—social unrest, volatility, poor public health, political inequality, and even the rise in authoritarian nations, all things that would be better for the poor and also the wealthy to remedy or avoid entirely, he said.

I got up for cross-ex.

"The resolution we're debating is that a government has the obligation to reduce the economic gap between its rich and poor citizens," I said. "Right?"

"Obviously," he said with a smirk, insinuating that I was wasting his and my time.

"For the purposes of this argument, are we focusing on governments in which there are free markets, in which everyone can participate and make money?" I asked. "Or are we considering all governments across the world and possibility?"

His smirk faded. "We are focusing on governments like that in the US, where there is both a free market and a tremendous amount of wealth disparity."

I nodded. "How does meritocracy fit into your argument?" I asked. "The underlying concept that people be rewarded based on merit . . . Will that be removed if the government reduces the economic gap? How will those who work harder or do more 'important' work—and by that I mean work that the society deems more important—be rewarded?"

"The reward will come from improvements throughout society," he said. "For instance, less crime. More education. Better schools. Arts programs. Things everyone can benefit from and participate in. Things that make everyone happier."

"What about Harvard—will everyone be able to go to Harvard?"

No one was on their phone this time. Francine was writing furiously in her notebook.

He flinched. "Maybe."

"How will everyone afford to go to Harvard? Will it be free?"

"This is a theoretical discussion about whether a government should be obligated to make these changes. It's Lincoln-Douglas, not policy. I don't need to elaborate on how, only if it should be."

"If Harvard is free . . . is it still Harvard?"

"I don't see why it wouldn't be," he said, shrugging.

"How much is tuition these days, anyway?" I asked. "Just out of curiosity."

"Fifty thousand dollars a year . . . give or take. That's without financial aid, though."

"Is that with or without room and board?"

"Is this line of questioning necessary?"

"I'm getting somewhere, I promise."

"With room and board, it's more than seventy thousand. But Harvard recently announced that families earning less than sixty-five thousand a year won't have to pay anything," he said. He stood up a little straighter and looked out at our audience with his most authoritative gaze. "So, you see, measures are being made to fight income inequality in some of our most important institutions. If a private institution like Harvard can do it, why can't the government?"

"Interesting," I said. "That will be all." I looked at Francine. "I'll skip prep and save it for later—if I need it."

I went to the middle of the room and stood.

"Income inequality is damaging to both the wealthy and the poor," I began. "With that, I am in agreement with my opponent. But that doesn't much matter when it comes to the resolution itself, and our debate here today. As Rajesh noted, in this round, we're talking about 'governments like that in the US, where there is both a free market and a tremendous amount of wealth disparity.' We are, therefore, dealing with capitalist systems.[46] But income inequality is an *inherent reality* in a capitalist system—you simply cannot have free market competition without inequality. Thus, I would contend that any government of a capitalist system, like in the US, is fundamentally *incapable* of reducing the economic gap between its rich and poor citizens, as that would cause a denial of the entire system, a breakdown of the governmental and societal structure itself. You cannot be morally obligated to do what will destroy you; self-immolation is immoral. The affirmative cannot win because the resolution is effectively meaningless. You must reject the capitalist bias in this resolution and vote for me."

The team stared at me. I wasn't sure if this was good or bad.

"Also, Harvard costs seventy grand a year now? That is insane, and supports my point. The institution isn't so much fixing income inequality as it's just charging more for certain people so it

---

46 Capitalism: "an economic system characterized by private or corporate ownership of capital goods, by investments that are determined by private decision, and by prices, production, and the distribution of goods that are determined mainly by competition in a free market." (*Merriam-Webster*)

can charge less for others. It's a PR move. Because it fundamentally cannot change itself, as a system that relies on capitalism to exist, just as we cannot fundamentally change our own capitalist natures, unless we step outside the box they've put us in. The only way out is not through the government. It's through a disruption of the entire system. Thank you."

I sat down.

"What was *that*?" Rajesh hissed at me.

"It's a kritik," I said.

"Hey, everyone, grab a partner to practice cross-ex with. Tag—a word?" Francine motioned for me to follow her into the hallway, shutting the door behind her. "This thing you're doing. I can't tear my eyes away. But . . ."

"You don't like the kritik?" I asked.

"It's not a matter of like. We're all riveted. I'm just not sure it's a good idea. I wonder if you could adapt your thinking to more directly focus on the resolution instead of saying it's wrong . . . I'm sure you could break what you're saying into actual affirmative and negative arguments."

"But it *is* wrong," I said. "A purely capitalist system can never redistribute wealth based on the principles of equality. What's the point of arguing both sides to something that's impossible?"

"As your debate coach, I'm not sure I can agree with that," she said. "There's *always* a point to considering both sides. But I'm not going to force you to do anything. I just want to make sure you know what you're in for. A kritik is a hard road in this circuit, especially in L-D. And you've been doing so well. I think you'll have an easier chance of breaking with a traditional argument."

"I don't want easier," I said. "I want to do it the way I believe in."

"Okay, then," she said. "It's your choice." She paused and looked at me. "How's everything else? We haven't had a chat in a while."

Why were adults always wanting to "chat"? "Fine!" I said. "Best I've ever been."

"Any lingering effects from Montgomery Hills?"

"Not really," I said. That wasn't exactly true—I still woke up in the middle of the night with my heart pounding every so often—but I didn't want to get into it.

"It's normal to keep processing for a long time," she told me. "What about you and Millie, things are okay there?"

"Yeah," I said. "Better than okay."

She smiled at me. "Just don't get sucked up in the idea of being a twosome and lose yourself."

"Millie's not making me run the kritik, if that's what you mean," I told her.

She raised her eyebrows. "I also noticed you haven't tweeted in a while, ever since Millie's debate against Blanton Bodie. Their words, not yours."

"Twitter just feels stupid," I told her, shrugging. "All these people vying for attention, and for what? There are more important places to say things."

"I get that. But promise me that when you do have something to say, you won't hesitate to say it. Wherever it needs to be said."

"That's what I'm trying to do with this kritik!"

"Then I support you."

"Thanks," I said. "Should we get back to the debate?"

"Let's give Rajesh a little more time to cool down." She paused. "Look, I wanted you guys to work this out on your own, but since both of you appear to be as stubborn as goats: This freeze-out you and Rajesh have going on isn't great for the team. Can you talk to him, please? You guys used to be such good friends. I'm sure you both miss each other."

I groaned, rolling my eyes. "He started it," I said.

"I don't care who started it," she said. "Rajesh needs you, and you need him. Just talk to him. You might find out some things you didn't know, even though I know you teenage boys; you think you know everything. You're seniors, and you represent the team. The others look up to you. Can't you make up with each other for the last semester of high school? I think you'll regret it if you don't."

"I don't think I know *everything*," I told her. "You have to be bad at some stuff in order to get better, right?"

"True," she said, and looked at me, waiting.

"Fine, I'll talk to Rajesh."

"Thank you," she said. "And also, I'm here for you, if you ever want to talk about anything."

"I know," I said. (Maybe I did think I knew everything.)

I caught up with Rajesh in the school parking lot as he was getting into his Corolla.

"Hey, wait!" I said as he slipped into the driver's seat and closed the door. He looked at me. I gestured for him to roll the window down.

He ignored me.

I stood there, waiting.

He started the car. Was he really just going to drive away from me?

I had this brilliant, stupid idea: I stood in front of the car.

He leaned on his horn. He inched forward until he almost touched my kneecaps.

"Really?" I asked.

Then he started backing up. I realized he was going to back his whole way out of the parking lot if it meant he didn't have to talk to me.

"Wait!" I shouted. "Please?"

He stopped the car and rolled down the window.

"What's that?" he asked. "I'm not sure I heard you."

"Rajesh. Can we talk?"

"Do you really want to hear what I have to say or do you want to just tell me I'm a jerk and accuse me of things I haven't done, and then throw Harvard in my face during a debate cross-ex? Newsflash: I didn't get in," he said flatly.

"Oh shit!" I said, and I really did feel bad. "I can't believe that! When did you hear? Rajesh. I'm really sorry. I had no idea."

He unlocked the doors. "Let's drive. Easier to talk that way."

I slid into the passenger seat.

"Found out just before winter break," he told me. "Kinda ruined the holidays. I haven't really told anyone. When you brought it up, I figured you'd heard and were calling me out for it."

"Man," I said. "I had no idea. I wouldn't have done that if I'd known. Bummer. Seriously."

"Whatever. I do have another shot, I guess. I got deferred, not full-out rejected. But it still stings."

"But you have another chance!"

"Or I wasn't good enough the first time, and won't be the second, either."

He started driving around the parking lot, making loops.

"So that thing you're doing, is that really how you're going to debate this time?" he asked me, his eyes on the road.

"I think so. I want to try something new."

"It's better than when you just argued the wrong side," he said. "Parts of it were kinda interesting. Even though you're still an asshole up there." He punched me lightly in the arm. "Oh, this song slaps." He turned up the volume and started singing along. As always, he was completely tuneless. I waited. When it was over, there was a second of silence, and I took that opportunity to speak.

"You're still a horrifically bad singer," I told him. "Will those dreams of being a rapper ever die and take your voice to the grave with them?"

He turned to me. "And you still have terrible taste in music. How's that classic rock fandom going for you?"

"Pretty good, pretty good," I said. "Once I get my time machine operating again, I'm going to totally kill in the eighties."

Rajesh laughed. "Bud."

"Dude," I responded.

The music surged again. He turned it off.

"Accusing me of doing that to Millie was really messed up. I would never make a video like that. I do care about other people. I'm not a monster just because I want to go to an Ivy, just because I want to win debates, and for the whole team to do well, too. Goals are important!"

"I know you're not. But, Rajesh, it felt like you just stopped being my friend, just because I wasn't winning. Do you even like me anymore?"

"I don't think you get how easy you have it sometimes. That can be hard to take," he said. "You can throw debate rounds for fun, and no one yells at you. You can try kritiks out on a whim just because you feel like it. You get away with everything."

"That's not true. It might seem like it, but it's not. Earlier this year, my parents were on me about debate, and college, a ton. I finally applied to Alabama just to appease them and Merwin."

Now we were circling the high school, over and over again.

"I mean, I don't even want to go to college," I told him.

"That's so you," he said. "What *do* you want to do?"

"Maybe I'll build a pizza truck that runs on vegetable oil and drive around the country plying my trade," I told him.

"Whatever you do, everything works out great for you. You even got a girlfriend, somehow, by being bad at debate!" he said. "And the one thing I want, I don't get. Why does *my* life have to be the one that gets ruined?"

"Not going to Harvard has not ruined a single person's life."

"How do you know that?"

"I guess I don't," I said. "But given that the acceptance rate is less than five percent, that's a whole lot of ruined lives to keep you company."

He laughed.

And then I said it: "Dude. I miss you."

In the background, a familiar song was playing. He turned it up. "Remember this?"

"Our choreographed kindergarten dance!" I said. "Which, as I recall, was really, really good. Until Ms. Casey called in our moms to talk about the appropriateness of the 'It's Tricky' lyrics."

"But they totally had our backs," said Rajesh.

"They still do," I said.

"Damn, Run-DMC still slaps." He turned the music up louder, and we chanted along to the words. "Micky-D's drive-through?" he suggested.

I nodded. "Remember when every single elementary school birthday party was there and we worked out that plan to steal as many balls as we could?"

"So we could re-create a ball pit in the living room of one of our own homes?" he finished.

"And at Jacinta Thibodeaux's birthday party when the cake was being served we managed to stuff our giant Minecraft backpacks full of balls, and we put as many as we could in our cargo shorts, too, and then we waddled out of the building and tried to convince our parents that the balls were party favors and we were supposed to take them home?"

"Our first heist," said Rajesh. "We had so many plans!" He looked at me and then back at the road. "Including being cowinners on the debate circuit. Remember that plan, freshman year?"

I nodded. "I'm sorry I let you down with debate. I'm sorry I yelled at you that night in my driveway. And I'm really, really sorry about Harvard. But I do think you'll end up where you need to be."

"I'd like to believe it," he said. "Hey, now that you're winning more, our team has gone up in the rankings. Maybe I have a better chance!"

"Maybe," I said.

"And, look, I'm sorry I said what I did about Millie," he told me. "I'm sure . . . if you like her . . . there must be something cool about her."

I stared out the window for a minute, thinking. "Neither of us liked her when we didn't know her. It's easy to hate someone you don't know."

"Especially if it's someone who beats your ass," said Rajesh. "It's really easy. That's, like, how wars happen."

"Someone's gonna ace that AP history exam!" I said. "But, you know, I really do like Millie."

"I know, she's your girlfriend." Rajesh punched me gently in the arm, again. "And maybe I'm a little bit jealous, okay? I wouldn't mind a cool, smart girl who likes me, too."

"Someone like . . . Rose?"

"What do you mean?" he said, but his face had taken on a pink hue, the way it used to when he was trying to keep a secret.

"She talks about you sometimes, too."

He smiled.

"I'll tell you this: If you like someone, you should go for it. What do you have to lose?"

Rajesh shook his head. "Yeah. You're right."

"Do it!" I said. "And this Harvard stuff, whatever happens, you're gonna be fine. You know that, right?"

"I do have a couple of backups," he said. "The University of Chicago actually sounds kinda cool."

"The pizza there is supposed to be epic," I said. "I'll come and visit."

We'd reached the drive-through. "Want anything besides a Coke?" he asked.

But I'd already leaned across the car and was speaking into the microphone. "We'll take two Happy Meals with chicken nuggets, two Cokes, and . . . how's the ball pit? Is it open?"

"Permanently closed," said the drive-through clerk. "Too much of a germ risk, they decided. Thank God; we all hated cleaning that thing."

"Can we get a couple of balls as souvenirs?" I asked. "Just chuck 'em through the window—we'll catch!"

" 'Scuse me?"

"Pardon my friend," shouted Rajesh. "Just the Happy Meals and Cokes, please."

"Drive around."

He turned to me then. "Dude. I missed you, too."

MILLIE

It was the day of the Strong family dinner, and I was the opposite of calm. My mom was at the hospital, so Tag picked me up at my house to take us to the library, where he helpfully dropped another bombshell:

"Rajesh is coming over for dinner tonight, too."

I stared at him. "Rajesh who—hates me? And, for that matter, you?"

"Remember how you told me to give him the benefit of the doubt? Well, I did—after Francine told me I better fix things, for the team. We talked. You were right. He's been stressed about college and stuff. And he didn't get into Harvard, which has made it a million times worse."

"Poor baby, no Ivy League, guess he'll have to just go somewhere cheap and horrible like the rest of us," I said, surprising even myself.

Tag gave me a funny look. "I don't think he thinks the other options are cheap and horrible. But he really wanted to go to Harvard. Like, it was his dream."

"I'm sorry. I'm just really nervous about meeting your parents." I was already anxious enough, and now Rajesh had to be there, too, giving me resentful stares?

"It was really great, honestly. We talked about everything. I told him how awesome you are." He squeezed my hand, and I squeezed back. "Y'all will like each other once you get to know each other."

"After we go to the library, can we stop by my house again so I can change?" I asked. I was wearing my standard hoodie and jeans for practice. What did rich people wear to dinner, anyway? Diamonds? Furs? Outfits made of credit cards.

"If you want," he said. "But it really doesn't matter what you wear. They're going to love you! How could they not? You're Millicent Chalmers!"

Tag kept being reassuring the entire day, and that plus debate practice really did help take the edge off. By the time we finished, I was about ready to show up in what I was wearing, but I thought better of it, plus Tag wanted to see Beau, and Mom was working a double, so it was safe.

We ended up in my bedroom. Tag perched on the edge of my bed, petting Beau, and looked at my walls, studying my banner from Nationals last year and the new DEBATE YOUR <3 OUT poster that my mom had given me, as I rifled through my closet. I watched him turn to take in my desk with its neatly arranged highlighters and philosophy books and yellow legal pads and multicolored Post-its.

"I never knew you were so messy," he said, teasing me.

"What do you think of this?" I said, showing him a dress my mom had found on sale recently. It wasn't really debate appropriate (it would have judges taking off points for "girliness"), but it was really pretty, with a high neck and a little bow that tied around it. "She was thinking it could be a good graduation dress. But I could wear it tonight, too."

"You don't have to dress up," he told me. "Unless you want to."

"I'll try it on," I said, and went to the bathroom to change. I came back to find him digging through his backpack, throwing stuff out left and right on my bed. "I can't find my AirPods," he said. "Maybe I left them at the library? Wait, oh my God, you look incredible. You should definitely wear that."

"You think?" I said, twirling around. I felt so pretty.

"Yes," he said. "And I'll wear the pizza shirt you gave me. And maybe even a tie. We can dress up together. My mom will love it."

I walked over to him and sat down. "It appears that *you're* the one making a mess here." I pointed to his belongings scattered all over my bed. "Is that your pumpkin tie? Do you carry it around with you everywhere? You know it's way past Halloween."

"Maybe," he said. "Or maybe just when I'm hanging out with you. It's my lucky tie, you know. A lucky tie knows no season."

"So you want to get lucky, huh?" I teased.

"No," he said. "I already did, when I ended up stuck in a closet with you."

"Tag!" I pushed him gently, and he pretended I'd shoved him to the floor.

Beau barked and tried to lick his face.

"I didn't mean it like that!" he said, laughing and warding off dog drool. "I promise! Hey, look, I found my AirPods!" He held up the little case, which had been hiding in my carpet. "See, I'm so lucky."

He sat next to me on the bed again. And then we were kissing, kissing, kissing.

On the drive to Tag's, I felt pretty good. I was wearing the dress, and he kept holding my hand at stoplights, and we sang along to the Steve Miller Band playing on Hector's sound system, and he told me about the menu he'd planned with his mom: roast chicken with lemons and herbs, a baked cauliflower dish with gruyère that, he promised, "tasted like mac and cheese but *better*," brussels sprouts with crispy bacon and sriracha, and a green salad. Plus assorted crostini on homemade sourdough to start (mushroom and goat cheese! tomato and mozzarella and basil!), and a special layered chocolate-caramel crepe cake he'd come up with for dessert. My stomach growled hearing him talk about it.

Then we pulled up to his house, a sprawling three-story with a Tesla in the driveway.

I gulped. He squeezed my hand.

Mason came running out of the house, wearing jeans with ripped knees and a cozy wool sweater. That didn't help. Was I going to look like an overdressed jerk? But when I got out of the car she hugged me, which made me feel better. "I'm so glad you're here!" she said.

"Me too!" I said back. "Have you heard the new resolution?"

"Yes!" she said. "I wrote up some practice arguments." She chewed her bottom lip for a second. "Would you . . . maybe want to look at them and tell me what you think?"

"I'd love to," I said.

Mason clapped her hands. "This is the best."

"All right, all right, Millicent Chalmers's number-one fangirl," said Tag. "Let us get inside." He'd grabbed my bag and was carrying it in for me. "I gotta help finish cooking."

"Guess what!" Mason said as we headed up the walk. "There's a winter storm warning. Mom says if we really get all the snow they're predicting, Millie should stay the night. She doesn't want you driving on icy roads."

"Is it really going to snow?" I checked the weather app on my phone, and there were snowflakes forecast for later that night, along with an ice warning. "Oh jeez." My mom was working late again, so I had some time, but there was no way to play off me not coming home at all. I'd have to call her and explain—but how was I supposed to explain I was staying at my boyfriend's house when she didn't even know I had a boyfriend, which, of course, was very much against our agreement? She would lose her shit. "When was the last time it snowed around here, that you can remember?"

Tag shook his head. "I don't know, but I like it. It's so homey and wintry."

I tried to push my worries to the back of my mind.

Tag's house was also homey and wintry, with tasteful white Christmas lights and a festive front-door wreath. Inside, it smelled like holiday candles and deliciousness.

"Tag?" called a woman from the kitchen. "Come tell me what to do with these brussels sprouts!"

"Hey, Mom," he called back, and we headed that way. I took a deep breath, wishing I had a pen in my hand, a card with some thought-provoking statistic I could pull out, or even a *Black's Law Dictionary*, anything that would remind me that I was a star Alabama debater and why in the world was I terrified of someone's mom?

She appeared, picture perfect with a dark bob and a big, toothy smile, wiping floury hands on her apron, which covered up a bright silk blouse and trim black pants, before she reached out to shake my hand. She had a diamond necklace around her neck and a matching diamond bracelet around her wrist. She wore them like she didn't think about them at all; in fact, the bracelet had little floury bits hanging from it. "Finally we meet! I've heard so much about you," she said in one of those southern accents that sound like liquid honey. "I do apologize that we haven't made it to one of your debates yet." She looked me up and down then. "What a gorgeous dress!" she said. "I love dressing up for dinner. It's a lost art, truly. The rest of these hooligans who live here will never join me, so I'm glad you are."

A little orange cat appeared next to her and meowed.

I smiled. "Is this Orion?"

He meowed again. I put out my hand for him to sniff, and he rubbed his face on it.

"He's such an attention hog," said Tag's mom, and Mason laughed. "He is!"

Tag was pulling on an apron. "Thanks for getting all this started for me, Mom," he said. "The cauliflower bake looks perfect, just needs another half hour or so. Mason, can you help me with the sprouts for a second? Add a few pats of butter."

"Sure," said Mason, grabbing butter from the fridge and walking over to the stove. It was one of those state-of-the art ones, like the kind they had in actual restaurants.

"We're his sous-chefs," said his mom. "I taught him everything I know, but he's surpassed me. He's always loved cooking."

Tag was opening the oven, pulling the chicken out and basting it with its juices—it smelled so good—and his mom took a seat at the kitchen island, waving me over to join her.

"I'm so excited to finally meet you and Mr. Strong," I said, sitting down.

"Did someone call my name?" asked the man entering the kitchen. "Is this the famous Millicent Chalmers? Hey there!"

Tag's dad had on a red-and-black-checked flannel shirt and a pair of jeans. He reached his hand out and shook mine energetically. His hair, like Tag's, flopped over one eye, but it was salt-and-pepper rather than dark brown.

"Hi, Mr. Strong," I said. "And Mrs. Strong."

"Call us Lawson and Emily," said Mr. Strong.

"Um, okay," I said. The doorbell rang.

"It's probably Rajesh," said Mason. "I'll get it!"

"So, Millie, what do you think of the new resolution?" asked Mr. Strong—er, Lawson. "'A government has the obligation to reduce the economic gap between its rich and poor citizens'—that's pretty interesting stuff, huh?"

"It is," I began, wondering how much I should come out and say in front of the wealthy parents of the boy I adored. Luckily, Mason returned, leading not one person but two into the kitchen. "Rajesh brought his friend Rose," she announced. "She's also on the debate team. I told them there was plenty of room for them both."

"Hey," said Tag to Rose and Rajesh.

Rajesh put a container of food on the counter. "My mom made samosas today," he said, and looked at Tag. "I know you love them. And Dad said to come over for dinner soon."

"I definitely will," said Tag, and grinned.

"How lovely," said Emily. "Please tell them both thank you. I'm so glad you two could join us! Rose, I just love that purple streak in your hair. It's so *chic*!"

"Thanks," said Rose.

"A whole house of debaters!" remarked Lawson. "This could get *rhetorical*!"

"Is that a dad joke?" asked Mason. "Because it's not even really a joke."

"It's more punny than funny," said Lawson, giving his daughter a head tousle.

"I don't think it's that, either," said Mason, rolling her eyes.

"Oh, are you gonna debate me on that?" asked Lawson. He pointed to his daughter and looked at us: "Wait till this one goes to camp. She'll be running circles around us all!"

Over at the oven, Tag smiled at me, and warmth spread through my body.

I don't just like him. I love him, I thought. *How did that happen?*

"Lawson, can you and Rajesh set the table?" Emily asked her husband. "Light the candles, please. Now, what does everyone want to drink? We have Coke, Sprite, iced tea, sparkling water, apple cider . . ."

"Apple cider!" said Mason.

"That sounds good to me, too," I said.

"Me three," said Rose Powell, who smiled at me. "I'm glad you're here," she whispered.

Dinner was like the food you get in a restaurant. We all kept going back for more. Then Tag brought out his cake, and I took pictures of him holding it, wearing his pizza shirt and a red tie that matched perfectly. After we dug in, we just sat there, smiling at one another in satisfaction. "I don't think I can move," said Rajesh.

"Me either," said Rose.

"You have to. Check out the snow, y'all!" shouted Mason, so we made ourselves get up and look out the big bay window that faced Tag's backyard. Everything was covered in white. It was so beautiful. Orion twisted around our legs, purring his appreciation for the evening.

"Millie, I really think you should stay here tonight," Emily said. "You know Alabama, less than a handful of snowplows for the whole state. I don't want you and Tag on the road when it's like this. We have a lovely guest room, and plenty of extra toothbrushes. Follow me, I'll show you."

"Okay," I said, and walked down the hall with her to a room with a four-poster king bed covered in overstuffed pillows. "There are plenty of clean towels in the attached bath," she told me, pointing it out. "And extra pillows and blankets in the closet. Do you want me to give your mom a call as well, to tell her it's fine with us if you stay?"

I shook my head. "No, no, this is so nice of you, thank you. I'll let her know." I was racking my brain trying to think of what I could say—I was sleeping at a friend's house? I hadn't slept over at anyone's house in ages; I was always either at debate tournaments or working on debate—when Mason came to join us in the room.

"Millie, want to talk now?" she asked. "About the resolution?"

"Uh, sure," I told her, and Emily smiled at me.

"Yay! Let me get my stuff. Meet me in the kitchen!"

"Okay," I said.

"Thank you so much for working with her," said Emily. "She is obsessed with debate—and you! In a good way."

"I'm pretty obsessed with debate, too, so it's a perfect match," I said, and we walked back to the kitchen, where Mason was waiting with a big folder of materials.

"Have fun!" said Emily, leaving us to it.

"Here's what I was thinking so far," Mason said, showing me a paper with the early flow of a case. "I like the value premise of morality. It seems like instead of just being just, morality is also about doing what's right and good for people. And there's so *much* in the world, but so few people have it. If we shared it, wouldn't that be better for everyone, which would then be more moral overall?"

I nodded. "I like morality a lot, too. And sharing what we have. Also, an obligation is directly tied to the moral action, or you can define it that way."

"I'm just not sure where to go from that," she said. "I have so many ideas!"

"I'm going to share one of the best tips I ever got," I told her. "Have you heard of K.I.S.S.?"

"No," she said. "Kiss?" She wrote it down.

"Hey!" Tag peeked into the kitchen at us and grinned. "There you are. We'll be in the basement," he said. "Come on down when you're done."

"Okay," I said, and turned back to Mason.

"K.I.S.S. stands for 'keep it simple, stupid,' or 'keep it stupid simple'—personally, I like the latter since it's not quite so insulting. It was a design principle the US Navy created in 1960," I explained. "Basically it means that most systems work better if they're kept simple. Avoid unnecessary complexities; always look at your arguments and see if you can pare them down and make them easier to understand."

Mason nodded. "I like that. K.I.S.S. Easy to remember."

"Very easy," said Tag, who was still standing there.

Mason stuck her tongue out at him.

"I thought you were going downstairs?" I asked.

"I'm going, I'm going!" he said. "It's just fun to watch y'all. But, Mason, don't keep Millie too long, I might kinda miss her."

"Then leave us alone so we can work!" said Mason.

"Fine!" said Tag, laughing as he left.

"You like him, don't you?" Mason asked me in a whisper.

I smiled at her and nodded.

"Good," she said. "Now tell me more about this K.I.S.S. thing."

"Now that you have it in your head, it's there to stay. A lot of times junior debaters will fill their cases with big words and complicated arguments, but the thing that will resonate most with a judge is probably the thing that is the easiest to understand," I said. "Even now, I look at every case and try to apply that principle."

Mason nodded and made more notes.

My phone rang. It was my mom. I sighed. Might as well get it over with.

"Just a second," I told Mason. I walked down the hall back to the guest bedroom and sat on the bed. "Hello?"

"Millie. Where in the world are you?" She sounded panicked.

I looked at my watch. It was 8:00 P.M. "I'm— Did you get out early?"

"They called me off because I'd already done so many back to backs. I have the night free, and I was planning to spend it with my daughter. I thought I'd surprise you. I didn't know you were going to be somewhere else . . ."

"Mom," I said, but she was still talking, and her voice was getting louder.

"So I went into your room looking for you and instead I found this boy's tie—it's got pumpkins on it? *Was there a boy in your bedroom?*"

Shit. Shit. Shit. Tag forgot his tie. And now my mom was assuming . . .

"Millicent M. Chalmers, I want you home this instant."

I looked outside, where an increasingly thick blanket of snow lay over everything. "That's not possible."

"May I ask why not?"

"I'm having dinner with my boyfriend's family at their house in Birmingham," I whispered. "That's the boy who left his tie. We were just in my room for a few minutes. Nothing happened. I'm sorry."

"Millie. Your what?"

"It's snowing and the roads are icing over and his mom won't let him drive. But his family is super nice and I can sleep over in the guest room and it will be fine. I promise."

"Did you say *boyfriend*?"

"Yes. I'm in Birmingham, where they live . . ."

"I heard you, I just can't believe what you're saying. Millie, what about our agreement? What about debate? What about college? Did you just forget about *everything* that's important when you decided to start lying to me?"

"I haven't forgotten," I said. "It just . . . other things happened. I didn't want to lie. I just didn't know how to tell you—"

"Text me the address so I know where you are," she said. "And send me the name and phone number of this boyfriend's mother. What's his name?"

"Tag," I said. But I'm not sure if she even heard me, because you know what she did? She hung up on me. She'd never done that before.

I tried to call her back, but it went straight to voice mail.

I went to the bathroom and splashed cold water on my face and tried to shrug it off. I sent her Tag's address, hoping she wasn't going to show up and drag me back home—the Honda didn't even have snow tires—and I headed to the basement. What else could I do? She'd hung up on *me*.

Downstairs, Rose was sitting on a leather chair, alternating between looking at her phone and watching Tag and Rajesh play *Call of Duty*, or, as she put it, "one of those first-person shooter games set in a semireal environment in which the players can do completely unreal things."

I hadn't had shooting nightmares in weeks. But now I was on edge. "I thought you were so antigun," I said to Tag. "What about all those things you tweeted?"

"Oh shit, YOU LOSE!" screamed Rajesh, jumping off the couch and doing a victory dance that involved shaking his butt and waving his arms in the air wildly. "HAHAHAHAHA."

Tag put down his controller and turned to me. "Trust me: I am antigun. Very antigun in real life, and anti–shooter scares. But Rajesh and I used to play this a bunch, so we were kind of just . . . going back in time, you know?"

"Ah," I said. "So was I. Specifically, to a tournament where we ended up in a supply closet, terrified."

Rose looked at me. "Wanna try it? Women are actually better at video games; we have more dexterous hands," she said, wiggling her fingers.

"That's okay," I said, shaking my head. I perched on the arm of Rose's chair. "Do y'all ever think about how things would be if it hadn't been a false scare?"

"Yes," said Rose.

"I've tried to block it out, and it's worked, mostly," said Rajesh. "Mind over matter, right?"

"I do, sometimes," said Tag. "But, Millie, this is obviously fake, and fun. It might even make you feel better, in a weird way. You get to feel in control when you play it."

"Maybe fun for you," I said. "You who gets to see it all as a game."

"Are you mad at me?" he asked. "Did I do something wrong?"

"I just thought, since you were this antigun voice on Twitter, you'd be that at home, too."

"You can feel differently about different things. Everything has layers. I don't think video games necessarily make kids violent, either."

"But having the goal of shooting a bunch of other people . . . I mean, isn't it nicer to read a book?" I asked.

"Depends on the book," said Rajesh.

"We should play *Animal Crossing*!" suggested Rose. "It's super cute." She leaned over and whispered to me, "I get it. I only play sometimes because it's boring to have to sit on the sidelines and watch."

Rajesh looked at me. "We don't have to play video games. We were just messing around. What do you want to do instead?"

"How about we watch a movie?" Tag suggested, putting his arm around me. I felt myself relax a little. "Or play a different kind of game . . ."

"Not Spin the Bottle," said Rose. "I refuse to be a part of a teen cliché."

"Never," said Tag.

"How about Two Truths and a Lie?" offered Rajesh. "We used to play that all the time. It's even better nostalgia than *Call of Duty*."

"How do you play?" I asked.

"We sit in a circle, and one at a time each person says two

truths and one lie, and we guess which are which. It's kind of like debate in that you have to cut through the rhetoric and figure out the truth, or try to convince others what you want them to believe." Tag grabbed a notepad from the coffee table and a pen. "If you get away with your lie, you get a point."

"Hang on, we need some good background tunes," said Rajesh. "Have you heard *The Mixes*?" He cued up his iPhone to play via Tag's basement's Bluetooth. "You're never gonna change that Wi-Fi password, are you?" he said, laughing, as music came blasting through the speakers. "It's still NACHOINTERNET!"

"It's one of my best puns," said Tag. "And it's not like you've ever changed your taste in music. You've loved Run-DMC since second grade."

"True," said Raj. "Can that be one of my truths?"

"Sure, you go first," said Rose.

"Okay. I've loved Run-DMC since second grade. Rose and I are . . . hanging out." (Rose smiled slightly at this, but it was hard to say if it was a truth smile or a lie smile.) "And . . . for a very long time I have been both terrified of and jealous of you, Millicent M. Chalmers."

"You and Rose?" asked Tag.

Rose smiled again. "Do I get to recuse myself from this one?"

"You're totally together," I said. "And, Rajesh: You're lying about loving Run-DMC since the second grade."

He looked at me, shocked. "How did you know that?"

"Because Tag told me the 'It's Tricky' story. Which happened in kindergarten."

Rajesh smiled at Tag, and Rose reached over and took Rajesh's hand.

"So you *are* together! I get a point!" I said.

"Yep," she said.

"Are you still terrified and jealous of me?" I asked Rajesh.

He shook his head sideways and then shrugged and grinned. "Maybe a little bit."

"How did you guys end up together, anyway?" asked Rose. "The closet, was it the closet? They say if you go through a traumatic incident like that you can really bond . . . You shared something so meaningful, you're connected for life!"

"It was kind of that," I mused. "But Tag was different from any other guy I've met. He was . . . special. He *is* special."

"Mmm-hmm," said Rajesh. "Tell that to his debate style."

Tag threw up his arms in pretend anger. "Are we playing this game or are we mocking me?"

"Can't we do both?" asked Rajesh. "But I have a question: Is it weird for y'all to practice so much together, knowing that only one of you can win state?"

"Not really," Tag said. "I mean, only one of any of us can win state."

"But if Millie wins, it's a huge deal," said Rose. "Fourth time in a row, and she'll get the Martha Linger Scholarship."

"I just want Tag to be as good as he can be," I said. "Who wants to debate a dud?"

"True—except when the final round comes along and full tuition is on the line," said Rose. "That's when I'd be fine with a dud."

Tag shrugged. "Dud or not, I just want to say what I really mean."

"My turn," said Rose. "I once baked a loaf of bread the size of a school bus. I was a cheerleader at my old school. And . . . I have a tattoo of Abraham Lincoln on my butt, which is why I decided to do L-D."

"Shut up," said Rajesh. "You do not."

Rose shrugged. "Wouldn't you like to know?"

"I really would," he said.

"A school-bus-sized loaf of bread . . . ," Tag said. "How do you even get an oven that big?"

"You don't seem the cheerleader type," I said.

Rose smiled. "Those two are true," she said. "The school-bus bread was part of a charity project we did at my old school to collect funds to feed the hungry. We baked it in sections in a giant industrial oven. And, my friends, I can rah-rah-sis-boom-bah even though I have a nose ring. Not all cheerleaders are alike. But wouldn't an Abe Lincoln butt tattoo be rad?"

Tag threw a pillow at her. "Point for Rajesh. You go, Millie."

"Hmmmm," I said. "I have a hundred-pound pit bull named Beau who is all mush inside. I eat the same thing every morning for breakfast. And I have a trophy room at home where I keep all my debate trophies."

"I recuse myself from this one," said Tag.

"You don't seem the pit bull type," said Rose.

"Not all pit bull types are alike," I said, smiling at her.

"Hang on, can we go back to 'trophy room' for a second?" asked Rajesh. "How many freaking trophies do you have?"

"I unrecuse myself," said Tag. "You would never, ever eat the same thing every morning for breakfast because you never eat anything for breakfast, unless I bring you something. Otherwise it's just black coffee, which doesn't count as food."

"Correct!" I said. "Your turn."

"Um. Let's see. I used to be the very worst debater in Alabama history. I'm pretty into a girl named Millicent Chalmers. And . . . it's snowing outside right now."

"The worst in Alabama history is a pretty tall order," I told him. "Someone had to be worse than you at one point or another."

"Probably," he said. "Or maybe not. I can't tell a lie, remember? That's always been both my worst and best quality as a debater."

"How do you know it's still snowing? There are no windows in the basement," said Rose.

"Some things you just have to believe," he said.

"So those were all truths?" asked Rajesh. "I think you might be playing this wrong."

"Your turn again," said Tag.

"Okay," said Rajesh. "My favorite character in *Saving Private Ryan* is Captain Miller. If I didn't do debate I would definitely be a sidewalk chalk artist. And . . . Tag knows this already, but I didn't get into Harvard."

"What?!" Rose seemed truly shocked. I did a good job faking it.

"Shh. I already feel bad enough."

"But that was just early action, right?" Rose asked. "You have another chance."

"Yeah, I'll move to the regular pool as a deferral. And maybe I can up my debate game in the next couple of months and maybe Francine will write me another letter and maybe something amazing will happen, like I'll figure out a cure for cancer or fix our broken political system or end climate change. Stop giving me the sad face; y'all are making me feel worse."

"I'm sorry," said Tag. "We know how much you wanted to get in."

"I'm sorry, too," I added.

Rose was holding his hand, rubbing her thumb on his.

"It just sucks when it becomes clear that the thing you've

worked your whole life for might not happen, and you don't know whose fault it is, exactly: Was I crap in comparison to the other kids who wanted to get in? Did they already meet their quota for Southeast Asians from Alabama? What if I'd gotten farther at Nationals last year? What if our whole team had a better record?"

Tag frowned.

"And it really sucks to feel like I'm disappointing my parents. They were so excited about Harvard," said Rajesh.

"What you want is important, too," Tag said. "They want you to do what you want to do."

"No, they don't. None of our parents do. What they want is for us to want to do what *they* want us to do," Rajesh said.

"Dang," said Rose. "I have never heard something so true in my whole life."

"Wait, does this mean you *don't* want to be a sidewalk chalk artist?" I asked, and everyone laughed.

"No, I mean, yes, you're right," he said. "I don't. But we're teenagers! What if we don't *know* what we want to do, exactly? What if we want to do a whole bunch of things to figure it out?" he asked. "What if, instead of being a doctor or lawyer or diplomat, I really *could* do something with music?"

Tag nodded. "I'm sure you could. Maybe not sing. But something."

"Like, I could so get down with a History of Hip-Hop class," said Rajesh.

"I know how you feel," I told him. "My mom has it all decided for me. This year, I was supposed to stay away from boys, and win state, and get a college scholarship, and win Nationals, and what else? I don't know. It never ends. I want those things, too, don't get me wrong. At least I want some of them. But then I met Tag. And I kept it a secret, because I didn't want to tell her."

They all stared at me silently.

"She called a little while ago asking where I was, and now she knows everything, and I'm terrified about what's going to happen next," I confessed.

"I'm guessing that's a truth," said Rose.

"She yelled at me and hung up." I looked down at my phone. Not even a text from her. "She found your tie in my room, Tag."

"Whoa," said Rose. "That sounds like *a lot*."

Tag hugged me. "I'm sorry," he whispered in my ear.

"Ouch," said Rajesh. "That's almost as bad as not getting into Harvard. "

"It's not a competition!" I said, which struck me as funny, so I started laughing, and then we all started laughing, which made me feel a little bit better.

Rose looked at her phone and jumped up. "Oh crap, I gotta get home," she said. "It's almost my curfew. My parents will freak if I'm late."

"Text them and say it's snowing—that gives us a fifteen-minute window," said Rajesh, getting up as well.

"Give me your phone," Rose said to me. "I'll put my number in it. We can talk about things that aren't first-person shooter games when we're tired of hanging out with these two." She nodded at the boys.

I handed it to her. "Yes, please."

"You're cool," said Rajesh, assessing me. "Millicent M. Chalmers. Even if you don't like *Call of Duty*."

"Thanks," I said. "That, uh, means a lot. I'm sorry about Harvard."

He shrugged. "I'll just try again. That's all I can do, right? Hey, I've been wondering forever: What's the *M* stand for?"

"She'll never tell," said Tag.

"'Bye, y'all!" said Rose, waving at us.

And then it was just the two of us. There was a knock on the basement door, and Tag's mom appeared. "Dad and I are going to bed," she told Tag. She gave him a serious look. "You two *will* sleep in your appropriate rooms. Remember who you are, please."

"Yes, ma'am," he said.

"Mrs. Strong—I mean, Emily?" I asked. "Can I have your phone number, to send to my mom?"

"Of course," Emily said, rattling off her digits. I put them in my phone and texted the contact to Mom. "Tell her she can call me anytime. I understand being worried about your kids."

She headed back upstairs, and Tag and I sat facing each other on the couch.

"So I'm sleeping over," I said.

"You're sleeping over." He grinned at me.

"Which doesn't mean what it sounds like," I said.

"What it means is, we get to hang out longer, and make out for a while, and then I get to see you first thing in the morning. Which sounds great to me."

I was blushing. "Me too."

"Not to ruin the mood, but . . . what are you gonna do about your mom?" he asked.

"I don't know," I said. I looked at my phone again. Nothing. She was really angry. And I couldn't blame her, exactly. I thought about how when I was little I told her everything. It hadn't been that way for a long time now. I sighed. "I think her biggest thing is making sure I don't have the life she had. She missed out on all these opportunities. But she can't force me to be the person she wishes she'd been. You have to let people find their own way."

"You know how you told me to talk to Rajesh? I think you need a real heart-to-heart with your mom. Really tell her everything."

"Probably," I said. "That's going to be so hard, though. She's not going to like what I have to say very much."

"When has that ever stopped Millicent Chalmers?"

He brought his mouth to mine, and I let go of all the rules, every worry about debate and college and our futures and expectations, of my fight with my mom and how I'd fix it. I was just there, in a beautiful basement in the beautiful home of my beautiful boyfriend, and that was the only place I wanted to be.

Outside, snow kept falling, and inside, we kept kissing, until our eyes got heavy and we pulled ourselves off the couch and made our way to our separate rooms. I got into the soft, comfortable bed and pulled the blankets around me and looked at my phone. **I'm really sorry**, I texted my mom. **I'll explain everything when I see you tomorrow. I love you.**

I heard a gentle knock on the door to the guest room and tried to make myself look as presentable as possible while in bed wearing one of Tag's old T-shirts, which said CHICKENS: THE PET THAT POOPS BREAKFAST. It was Tag, in a chef's apron. He looked adorable.

"Do you like pancakes?" he said from the doorway, waving a spatula.

"How long have you been up?" I looked at my phone. It was 9:00 A.M.

"Hours!" he said, and laughed at my horrified expression. "Twenty minutes. Want some coffee?"

"Yes," I croaked.

"You look cute," he said. "So mussled and tousled!"

"Mussled is not a word. Unless you mean *muscled*. Which I am not, particularly."

"Whatever, lexicographer. Get ready and meet us in the kitchen! I have something to show you."

"Okay," I said. I glanced at my phone. My mom had written back, thank God. "Be there in a second."

"I'm pouring you coffee," he said, and closed the door.

I read her text. **I'm angry, honey, and we definitely need to talk. I spoke to Emily. They seem like a nice family. Thank them for their hospitality. I love you, too. I took the day off work. I'll be there to get you at 11 A.M.**

I had two hours to figure out how to handle that.

I brushed my teeth and pulled my hair into a ponytail and hustled to the kitchen, where his parents, both in robes, and Mason, in her pj's, were waiting. "'Morning!" they said. "'Morning," I mumbled back, embarrassed about my dirty hair and Tag's T-shirt and sweatpants, which I was still wearing, and the fact that my mom had called Emily at some point this morning (or last night?) and was a couple of hours from showing up at their doorstep, but they didn't act like anything was unusual at all. Tag handed me a coffee, and then set a pancake down in front of me. "Here's my first test pancake."

"Why does it look like . . . Hillary Clinton?" I asked. "You made this? On purpose?"

"I didn't ever mention I was a pancake artist?" asked Tag.

Emily laughed. "He's been doing celebrity face pancakes like these since he could cook."

"At first I used these designs you can find online, but then I started to just free hand it," he said. "Which opens up way more options."

"Make me an RBG!" said Mason. "And take a picture of it this time and put it on Twitter and you'll totally go viral."

Tag shrugged. "Some stuff that's great in real life just doesn't translate the same way online." He turned to Emily. "Mom, any requests?"

"I'll take a Frida Kahlo," said Emily. She looked at me and smiled. "He does the eyebrows out of chocolate chips."

"Who do you want, Dad?" asked Mason. At the end of the table, Lawson lowered his paper. He'd been quietly reading. He smiled at me, too.

"Since we're on a power woman roll, how about AOC?" he asked. "The congresswoman from New York?"

"You know AOC?" asked Mason. "Dad!"

"Seems like she's saying some interesting stuff," he said. "Not that I necessarily agree with all of it. But I'm listening."

I was admiring my Hillary pancake. "How do you make these? They're art!"

"I've been practicing for a really long time," Tag said.

"I don't want to eat her, but I have to." I took a bite. "She's too good."

"Don't worry, I can always make more," said Tag. "There's room for a lot of power women in this pan."

TAG'S NOT-FROM-SCRATCH[47] (BUT DELICIOUS) PANCAKES

- For 6–8 pancakes that are around 8 inches across, pour two cups of packaged all-in-one complete pancake mix (I like Krusteaz) into a bowl, and instead of using water like the mix says, add a cup and a third of whole milk—it'll make your pancakes super rich and good. Mix until your batter is the consistency of cake batter, stirring the whole time, until most of the lumps are gone.

- Heat up your pan on medium high (hot enough that when you put a drop of water in the pan it jumps around a little).

- Add a thin slice of butter to the pan or griddle and move it around with your spatula to coat the bottom. Make sure the whole pan is coated thinly so your pancake doesn't stick.

- Pour in your batter to the size of the pancake you want to make. If you're doing a face, it's easiest to use a squeeze bottle, like the kind you see at restaurants for ketchup.[48] If adding blueberries or chocolate chips, drop in by hand at this point, as many as you like.

---

47 Can you make these from scratch? Sure! But I like to keep things easy in the morning, and maybe it's the nostalgia factor, but these taste just as good, imo.

48 I recommend watching YouTube videos—google "Face Pancakes"—for pointers here.

- When you start to see bubbles appear on the top surface (after about a minute or two), flip the pancake to the other side. Lift up the pancake edges with your spatula to check for doneness (it should be golden brown on the other side). Important: Only cook once per side—do not flip back and forth!

- Put on a plate. Add whipped cream and chocolate chips or blueberries (or both!) and maple syrup to your heart's content. Serve hot.

MILLIE

By 10:00 A.M., we'd finished breakfast and the road in front of Tag's house had been plowed. His yard was still covered in snow, though. I thought about how, if you give it enough time, snow melts. Everything changes. People can change, too.

But sometimes you can't just wait for the snow to melt.

Part of me wished I could wait outside, to avoid the inevitable: My mom was coming to get me, and she was not only going to meet Tag, she was going to meet his whole family, all their money and privilege hitting her square in the face. I didn't know what she'd think. The Tesla, despite a layer of snow, was unmissable right there in the driveway. But it was too cold and going outside to wait would seem weird and antisocial. So instead, I sat at the table, making pleasant small talk with Tag's mom and dad until Tag excused us to go hang out in the basement for a while.

Once we got downstairs, I hugged him hard. "I don't know what she's going to do," I said. "This could be our last hangout for a while."

"You seriously think she'd forbid you from seeing me?" he asked. He held my face and looked at me intently.

"Well, that was our agreement. No dating this year until my college situation and money is squared away."

"That just doesn't seem fair. Or like something you would have agreed to—"

"Honestly, I didn't think I'd be giving much up," I told him. "It's not like there was anyone I was interested in dating . . ."

"Until me." Tag grinned.

"Shhh," I said. "Nobody likes a bragger."

"Yes they do," he said, smiling even bigger.

I laughed.

He always made me feel better.

At 10:58 A.M., we went back upstairs. At 11:00 A.M. on the dot, I heard her car door slam. We went to the front door, and through the windows you could see Mom walking up to the house, wearing her jeans and an old winter coat with a broken zipper. Sunlight glinted on the side of the Honda, hitting the FUCK YOU so I could just barely see the outline of the letters. I hoped Tag hadn't noticed at all.

"There she is," I said.

"She looks like you," he said.

He had the door open before she knocked. "Hi, Ms. Chalmers!" he said. "Come on in. Want some coffee? Or tea? Or anything? I can make you a pancake! I've been wanting to meet you for a really long time."

I looked at him and made a face.

My mom seemed a little bewildered by the onslaught of attention. "Ah," she said. "We really should be getting back."

But then Emily appeared, all smiles, the perfect hostess. "I made a fresh pot of coffee," she said. "Want to sit down for just a second?"

She poured us each a cup, offering us oat milk, almond milk, whole milk, and half-and-half (Mom and I stuck with black), and we sat in the kitchen table together, holding the mugs between our hands.

It was . . . awkward.

"It's so nice to meet the mother of this impressive young woman!" said Emily. "I hear you work at the ER?"

"Yeah," said my mom. "As a nurse. You never know what's going to happen. It's kind of like raising teenagers. I'm sure you know what I mean." She gave Emily a half smile.

Emily smiled back. "Never a dull moment!"

Tag and I shared a glance.

"I just wanted you to know that Millie's welcome back anytime," said Emily. "She's been so good for Tag, helping him focus his debate energies, and also for Mason, our daughter, who is pretty obsessed with debate right now. Last year it was horses." Emily laughed. "Anyway, we just love having Millie around. She's a breath of fresh air!"

My mom looked at me and raised her eyebrows. "Well, thank you," she said to Emily. "I didn't realize Millie had such an interest in coaching debate, but maybe that's something for us to consider down the line, once she's not competing on her own."

Emily nodded. "I believe it can be very lucrative, too."

"So can actually winning, assuming she still has time for that," my mom said. "What with everything else."

"Oh, she'll win," said Tag. "She's the best." Under the table, he reached for my hand, and squeezed.

"Time," said Emily. "That's the one thing you never have enough of, right?"

My mom nodded and took one last sip of her coffee. "Speaking of which, we should probably be going. Thank you so much for your hospitality. Millie, do you have your things?"

We drove in silence for a good ten minutes while I thought about what to say and hoped my mom would start first. Finally, she did.

"I don't like lies," she said. "And I especially don't like my own daughter lying to me."

"Mom. I'm sorry," I said.

"Why'd you do it?" she asked. "Not just the lying, but going back on our agreement. Hiding all this from me for months. I feel like I don't even know you." She looked at me, and instead of anger I saw hurt, which made me feel even worse about everything.

"At first I was really just helping Tag. I felt like I owed him, but there was more: I *wanted* to help him. I told you that."

"And I told you to buy him coffee or write him a thank-you note," she said.

"I didn't want to do that. I had a plan. And then it started to be more. I really like him."

My mom shook her head. "Which is what I warned you about. That's exactly why we had our rule . . ."

"But, Mom. It was never my rule; it was yours. I said yes, but I never should have had to! I'm seventeen. I'm allowed to like people. I want to be a person, not just a debate robot!" I said. "And you should know by now that I'm not going to mess up my future for a guy. I'm still winning debate! You need to trust me."

"Millie, I wish we had enough money that we didn't have to worry about how you're going to pay for college. But we're not like

Tag's family, with savings in the bank and so many fancy cars they have to keep one of them in the driveway. Things are just going to be harder for you. You have to make sacrifices. And take it from me: Romance at this age can really derail you." She stared straight ahead at the road, and she looked so tired suddenly.

"I'm not going to throw away my future," I told her. "I just want to have a life, and debate, too. Why do I have to sacrifice having a life for success?"

"Because, Millie, you want to have a life later."

"But I have a life *now*."

She laughed in this rueful way. "You think you do."

I turned on her then. "Mom. I am not going to get pregnant after a one-night stand and never tell the guy because *I don't even know what his last name is* and have to raise a baby on my own. I'm not going to ruin *my* life. I'm smarter than that."

She gripped the steering wheel hard but said nothing for a long time. We were pulling into the driveway when she finally spoke again. "Fine, Millie. I hear you loud and clear. Why would you listen to your mother when you have everything figured out? So, go ahead. Make your own decisions. Do what you want to do."

I could feel the rest of what she left unsaid, what she would never actually say, but what she felt in that moment, clear as day: "Just don't come running to me to help you pick up the pieces when it all goes to hell."

But it wouldn't. I wouldn't let it.

TAG

The Abraham Lincoln and Stephen A. Douglas Open in Hartselle, Alabama, was a key Nationals qualifier,[49] held in January each year. It was also my three-month anniversary with Millie, counting back from the supply closet moment. (Anniversaries were arbitrary, so might as well start where we began.) The night before the tournament started, I had reservations at Ciao!, the Italian restaurant where I'd worked as a dishwasher to save up for Hector's sound system. They had the best tiramisu I'd ever eaten. I couldn't wait for Millie to try it.

She kissed me on the cheek when she got in the car, and then she put her hand on mine on the steering wheel. "I'm so excited for dinner, and I hate to be a buzzkill, but ... can we just make sure I'm home by nine, or ten at the very latest?" she asked. "I want to make sure I get a good night's sleep. We're just two months from state! And I want to show my mom that I'm behaving responsibly after the whole sleeping-over-at-your-house debacle. We're still not really talking all that much. She says to go ahead and do what I want, but I'm waiting for the other shoe to drop."

"Not to worry," I told her. "We can have our tiramisu and debate, too."

She rolled her eyes, but she laughed.

I'd stayed up late the night before making a bouquet out of old

---

49 Various tournaments throughout the year were Nationals qualifiers; you had to place at several of them to be invited. Not surprisingly, Millie had already done that.

debate flowcharts. "Think that's corny? These are for you," I said, handing them to her. "Flow-ers."

She took them from me and brought them to her nose, smelling them. "I love them."

"For our first three months," I said.

"I didn't get you anything!"

"You didn't have to," I said. "What's that they say, your presence is my present? Your presence is my present."

"I think that's what you say to party guests."

"You're my one-woman party," I told her.

"That's more than enough cheesiness for one car ride," she said, smiling. She put her nose in the bouquet again. "No one's ever given me flow-ers before."

Dinner was perfect. The waiter, a guy named Tommy with a full sleeve of tattoos, remembered me from my dishwashing days and kept bringing over "amuse-bouches"[50] from the chef-owner, Roberto, who was tickled his former employee was on a date in his restaurant. Millie and I split a caprese salad, and I told her about how they grew their own basil and tomatoes in the greenhouse out back.

"You really should become a chef," she told me.

"It's always been kind of a dream of mine," I admitted.

"That's when stuff starts coming alive, when you say it," she told me, her eyes shining.

Millie ordered pappardelle bolognese, and I got the mac and cheese with truffle oil because, well, mac *and* cheese *and* truffle oil? Our dessert might have been cliché, but it was so good. We

---

50 Small appetizers or hors d'oeuvres, usually complimentary at fancy restaurants. The word means "entertains the mouth" in French.

held hands and stared into each other's eyes and shared every-thing. And then she checked her phone.

"Tag! It's almost nine," she said. "I don't want tonight to end, I really don't, but we have a tournament tomorrow."

"Your cases are perfect. I don't think you could lose even if you tried," I said.

I could see her wrestling with whether to stay or go, and I just waited, figuring it was her decision. When Tommy came by and asked if we wanted espresso, Millie said, "Why not?" He left to get our drinks, and she leaned in conspiratorially. "I've never had espresso before," she said. "Tag, this is why you're so good for me. You do what you want. And I should, too. My mom isn't telling me what to do. I can choose for myself."

"Well, in that case," I said, "the night is still young. Should we take advantage of it for a little bit longer?"

"What do you mean?"

"There's a karaoke place right down the block," I told her. "People from the restaurant always talked about it. We don't have to stay late or anything. But want to try singing into a microphone in a dark room to the musical accompaniment of your choice?"

"Maybe I do." She leaned over and kissed me again.

Tommy came by and dropped off our check. "Guess who's here?" he said, pointing at the bar, where an older white guy in a suit and tie sat talking to the bartender. "Senator Martin Leaney. He comes in here once in a while, says he loves Roberto's cooking more than his own mother's."

"I know that guy," I said slowly. "He's one of those old-school Republicans who's been in office forever. A total Second Amend-ment guy. He voted no on the gun safety bill they were trying to pass last year. He said teachers should arm themselves with baseball bats or books to fight off shooters. He's the worst! All 'thoughts and prayers' and never doing anything to actually prevent people from dying."

Tommy shrugged. "My policy is, stay out of politics and it's all good." He smiled. "No rush. Pay whenever you're ready," he added, and walked away.

"I'm going to go talk to him," I said, reaching into my wallet for the cash to pay our tab.

"Who?"

"The senator. Tommy's wrong. You can't stay out of politics if you want anything to change. I'm going to tell Leaney what happened to us. Maybe I can make a difference!"

"Tag!" she said, "I don't think . . . ," but I was already heading to the bar.

"Mr. Leaney," I said, tapping him on the shoulder. "I'm one of your constituents, and I wondered if I might have a word."

"I'm off the clock," he said, pointing to his whiskey. "Son, aren't you a little young to be at the bar? Are you a registered voter?"

"I will be next year," I said. "And what I have to say won't take any time at all. In October, I was at a high school debate tournament where there was a shooter scare. It was mass chaos. I had to hide in a supply closet for nearly an hour, and I've had nightmares ever since. Meanwhile, you voted against a bill supporting even the simplest background checks that would make it just a little bit harder for people to get guns. In Alabama, more than a thousand people die of firearm deaths yearly, an average of nearly three people a day! It's one of the highest rates in the nation. I wanna know . . . how do you sleep at night?"

"I sleep pretty well, actually," he said. "Got me a new Posturepedic mattress, and it treats me right. So does upholding the Second Amendment." He grinned and patted me on the back. "Son, sounds like nothing much happened to you—it was a scare, not an actual incident—so what's the worry?"

"What's the worry?" I couldn't believe what he was saying. "What about all the people who weren't lucky enough for their shooter situations to just be scares?"

"I have a tip: Try getting your anxieties out at the shooting range—you'll feel a whole lot better. Take some control. Be a man." He sipped his whiskey and turned away.

What an asshole. For a second, I almost let it all out, the way I had with Culhane in my round with Millie. I could tell him what I really thought about him and his ghoulish beliefs, and that would feel good, for a minute. But it wouldn't change anything, I realized. What if I approached it from another angle?

"But background checks and basic gun safety regulations aren't against the Second Amendment," I said slowly, and he turned to face me again, like he was surprised I was still there. "I'd think that as a Republican, you'd support responsible gun ownership that upholds American tradition, safety, and order. If people are going to have guns, shouldn't we make sure they're gonna use them responsibly, in a way that's consistent with family values? Don't we have rules about a variety of other things—like driving, or how old you have to be to buy alcohol, or wearing seat belts, that are about making the world safer for everyone? And shouldn't unlicensed vendors be prevented from selling guns? At the very least, the state should be making money from licenses!"

"That bill they were tryin' to pass was full of a bunch of other garbage, too," he said. "I couldn't agree with it. "

"Then why don't you write a new law?" I asked. "Background checks are a start. Don't you want that for your family . . . for your grandbabies?" (I was shooting in the dark—no pun intended—hoping that he actually had grandbabies.) "Don't you want to be one of the guys who did something good, who will be remembered for that?"

"That I do, my boy. That I do." He sipped his whiskey again. "But I already believe I'm doing something good. Our little talk ain't gonna change that."

Roberto had come out of the kitchen. "Tag, I'm going to have to ask you to leave. You really can't be in the bar area."

"He's leaving now," said Senator Leaney. He was so sure of himself.

Then Millie was right next to me. She grabbed my elbow and whispered in my ear, "You did it. Now let's go before they call the cops."

"I'm done, anyway," I said.

We left the restaurant and stood on the sidewalk, looking at each other.

"Tag. That was incredible." She grinned.

"It didn't change a thing, though. In fact, I might have just made him more anti-gun-control." I frowned. "I kinda hate that guy."

"But you said it. That counts," said Millie. "Do you really think that we just need background checks? I thought you supported banning guns altogether."

"I do. But I read this thing about how to convince people who are on opposite sides of the fence, and I thought maybe I'd try some of those tactics. I thought, maybe I can get him to change his mind one little point at a time, you know, if I make it about patriotism and safety and babies?"

"You used rhetoric," she said, beaming at me. "You really are a great debater."

"But it didn't work."

A twentysomething Black woman stepped out of the restaurant carrying a takeout bag. "Hey, are you that kid who was just in the bar talking to Leaney?" she asked.

"He is," said Millie.

I nodded. "Not that it did any good."

"He's a lost cause—forget him. He's not gonna last forever. There are plenty of others who need to hear what you have to say, who will actually listen. I'm looking to organize some mobilizing events for young and upcoming voters, and I'd love you to be a part of it." She pulled a card out of her bag and handed it to me. "Lila Johnston. I'm on the Birmingham City Council. Local government is where stuff really happens."

I took the card. "Thanks," I said.

A car pulled up, and she got in. "Email me!" she said as they drove away.

"Well, look at that," said Millie. "Someone said something that mattered, and someone heard it, and now maybe they're going to do things about it!"

"Oh my God," I said. "Karaoke? I can't end the night like this!"

She grabbed my hand. "Yes!"

Fifteen minutes later, we were in one of those private rooms karaoke places have, where you can croon to each other free from the embarrassment of others watching. She was paging through the binder of songs. I watched her running her finger down the pages and turning them thoughtfully. Everything Millicent Chalmers did, she did well.

"Found it!" she said, and looked up. "Why are you staring at me?" she asked. "Do you know what you're singing? You didn't even look at the book!"

"I've had it picked since this morning," I admitted.

"You knew we were going to karaoke this morning?"

"I hoped," I said.

I'd chosen this ballad from Guns N' Roses, a band my mom used to like, and I guess they were still around because I'd seen tweets from Axl Rose, their frontman. The guy used to be kind of an asshole, but nowadays he spoke in favor of progressive stuff and the band had even published a children's book. So maybe you really can reinvent yourself, become a better person, grow up and change? Was there hope, even, for politicians who'd chosen the wrong side of the argument? The song was "Patience," and it made me think about Millie, how I'd had to be patient and wait for her to get in touch with me, and she had. But maybe it was also about patience with the world, waiting for it to change. How patient, though, could anyone be? Sometimes the answer isn't patience. Sometimes there's literally no time for it.

I'd been practicing a slow sway-dance like Axl did in the video. Millie watched me, transfixed.

"Oh. My. God," she said when I was done, and clapped. "I love it."

"Now you!" I said.

"Close your eyes first," she said, and I did.

"Turn around," she said.

"Huh?" I said, opening my eyes. "I'm looking at you." But she was singing.

I knew this song—it was one that my mom played when she was on a break from the hair bands. I sat and listened, and when Millie was done with "Total Eclipse of the Heart," I stood up and cheered.

We kept going, mixing my favorite rock classics with Taylor Swift and The Weeknd and Billie Eilish and some K-pop, too. We even sang "It's Tricky" together. Just before midnight, the people from the karaoke place came and knocked on the door of our room and told us it was time to go home; they were closing up.

"It's so late!" said Millie, looking at her phone. "Oh my God."

"I know!" I said. "But it was so worth it."

"It really, really was." She kissed me.

I couldn't think of when I'd had so much fun.

MILLIE

He dropped me off at my door after midnight.

They say sometimes there are sparks when you kiss someone you really like, but this felt more like an electrical storm.

The next morning, I woke up smiling, which was funny. Who woke up smiling? Beau licked my face, and I pushed him away, still smiling. I got out of bed and walked to the bathroom, where I washed my face and brushed my teeth, gazing at this smiley person in the mirror. Who was she?

"Who *are* you?" I asked. But nothing came out.

Oh no. NO.

I ran to the kitchen, and my mom watched me as I rummaged through the refrigerator. Did we have orange juice? We were not juice-drinking types. Black coffee or nothing.

She knew something was wrong right away. "What's up?" she asked.

I tried again. Nothing. I pointed to my throat and shook my head.

She jumped up and felt my forehead. "Are you sick? You're not feverish. Let me put on some hot tea and take a look at your throat. I'll get my nurse's bag," she said. "Millie. Breathe."

I must have looked like death, or like someone just died. RIP, my debate career.

I thought about what Tag had said the night before, that I'd turned him into a winner. Maybe he'd done the opposite to me. Not on purpose. It couldn't have been on purpose.

My mom had warned me. And I had refused to listen. This was all my own stupid fault.

"Open wide and let me see," she said, coming back and putting a tongue depressor gently in my mouth. "Looks red, but not like strep." She pulled out the depressor and gave me a sharp look. "I didn't hear you come home; it must have been pretty late. Is this you doing what's right for you, what you're smart enough to decide for yourself?"

I tried to speak. Again, nothing.

"Don't talk," she told me, and handed me a pad of paper and a pen. "And don't whisper—it's harder on your voice. Write it down."

Mom, the tournament starts tonight. What do I do?

"Lots of fluids," she said calmly. "Rest, gargle with salt water, and hopefully by your first debate you'll be back in fighting shape."

I hung my head.

"Or not. Millie, I've been thinking about what you told me, about how you want to have a life along with debate. I get that. I do. And I understand wanting to make your own choices, and feeling old enough to do so. But there are repercussions for everything you decide."

"I know," I tried to say.

"Don't talk. I have to admit, I did a heck of a lot worse than you when I was young. But you're not me. *You* have a real chance here! Don't you see how important that is? For you. Not for me. For you." She sighed.

I DO SEE.

She patted my back. "Good. Now, one debate tournament is not going to make or break you. This isn't state. You still have a chance at that scholarship. But I think you should think about what you really want. What are the words you use in debate? Fallacy versus truth? What's the truth for you, and what's the fallacy?"

Oh God, now she was dropping Mom philosophy mixed with debate philosophy.

"Because you've worked really hard, and for a long time, on debate, and this boy has just come into your life, and I know how that changes things—trust me, I know. He's cute, he really is, I can see that . . ."

Awkward.

"But it's important to remember that you're still you, and the things you want and need are still there, too, outside of him. What we want is allowed to change and shift as we grow and learn. But when it comes to giving up money for education, or something you've worked on for your entire high school career, I really want you to think about that . . ."

OKAY.

"That's all. I just want you to think. Before you ditch it all for some hottie."

Good lord.

Mom went to work, and I stayed home, cuddling with Beau, drinking hot tea with honey, gargling with salt water, sucking on lozenges, googling laryngitis cures. I downed chicken soup. I took the hottest of baths, filling the room with steam and sitting there for as long as I possibly could.

By the afternoon, my voice was barely a crackle. I texted Kargle that I would have to forfeit. I texted Carlos that I was sick and to tell Tag. And I shut off my phone and buried myself in Netflix, where I didn't have to think about anything for a while.

TAG

I texted her when I woke up. A string of smiley faces and hearts. At first, when she didn't write back, I thought she was just busy getting ready for the tournament. But when I didn't hear from her by the afternoon, I started to worry. She didn't respond to any of my follow-up messages, either.

At the tournament, Carlos told me she was sick. That was weird. Why hadn't she written to me? Or called me? She'd been fine the night before.

He shrugged. He didn't get it, either.

I left her a voice mail telling her to drink lots of soup and stay warm and that I'd call her later.

Once the debates started, time kind of got away from me, because my kritik in which I pointed out that the government could never reduce an economic gap between the rich and poor because that was the very basis of a capitalist system . . . it actually worked. I couldn't believe it.

By the end of it all, there was a new winner. It was me.

Rajesh came in second. Without Millie in the picture, The Park School swept the tournament. Rose made it to semis and so did Carlos. So did Ricky Yee, who now had an official date with Carlos after the two of them happened to meet at the Starbucks around the corner from the tournament, reaching for the oat milk at the same time.

Angela Tennant was there. This time she had on purple lipstick and a purple dress. She complimented me on my "groundbreaking take" and asked me where my girlfriend—"the amazing debater"—was, but I didn't have an answer.

Francine was so happy when the finalists were announced, she did a little dance. She took a picture of me accepting my trophy, and I texted it to my parents and Mason. They sent me a slew of thumbs-ups and happy faces. I texted it to Millie and got nothing.

Cheater's Lake was there, but not a single one of them broke to finals. They glared at me when I went up to accept my award, and one of them muttered, "Commie." I wished I could send a picture of how mad they were to Millie. We would laugh and laugh and laugh.

Rajesh and I actually had a good time in our final debate, and when it was over, he high-fived me and said, "Man, this is why you're the GOAT! No one but you could pull that argument off!"

I texted Millie paragraphs about what was happening. Finally, she wrote back.

I lost my voice, she said. **Staying out and doing karaoke.**

And then I got it.

I had been really stupid, and selfish, again.

I'm so sorry, I wrote. **That was all my fault.**

She didn't respond.

I didn't know what to do about it, how to make it up to her. I mean, I wouldn't talk to me, either, if I *could* talk to me. And now she couldn't use the thing that made Millicent M. Chalmers the best debater in Alabama. Her voice.

Now, according to this tournament, the winner was *me*.

I hadn't done it on purpose, I really hadn't.

You believe me, right?

What should a person say to make another person believe they'll start listening, for real, this time? Or do you just have to wait patiently and listen as hard as you can?

MILLIE

After a weekend of thinking, resting, and finally getting my voice back, I decided I would have to cut Tag out of my life. My mom was right. He was too much of a temptation. I needed to stay focused and win. That was what mattered.

I'd tell him all that, in person, at the next tournament. It was just two weeks away. I couldn't break up with him on the phone. That wouldn't be right. I avoided his calls and sent a few texts saying I was just really busy dealing with some college stuff; I'd talk to him soon. I'm sure he was confused, but I didn't know what else to do.

Then, on the morning of the next tournament, the Renegade Round Robin of Rainbow City,[51] I really did have a fever. It turned out to be the flu. I texted Kargle, and I told Carlos I wouldn't be there, and I basically repeated my convalescence routine, with a bucket by my bed, while my mom texted reminders for me to hydrate and Beau cuddled with me.

I didn't want to lose too much ground. Missing two tournaments wasn't great, but I could still make it up. I had to get back out there as soon as I could.

But something had gone wrong. At home, I'd look at my cases and I'd choke. Literally, I'd cough until I had to stop and get a glass of water, and then Beau would nudge my hand and want me to

---

51 Alliteration! Debaters love it, too.

play with him, and I'd do that and be fine—until I opened up a debate case again.

The only thing I could read was the Wollstonecraft book, which was now overdue.

I tried to go back to the library to return it, but when I got to the bike rack I just started crying. I had to go home.

It was like something in me had broken.

I started to wonder why I'd spent so much of my life doing this thing that caused as much pain as it did pleasure. That I wasn't even sure I liked.

Why did I care so much about winning, anyway? Without debate, I could just be a normal teenager. I could do my schoolwork and go to football games and hang out with my friends. I'd have to get some new friends, though, because my debate crew was, well, debating.

Carlos thought I was depressed. He thought I should talk to Tag.

I caught my mom googling local therapists. I saw a missed call from Coach Kargle on her phone, and when she noticed, she walked into the next room to make a call and whispered the whole time.

Kargle kept checking in, telling me he was there if I wanted to talk. I didn't, really.

I missed Tag. That wasn't a fallacy. I missed him so hard my whole body ached.

I drafted so many texts to tell him how I really felt. But I could never actually send anything. I wanted to, but I just couldn't. I know it wasn't fair. He reached out about a million times. I stopped responding. Eventually he stopped trying. I couldn't blame him for that, but it hurt, too.

I'd missed two tournaments, and almost a full month of debate. Meanwhile, I heard he was winning with that kritik argument only he could pull off. Carlos told me Tag and Rajesh were now the two to beat. Maybe it was just their turn to win.

Someone should end up a winner in all of this.

TAG

By Valentine's Day, it was pretty clear I'd been dumped. She'd stopped responding to my texts and voice mails; she wouldn't take my calls. How long do you try before you get the picture? I didn't want to cross the line from ex-boyfriend to creep.

When I saw him at the second tournament she missed, Carlos told me Millie was going through some things. He didn't really understand it himself, he said.

"Do you think she's okay?" I asked.

"I don't, really," he said. "But I don't know what to do about it. I even called her mom. She thinks Millie just needs to commit herself fully to debate without distractions."

"But she's not even debating!" I told him. "One of the things that makes her *her*."

"I know," said Carlos. He made a sad face.

"You have to keep checking on her," I said. "Don't let her go through this alone."

"I won't. She's my best friend," he said. "I'm sorry; I really liked the two of you together. She seemed really happy. I'd never seen her like that in all my time knowing her. She was just, like, *happy*."

That's what I didn't understand at all. She *had* seemed happy. Was what I'd done so bad, so unforgivable, that she couldn't remember how happy we both had been?

She hadn't even given me a chance to say sorry.

What's weird is, everything else was going great: I was winning.

People kept throwing arguments at me, but I could always find a way to fend them off. Rajesh and I were both killing it. He kept asking if I wanted to hang out with him and Rose, but I couldn't stand to be around another couple.

Francine pulled me aside after class one day. "You're debating better than you ever have," she told me. "But that's the only place it seems like you're alive. If you need to take a break, or just talk, I'm here."

"It's just, what happened with Millie," I said. "She won't even talk to me. I can't make her understand."

"Sometimes you just can't and you have to let it go," she said. "But it will stop hurting so much. I promise."

"I guess," I said. I couldn't see how I'd ever get there, so it might as well be a fantasy.

Part of me wanted to stop debating, but I felt like I'd be letting Francine and everyone else down. I believed in my argument, but that didn't make me feel better. It was only talk. How did you actually start to change systems that were unfair and corrupt? Not through talk: through doing.

I wanted to do more. I emailed Lila Johnston, the Birmingham City Council member Millie and I had met that night outside of Ciao!, and arranged a meeting. That helped.

Then one day I was home, moping around and going back and forth between my debate cases and YouTube videos on how to hand-stretch mozzarella cheese when Mason popped her head into my room.

"Tag. I have something I need to tell you," she said.

I tore my eyes away from my screen. She looked nervous and was holding her laptop. "What's up?"

"Promise you won't be mad."

"How can I promise when I don't know what you're going to tell me?"

"Okay, well, this is going to sound kind of weird, but . . . I'm the person behind the Millicent Calmerzzz Twitter account," she said.

"You're the—what? That bot account?"

"I'm the bot," she said. "Or, I mean, I'm not a bot. I'm me. Don't be mad!"

"I'm not mad, but what the heck, Mason. That's a really creepy thing to do."

"I know," she said. "It wasn't supposed to be. I wanted to make it an anonymous fan account, to make Millie feel good. But then I never really had anything that felt right to say, and it started to feel weird that I had her picture up there. I don't know if you noticed, but I changed it to a puppy a while back. Honestly, I'm pretty embarrassed about the whole thing. I never even tweeted from it. Don't tell her, okay?"

"We're not even talking, so I definitely won't."

Mason frowned. "Can't y'all make up?"

"It doesn't work that way, unfortunately," I said.

She frowned harder. "But . . ."

"And you should probably delete that account."

"That's why I went on today in the first place," said Mason. "And then I saw I had a message. I think you need to see it." She handed me her laptop.

I had to read it twice. "Oh my God," I said.

It was a tip from someone with a throwaway account called

@NoMoreCheatinginLD. They claimed to be a former Alabama debater who'd left the circuit a few years ago and had solid evidence that Chatham's Lake had been plagiarizing cases back then, and still were. *If you're the real Millicent Chalmers, I thought you should know*, the person said. *You deserve to win state. Not them. Tell Speech and Debate to look into it. They have a repository of archives they keep pulling from. They never credit the original source. And they don't even change a word sometimes.*

"Wow," I said.

"Yeah," said Mason. "What should we do?"

"I think I should tell Millie," I said. "But first, let me screen grab this. We might need it as evidence."

"Maybe Cheater's Lake will finally get what's coming to them," said Mason.

"I hope so," I said. "Finally."

"Yeah," she said. "It's been too long."

I stared at that screenshot for a good fifteen minutes, and then I picked up the phone.

MILLIE

I was sitting at the table with my mom talking about what we wanted for dinner when my phone rang. Something made me pick up. I didn't even look to see who the caller was. I guess I should have.

"Hello?"

"Millie!" It was Tag. "Are you okay? I've been so worried—"

"Hi," I said as emotionlessly as I could manage. "You don't have to worry. I'm fine."

"Can I see you? Can we meet? Maybe at Nick's or the library? Can we talk?"

"I can't," I said. If I gave myself a little, I'd want it all. And there was no way to have all of what I wanted; I'd proven that already. "I'm sorry, Tag. I just can't see you anymore."

My mom put her hand on my shoulder.

"This just feels so wrong, Millie. And there's something I really need to tell you . . . it's important."

"I'm sorry," I said again, trying not to cry. If I started crying, I wouldn't be able to stop. "I'm really sorry. I have to—"

"Millie! Don't hang up! Promise me one thing . . . You owe me this!"

That helped. I got steel in my voice then.

"I don't owe you anything," I said.

"You're right. But please come back," he said. "I'll do whatever you want. You never have to talk to me again, but you could still win state. We can box out Chatham's Lake, and I'll step aside so you can take it."

Anger flared up in me then, hot and true, and you know what, it actually felt good. "Excuse me. Are you saying *you'll let me win*?"

"Well. Er. No, not that you need that—"

"No. I don't. Taggart Strong, don't forget that I taught you everything you know. You don't need to *let* me do anything. I'll see you in finals. If *you* can make it that far."

I don't know what he said next because I hung up the phone.

My mom looked at me, and I could see she was both impressed and maybe just a tiny bit afraid.

"No boys," I told her. "It's like you said. They just get in the way of everything."

Then I picked up the phone and called Coach.

PART FOUR

March

Resolved: Inaction in the face of injustice
makes an individual morally culpable.

MILLIE

I t was one of those late-winter days where you can just feel that spring is coming, it's going to happen, it really is. There's hope in the air.

I was meeting Coach at Nick's to go over the new resolution, and my cases.

I was back.

When I got there, Nick pointed to the booth where Kargle had set up shop. He was surrounded by papers. Typical Coach; he just got right back up and started coaching again. I had to respect that. "Tell him to make some room for the pie he's ordered, 'cuz it's coming right up," Nick said. "Millie, it's been a while. Nice to see you again."

"I'm sorry, I've missed this place," I told him. The last time I'd been there, more than a month ago, it had been with Tag. Looking around at the booths, I could almost picture us laughing and sharing a pizza. It made me ache, but I couldn't let that stop me.

"Things happen. No worries."

I slid in across from Kargle. "What is all this?"

"Millie," he said, smiling at me. "I have something to say."

"Never leave you in a lurch again?"

"No," he said, looking at me seriously. "We all deserve a moment to reconsider the path we're on. But presuming you're serious and want to get back out there—"

"I am," I said. "One hundred percent."

"There's something we should talk about. Chatham's Lake—"

"Pizza!" said Nick, setting down the wire rack.

"Thanks, Nick," said Kargle, sweeping his pages over to the side. "I'm famished."

I took a slice, too. Eating always helped.

We both chewed contentedly for a few minutes.

"You were saying?" I finally asked. "Something about Chatham's Lake?"

"Yes. I had this idea. What if you did a kritik?" he asked.

"About what?"

"About them."

I almost spat out my pizza. "Really?"

He showed me the pages he'd been working on. He'd written out a list of everything the Chatham's Lakers had done to me, from the nude photos to the harassment from Culhane and the video, which, while we couldn't prove it, exactly, had their fingerprints all over it. And everything in between. A million tiny cuts, some larger than others, that, along with laryngitis, had very nearly resulted in me quitting debate forever.

"You could use all this," he said. "Say it. I think people would listen."

"I don't know," I told him.

Kargle looked at me. "You're still up for the Martha Linger Scholarship. If you win, that sets you up for something even bigger. The opportunities are there for you. You deserve them. And the world will benefit from you having them. I want a future where Millicent Chalmers is, pardon my French, getting shit done! Why don't you call those pieces of you-know-what on their behavior and really show them who's boss?"

I thought about fear and how it could keep you down. How doing *nothing* would never really keep you safe. How I didn't want to have to depend on others to get what I wanted. And how much I really did want to take home that state trophy, and the scholarship, too. "That's why I'm here," I said. "I want that, too."

"So, you'll do it?"

"Here's the thing about that," I said slowly. "Remember how we reported them for what they did with those nude photos freshman year? And any number of other things they've done wrong—"

Kargle was nodding. "They got slapped on the wrist and just kept debating?"

"They're still debating, they could still win state, and they could still go to Nationals. Nothing has ever changed with them. I just don't know if calling them out is going to have the effect we want. Usually it just makes them mad, and then they go after me harder."

Kargle looked at me sadly. "I'm kind of wrecked this is the lesson you've already learned in life."

"But it does make me want to beat them even more than ever," I admitted.

He considered me for a moment.

"I just want to win on my own terms," I told him. "The way I want to do it. And not because of anyone else. Because of me."

"A running play, if you will," he said. "Instead of a quarterback sneak. I understand that completely."

"Me too," said the same football player who'd asked if I'd seen Kargle when I was at Nick's with Tag months ago. He had a way of creeping up on you. "Though the rest of y'all's debate talk is over my head half the time," he admitted.

"Hey, Brian," said Kargle. "What's up?"

He pointed back at the girl in the booth who was looking over at us. She blushed and gave a little wave. "That's my sister," he said. "She's going to be a freshman. She's pretty shy, which is why she got me to come over here first. Anyway, she's interested in joining the team and wants to talk to you about it, Millie."

"Really?" I said.

"Yeah, I tried to ask before, but you were with a dude and it seemed personal, so I didn't want to interrupt. I hadn't seen you in a while, and then you were here today. Sorry if I barged in on something important."

"No worries," I said. "What's your sister's name?"

"Cleo," he told me.

"Cleo!" I yelled across the room, making a megaphone with my hands. "Text me! I'm giving your brother my number." I wrote it on a napkin and handed it to him. "Once you start, it gets easier and easier." I pointed to Kargle. "This guy helps."

"Thanks," she mumbled back, turning bright red. But she smiled. "I will."

"Thanks," Brian echoed. "Good luck with your tournament and stuff. Later, Coach."

As Brian walked back to his table, Coach reached for another slice. "Listen, if I eat the whole pie, we can order another," he said.

"Coach Kargle, I may have underestimated you," I said.

He smiled. "A lot of people do."

My first tournament back, the Ardmore Rumble, was hard. The two hardest parts were (a) seeing Tag (ugh), and (b) going against Blanton Bodie in semifinals. I stepped into that room, and Edmund Culhane and a bunch of other Chatham's Lakers were there watching. Culhane sneered at me, and I felt sick to my stomach. I felt even worse when Blanton started talking. It turned out, kritiks were all over the place now: Blanton was trying one out, and it was against me. He called my behavior "antagonistic" to the values of debate society. I asked what behavior, exactly, he was talking about. He said that the proof was everywhere—I'd had a relationship with a competitor on the circuit; what other improprieties might there be? You could see the judges grimace, but they didn't tell him to stop. My recent absence also showed lack of proper dedication to the debate cause, Blanton said. I was not worthy of a win at this tournament and certainly not at state, he claimed.

I got up. "As the honorable Supreme Court justice, the late, great Ruth Bader Ginsburg, once said, 'I ask no favor for my sex; all I ask of our brethren is that they take their feet off our necks.'" I gave Blanton Bodie the kind of death stare the Chatham's Lakers were so fond of delivering and then turned back to the judges. "Regardless of the many unsubstantiated rumors my opponent is throwing at me, I offer that this debate, all debates, must be considered on the merits of the debate itself. If we start turning debate into a referendum on personal morality, trust that my opponent will himself face all sorts of difficulties. The burden of debate must be upheld. Also. *I only missed two tournaments, for the love of God.*"

I won.

Luckily, Tag lost in semis, so I never had to debate him.

I won the entire tournament. Still, the rumors didn't stop. I could hear the whispers while I was onstage accepting my trophy. *I was a slut with daddy issues who was sleeping with Tag and my coach and the tournament director. I was a dude. I was pregnant. I'd had an abortion. I gave blow jobs to win. And had you heard about the nude pictures?*

How in the world could all these things be true at the same time? It didn't matter. You had to give Chatham's Lake credit for one thing: They were always just as gross as you imagined. They were allowed to be just that gross, and I had to take it. This was my punishment for doing what I wanted to do, for winning.

It's like people say: When someone shows you who they are, believe them. But what if you also have to keep interacting with them?

I did think about coming back with a kritik like Kargle had suggested, but it just didn't feel right. Would anyone believe me, or care enough to change things? They never had before.

So I steeled myself and worked even harder. Millicent "Machine" Chalmers. That was me.

TAG

Y ou could have predicted the backlash when Millie came
back and started winning everything again.

I'd see her across the cafeteria, sitting with Carlos. I
cheered her on from afar, not that she knew it. She wouldn't talk
to me; she wouldn't even look at me. I couldn't believe Blanton
Bodie did that kritik about her reputation. I was proud of her for
how she responded, but I kept thinking about how much it must
have hurt. I couldn't focus in semis, and lost to this novice from
Decatur High.

Oh well. At least Millie took home the whole damn thing.

After that tournament, I'd had enough. I called Speech and Debate administration and reported Cheater's Lake for plagiarism.
The woman who answered the phone said they'd look into it.

"Look into it like actually *do* something about it?" I asked. "Because there's been a whole lot of talk and not enough action when
it comes to these guys and their bullying, misogyny, and, apparently, outright cheating that's been happening for decades. Please
do more than look into it. Stop them."

"I'll include that in the note to the director," said the woman.
"Thank you for your concern. What's your name, son?"

"Uh, Blanton Bodie," I told her.

I started having this new nightmare. I'd watch as a group of
guys who looked a lot like Cheater's Lakers surrounded Millie
and started taunting her. One of them would pull out a gun.

I'd wake up covered in sweat, my head pounding.

At least there was some good news: Rajesh got into Harvard! But now he was second-guessing his choice. The University of Chicago seemed like it might be awesome, and Chicago was such a cool town, he kept telling me. Or what if he went to the University of Alabama, and then he could see Rose every weekend? What if he did something different from what everyone expected—from what even he had expected for himself? The possibilities were suddenly endless.

I told him to follow his heart. "That's the problem," he said, making a face. "My heart wants so many things. How do I choose?"

I could hardly relate. After all, my heart only wanted one thing.

But somewhere along the way, it started to want something else. To win. On my own. To show her, and, I guess myself, that I could.

I started by going to the library. My own, not hers. It was pretty decent, too, even if there was no Mrs. Mendez, and I only had one sandwich, not two halves. I read so much in those weeks. Around that time, I found out I got into Alabama, too. My parents were thrilled.

MILLIE

Sometimes winning had its drawbacks.

People stared at me when I walked through the halls. Some of them snickered or made rude noises. I heard "nude photos" in whispers when I entered rooms.

I just kept debating.

At one competition, a kind-looking woman judge in a floral dress took me aside to ask if I knew about all the rumors and how they made me look. "What about how they make the people who *started* them look?" I asked.

"Oh, darlin'," she said. "But you're the girl. Even if it's a lie, it's worse for you."

That didn't help.

Blanton Bodie didn't dare try a kritik again, but the harassment continued. Most weekends, my hands were covered in ink.

I avoided Tag. I'd see him at tournaments, trying not to look at me. That hurt, but a lot of things hurt. I hunkered down, and I kept debating.

And I kept winning.

State was at Chatham's Lake. All the schools took a turn, and it was theirs. There was nothing I could do about that except play the game. When I won, *then* I could celebrate. My mom had the day off and was going to come see me in final rounds. We could *both* celebrate.

For the record, I did enjoy how someone edited the signs posted at the tournament.

WELCOME TO THE ALABAMA STATE TOURNAMENT

❀

Greetings, students, coaches, and judges!

We're happy to share our beautiful school with you this exciting debate weekend.

Please await your first assignments in the cafeteria.

There are many fine catered foods for sale: We accept cash, credit, and Venmo.

Garbage bins are placed handily around the building; please use them.

It's our pleasure to host you.

May the best debater win state!

CHEATER'S
~~Chatham's~~ Lake Boys' ~~Preparatory~~ School
Harassed ~~Hosted~~ by the Predatory

#1 in Ivy League acceptance rates in the state
"WHAT OTHERS FEAR, WE DO FOR FUN"

TAG

Cheater's Lake was one of those schools with a *very* active alumni association, and when we arrived, it appeared that they'd all been summoned for a meeting. Their parking lot—marked ALUMNI ASSOCIATION ONLY—was full of BMWs. A bunch of guys were running around in suits, looking worried. I could only imagine it had something to do with covering their asses.

Maybe all the bad guys would, in the end, just take themselves right down with their own hubris and stupidity, I hoped. In the meantime, we'd have to do our best to challenge them.

At the coffee stand in the cafeteria, I ran into Joe Keller, who was adding sugar to his travel thermos. "Hey," I said. "I haven't seen you in a while! You shaved your beard."

He rubbed his face. "I always do in the spring. It's my renewal ritual."

"Ah," I said.

"Work's been a bear," he added. "But I got called in on kind of an emergency." He seemed a little amped. "Chatham's Lake has been disqualified from state due to plagiarism."

I tried to remain cool. "Oh, really?"

"Yes. Speech and Debate got a tip and found, and I quote, 'undeniable proof' that a 'purposeful history of plagiarism' has been underway at the school for at least a decade. Their coach is now under investigation for cheating *and* mishandling of the forensics budget. So I'm the de facto director this weekend. When it rains, it pours! Luckily, nothing I can't handle. Law, especially the non-profit world, prepares you for pretty much anything."

"What do your socks say?" I asked him, and he lifted one foot out of his loafer to show me. "KEEP CALM AND CARRION"?

"It seemed right, somehow," he said. He looked around the cafeteria. "I used to go to this school. How weird is that? Actually, I really hated it. Debate was the only good thing about it, and even that had issues. Get it? Debate, we got issues.[52] . . . Not that I ever plagiarized a case myself. But, you know, I remember a few kids who did. I didn't say anything back then. Didn't want to deal with the fallout. I guess it just kept happening, even after I left . . ."

I nodded, but my attention was elsewhere. Millie had just walked into the room, and it appeared that first-round schematics were being distributed.

The show would go on. Without Cheater's Lake.

---

52 Like I said. Debaters.

MILLIE

Cheater's Lake was out, disqualified for plagiarism, but I didn't have time to do much more than high-five Carlos and Kargle about that.

I kept debating. And I kept winning.

Tag was winning, too. That was fine, I told myself. I'd take him down just like the rest of them. Kritik or no kritik.

I knew how he worked.

Alabama State 67th Annual Tournament Finals Bracket

Carlos Gonzalez-Claremont

Grant Sturgess

Carlos Gonzalez-Claremont

Tucker Treadwell

Josh Coody

Tucker Treadwell

Carlos Gonzalez-Claremont

Blanton Bodie [DQ]

Taggart Strong

Taggart Strong

Howie Wilson [DQ]

Niva Prithee

Niva Prithee

Taggart Strong

Millicent Chalmers

Ricky Yee

Millicent Chalmers

Rajesh Shah

Renee Simpkins

Rajesh Shah

Millicent Chalmers

Olivier Fernandez

Fentress Jackson

Olivier Fernandez

Rose Powell

Casey Cratchett

Rose Powell

Rose Powell

53

53 FINALS!!!!!!!!

TAG

Rose and Rajesh came running toward me in the cafeteria, waving the paper listing the two debaters who would compete in the state final. "Tag. It's you!" Rose said.

I had a thought that made me laugh. At least she would talk to me now. She had to.

"You can do this!" Rajesh patted me on the back. "Bring it home, dude!"

Another voice came through. "Tag? Tag, can you come with me?"

I turned to face Francine.

"Let's go somewhere quieter," she said. I glanced around the cafeteria, where, beyond Rajesh and Rose and my whole team's concerned faces, I saw Edmund Culhane shouting at Blanton Bodie while the rest of their team looked on and their coach talked angrily into his phone. Even though they'd been disqualified, they'd stuck around, trying to fight the ruling. They kept saying it was their school, and if we wanted them out, we could try to make them leave. No one had time for that. We were here to debate.

Beyond them, Carlos was standing in a crowd of debaters who were clamoring over the schematics, freaking out when they saw that the former couple who didn't speak to each other were going to have to debate in the state final. *This* was the sort of drama people lived for. Carlos looked over them at me, and I looked back. "You okay?" he mouthed.

I didn't have a response to that.

Francine led me to a nearby classroom, where she sat me in a chair and told me to listen.

"Right now, this probably feels like the hardest thing you've ever had to do," she said. "I know. I've been there. But you just have to go out and debate the same way you've been debating all spring. You really do have a chance at this. Everyone's been saying your cases are incredible this resolution. Negative *and* affirmative. You're really doing it."

This time, I'd abandoned the kritik to go old-school. So many people were running them at this point, the technique had lost some of its magic. And I'd learned how to stand by my arguments on both sides, even if there *was* one I preferred to the other. *Could I actually win?* I wondered. *The Alabama state championship?* In the fall, it would have been unimaginable. But now, I *wanted* to. My parents and Mason would be in the audience watching me, and that made me want it even more.

My phone pinged. I ignored it.

"And, Tag. Isn't it better that it's you than one of those sexist, plagiarizing jerks from this very school? They're out! You can show them what the right thing to do really is!"

That had been the plan all along, hadn't it? Me and Millie, together in the state finals.

"Tag?" Francine asked. "Can you do this?"

"I think so," I said. "But I have a question. You said, 'I've been there.' What did you mean by that?"

"When I was in high school, I had to debate my ex in the final round of state," she said. "He dumped me right before, when I told him I wouldn't just let him win. He said it was more important for his future than mine." She made a face. "I never really talked about how wrong that was until now."

"Who won?"

"I did," she said, and grinned. "And I don't regret a single thing about handing his ass to him on a platter."

"I'd high-five you if I didn't feel a little bit like puking," I told her.

"Why don't you prep in here?" she suggested. "It's nice and quiet, and you still have almost a half hour to clear your head before the debate starts. I'll tell Rajesh to come and get you in plenty of time to make it to the room. How does that sound?" She looked at me. "Take some deep breaths."

"Okay," I said. I breathed, and then I pulled out my three-ring binder and got to work.

A minute later, I remembered the text that had come through. I grabbed my phone and looked at it.

It was from Millie.

MILLIE

They found me in a classroom where I'd sneaked away to get a little quiet time before the final, in an area of the school that wasn't being actively used this weekend. It wasn't so much that I needed to review my cases—I had those under control. But I was nervous about having to stand in the same room as Tag. Would I reach out and try to grab his hand during cross-ex? Would how I felt be clear to everyone in the room?

I still missed him.

But winning, and getting that scholarship, was way more important.

I had my head bent over my notes when Edmund Culhane walked in, followed by Blanton Bodie and three other Chatham's Lake debaters. They stood together, trying to intimidate. I wouldn't let them scare me.

Then they shut the door and locked it. *That* scared me. Not that I was going to show it.

"Why are you here?" I asked Culhane. "You're not even on the team anymore. Don't you have anything better to do? And Blanton, aren't you suspended? Aren't all of y'all suspended at this point?"

Culhane smirked at me. Blanton rolled his eyes.

"Don't *you* have anything better to do?" he asked. "Like get your nails done or something? Be an actual girl instead of competing in a sport that doesn't want you?"

"Debate is for people who want to *think*, so I have no idea why any of you do it," I snapped back. "It's for anyone who wants to have a voice."

They were clustered around me now. I thought about what I could do, who I could call for help. *Don't panic*, I told myself. One of them picked up my phone and pretended to talk into it.

"Oh, DebatrGrl, do you think Taggart Strong can save you this time?" he said in a falsetto.

Was this the moment they tried to use @MillicentCalmerzzz against me? I felt nauseated. And I couldn't even check my phone, since it was in one of their grubby hands. I'd have to sanitize it when I got it back.

"What are you talking about?" I asked. "Why are y'all such *creeps* all the time?"

"Bet I know her passcode," said Culhane. "Try 6–3–7–3. You know, the first four components of a debate."

"Nope," said the guy fiddling with my phone. He looked at me. "Wanna just tell us and make it easier?"

"Hell no," I said.

"Then it's the last four: 3–4–6–3," suggested Culhane.

"I'm in!" the guy said.

"DebatrGrl, so predictable," said Culhane. "You really should come up with something that isn't so easy to figure out."[54]

"Give me my phone back!" I yelled, trying to grab it, but the guy was typing something and pressing send, and then they were shoving me into a little supply closet that, yet again, I hadn't even noticed at the front of the room. I kicked and screamed and scratched—I got a nail into one of their faces, and that felt good— but they were too big, too strong, and we were so far away from

---

54 Point taken.

anyone else at the tournament. *Why had I chosen to come to this part of the building, stupid, stupid Millie!*

"Lock her up!" one of them said, and they all laughed. The door closed, and I heard a click. Relief that at least I was on one side of the door and they were on the other faded. I was their captive.

"Let me out!" I shouted. "You—fucking—assholes!"

"Shhhhh," said Culhane. "You don't want to interrupt the debate. It should be starting soon. It's the state final!"

They all laughed again.

"Conrad, you're bleeding," said Blanton Bodie.

"That bitch," answered Conrad. "Probably gave me hep C."

"Low-class trash. She deserves everything we're giving her, and more," said Blanton Bodie. "She brought it all upon herself. Probably the one who reported us for plagiarism, using my name!"

"She *wishes* she was a man," said Conrad, and laughed to himself. "Millicent Manboobs Chalmers."

"Okay, guys, part two of the plan. Let's go," said Culhane.

I could hear their voices fade and their footsteps grow quieter as they walked away.

I screamed as loud as I could, over and over again.

But when I heard them coming back, I stopped screaming and listened.

TAG

She'd written this: **Can we talk? Meet me in classroom 336.**
Sure, I wrote back. **Are you okay?**
Yeah, she wrote. **Just wanna clear the air bf we debate. U kno?**

Outside of classroom 336, I straightened my tie and knocked. Someone opened the door, grabbed me by the shoulders, and yanked me into the room.

It was Blanton Bodie. Culhane and some other creeps were with him.

"What are you doing?" I asked.

"If you're the assturd who reported us for plagiarism, fuck YOU," he said. "Someone used my name, and I know it was either you or your stupid girlfriend. Like it even matters—those cases were four hundred million years old. Whoever wrote them is probably dead by now."

"I don't think that's how plagiarism, or time, works," I told him. "And I'm hardly the only one who might be aware of your instincts to cheat before actually doing any work. Also, she's not my girlfriend."

"Fuck you, anyway," he said. "For fucking me over. For winning. And for fucking Millicent Chalmers," he added, and before I could explain that only two of those things were remotely true and one was a lie, he had punched me in the eye, which really, really hurt.

"You should have left Millicent Chalmers alone," said Culhane. "But since you had to go there and try to mess with us, too, you should know that Chatham's Lake *does not back down.*"

"Yeah! It's payback time!" shouted a red-faced Blanton Bodie like he thought he was in a Steven Seagal movie. I thought of Rajesh and *Saving Private Ryan*, and how that was a much better film than anything Seagal ever did, and boy, was I glad my best friend was Rajesh Shah and not Blanton Bodie.

The rest of the Chatham's Lake crew laughed, and one of them, who appeared to be bleeding from the face, said, "We just have to wait ten minutes now. If they don't show up, they're both disqualified."

They?

"You liked it when you were in a closet last time, when you freaked out from the sound of a *scawy motowcycle,*" said Blanton Bodie.

"Yeah, what a bunch of loser babies, wah, wah, wah," said Culhane.

The group of them shoved me into a dark supply closet, closed the door, and locked it from the outside.

"Okay, guys, let's go," said Culhane. "As far as anyone knows, Millie lured him into the closet for some sexual *flavors* so he'd let her win. You still have her phone?" he asked one of his cronies.

"Yep," the boy said.

"Set it up," said Culhane. "Take a picture of the messages after you press send. We'll destroy the phone later, and we might need the evidence."

There was more laughter, and footsteps. A door closed. Silence.

They? Was I alone in this closet or . . .

"Hey," said a voice in the dark.

"Millie?"

"Yeah."

"Did he just say *sexual flavors*?"

MILLIE

I flicked on the light. "Tag! Your eye!"

"Yeah. It really hurts to get punched in the face. That's something I wish I didn't know."

"I didn't text you that message," I said.

"I should have figured that out. You never write things like 'U kno.' Or, I mean, you never used to. When you wrote to me."

"Tag."

"It's okay," he said. "I'm a big boy. I can handle it. No one is entitled to have someone else like them just because they want it to be the case. But I do wish you'd at least dumped me in person. The ghosting really hurt. And then I had to keep seeing you, but I couldn't talk to you, and . . ."

"I didn't want to dump you at all," I said. Tag was supposed to be my competitor, and you could never let them see you break down, but suddenly I felt like crying. "That's why I could never say anything, even when you called me that day. It all just got so messed up. Like, if I didn't win, who was I? And you didn't understand how much I needed to win!"

"I did!" he said. "I wanted you to!"

"Well, I wanted to, too. But instead, the opposite happened. I fell apart. And now, when I just need to get out there and win, I have these assholes shoving me in closets and . . ." I put my face in my hands. "It's not fair. It's never been fair. I was *never* going to win, was I? They wouldn't let me. Why did I try so hard and give up so much when it was never going to happen in the first place?"

"Who says it was never going to happen?" said Tag. "It's not *their* job to decide who wins." He reached into his pocket. "It's *ours.* How convenient that Cheater's Lake didn't notice I had my phone with me. Does that sound like the kind of thing a winning debate team would do? Not to mention, framing two people for a supposedly orchestrated make-out session in a room where the door locks from the *outside*? And don't even get me started on the plagiarism."

"Seriously? You have your phone?"

"It's endlessly shocking to me to realize how *stupid* certain bad guys are," he said. "It's like they never did any of the actual work and have just gotten by on their money and privilege their whole lives. And then there are people like me, who aren't stupid, exactly, but who could admittedly stand to learn a little bit more about their entitlement and how that plays into how they treat others, too."

I stared at him.

"I'm trying," he said.

"I'm happy to hear that," I said. "Now, let's get out of here. We have a debate to get started."

TAG'S GROUP TEXT

TS RS RP

TAG: Hey y'all, it seems that I have been locked in a supply closet with Millie. Can you come get us out? Room 336.

RAJESH: How did everything go FUBAR? We've been looking for you everywhere.

TAG: DON'T TALK, RUN! THIS IS YOUR SAVING PRIVATE RYAN MOMENT!

ROSE: We are en route. Voice-texting as we sprint. What's this about Spielberg's epic war movie starring Hanx?

RAJESH: It's one of my faves. We should watch it together sometime.

ROSE: I'll make popcorn.

TAG: This is Millie on Tag's phone: Hurry, y'all! We'll be disqualified if we don't get there soon. Tournament rules.

ROSE: WHO DID THIS TO YOU? LET ME AT THEM.

TAG: Two truths and a lie—it was Cheater's Lake, it was Cheater's Lake, or we did this to ourselves because we wanted some privacy. Millie says don't text her phone btw! They still have it!

ROSE: ROGER THAT. But . . . wouldn't the lateness forfeiture be suspended if, say, you were locked in a closet by another team—WHICH HAD ALREADY BEEN DISQUALIFIED FOR PLAGIARISM—to prevent you from competing?

TAG: You'd think. But Millie still wants to get there on time. First impressions are important, she says.

RAJESH: She's right.

TAG: Millie again: They punched him in the face, y'all. He's going to have a black eye.

ROSE: I hate them so much.

RAJESH: WAIT. ARE YOU TWO BACK TOGETHER?

ROSE: Rajesh!

TAG: I mean, this just happened. We have a lot of things to talk about. This is Millie: Y'ALL. RUN!

TAG

I figured my Twitter account might be good for one more thing.

Taggart Strong · @TaggartStrong · 3 m
Any @alanews reporters out there? Something wild is happening at the
Alabama state high school debate tournament being held rn @chathamslake.
I've got a black eye to prove it #alabamastate #forensics #journalism

💬 1   🔁 10   ♡ 15

|

Taggart Strong · @TaggartStrong · 2 m
Seriously. Get here fast. Shit is about to go down #cheaterslake #debatenews
cc @bhamreporters @alabamabreakingnews

💬 1   🔁 8   ♡ 12

MILLIE

This closet didn't have a beanbag chair, or a dry-erase board. So we sat on the floor and talked.

"I owe you an apology," I started. "For never getting in touch with you to explain. That was shitty. I should have at least told you why . . ."

"I never should have kept you out late that night, making you do karaoke before a tournament," he said.

"You didn't make me. I wanted to," I told him. "That was part of the problem. I agreed with my mom that I should focus on debate this year, and for a while, that was okay. But then I met you, and I wanted more."

"So did I!" he said.

"But I couldn't have it. I messed up. And everything has repercussions."

"I guess that's why we're here in this closet," he said. "Repercussions." He was quiet for a minute, and so was I. Then he brightened. "But it's also why Cheater's Lake is disqualified. Which is why I was calling you that day you got mad at me and hung up. Mason was Millicent Calmerzzz on Twitter this whole time—"

"What?"

"She got the plagiarism tip from an anonymous account; I reported it. She was kind of obsessed with you. But she's really embarrassed about it now. She's deleted the account."

"Well," I said. "I guess it's a relief that they're not about to start using it to smear my reputation, not that they haven't already done that in a million different ways already."

"Yeah."

We sat in silence for a minute.

"I do have a question," he finally said.

"Yeah?"

"Was everything with us, well, was it just because of the trauma bonding, what we went through together? Or was it real? Were we . . . real? Because sometimes I feel like I'm not sure anymore." He looked so sad, and I wanted to put my arms around him, to kiss him on the cheek, to kiss his lips, to go back to what we'd been and what part of me still wanted, but I held back.

I thought about what Coach had said, that I needed to trust myself. But what was I supposed to trust? What if what the heart wanted was wrong? Winning state: That was real. But we had been, too. Tag and me. Regardless of what happened next, that was true.

Two things could be true at the same time, I thought.

"We were absolutely, one hundred percent real," I said, standing up.

Tag had been right all along: Debate should be about learning how to say what you really mean. What you really needed to say. And feminism, it wasn't about forcing yourself to fit into other people's boxes. It was about doing what you wanted and needed to do for yourself.

"Hey," he said, standing up and putting his arms around me. "Are you crying?"

"No!" I said, even though I could feel tears streaming down my face.

"The evidence contradicts that statement," he said. "Why are you crying?"

"You know how the supply closet at Montgomery Hills was the start of something? I just have the feeling like . . . this is the end of something," I told him.

"Well, it *is* state. The last tournament besides Nationals," he said. "And maybe the Winners' Tournament, if you go . . ."

"I meant more like us, I guess," I said. "The actual end of us."

"Oh," he said. "The end-end, you mean? Or the middle-end?"

I kissed him.

"Your tears are salty," he said.

He kissed me back, holding my face in his hands.

"But, listen," he said. "Ending one thing means beginning something else. I'll leave you alone forever, if that's what you want. But maybe it doesn't have to be?"

I shook my head. "I do think I need to be on my own for a while, after this. I've been so focused on one thing, but I've got my whole future ahead of me. I owe it to myself to think about who and what I really want to be."

"Okay," he said. "I get that."

He wrapped his arms around me again, and we just stood there for a minute, breathing.

There was a knock at the door. We jumped apart.

"You in there?" asked Rose.

"Ya both decent?" That was Rajesh. He unlocked the door.

Adrenaline flowed through me. I could do this. I would trust myself.

"Ready?" asked Tag.

"Hang on a second!" I yelled.

Tag did a double take. "Millie?"

I'd reached under my dress and grabbed the elastic waist of my pantyhose and pulled down, yanking those fabric casings from my legs. I left them crumpled in the middle of the closet. The air on my legs felt great.

I slipped my shoes back on and wiped my eyes and smiled. "Ready. Tag, you better do your best. And make this fun."

He gave me a thumbs-up and opened the door.

"It's three minutes till start time!" I yelled. "Let's gooooooo!"

TAG

We arrived, gasping, with fifteen seconds to spare. All our debate material was still in the rooms where we'd unwillingly left it, but it didn't matter; we were winging it now. At the front of the room, below the stage where we would debate, Carlos was talking to Joe Keller, gesturing with both hands. Francine and Coach Kargle were hovering nearby, looking worried.

"We're here!" I yelled, running to the front of the room, Millie next to me.

"What *happened*?" Francine asked. "Your face! Tag, are you okay?"

"I got punched," I said.

"Culhane and Blanton Bodie and a group of Chatham's Lakers locked us in a supply closet, hoping to get us disqualified," explained Millie.

"You're kidding," said Joe Keller.

"I wish we were," I said.

"Where are they now?" asked Francine, looking around the auditorium, where several hundred audience members sat, waiting for the final debate to begin. They watched our eyes settle on the back of the room, and their eyes followed ours. "Oh," said Francine. There was a collective intake of breath from the audience.

It must have been a slow news day because the journalists had arrived. They stood with notepads and iPhones in the doorway, recording as the shit went down as promised.

The Cheater's Lake coach had his finger in Culhane's face. "You said you had a foolproof way to win state! That's why I gave you this job!" he was yelling.

Blanton Bodie was standing nearby, whining. "We didn't know it was wrong—we thought the archives were there to help us!" he was saying. "Chatham's Lakers help Chatham's Lakers!" Several other Chatham's Lakers, including the ones who'd shoved us in the closet, were standing nearby with varying looks of disgust and pain. One of them had a Band-Aid on his face. It did not improve his appearance.

The journalists looked on, seemingly thrilled.

"They still have my phone!" said Millie, who ran over to retrieve it. I followed her.

"Can I get a comment?" asked one of the journalists. "Is it true that Chatham's Lake has been plagiarizing debate cases all year—and even longer?"

"Yes," said Millie.

"A tweet from a former debater helped crack the case," I explained, and showed the screenshot from @NoMoreCheatinginLD I'd saved on my phone.

Another journalist put her recording device forward. "Is it true that members of the Chatham's Lake debate team tried to fix the state final by locking the top two competitors in a closet?"

"Yes," I said. "And they punched me in the face, too."

"Ouch," said yet another of the journalists. "Can I take a picture?"

I nodded, squinting at the flash.

"Can I have my phone back, please?" Millie asked the Cheater's Lake coach. "Culhane stole it."

But Culhane had gotten loose of his former coach. He

slapped the journalist's recording device away. "So what if I did?" he said. He took Millie's phone out of his pocket and threw it across the room. "Catch it, DebatrGrl! Let us watch you run."

The phone swooped in an arc over several rows of auditorium seats. Bystanders ducked, and, miraculously, Ricky Yee, who'd been standing in the aisle, reached out and caught it. Carlos ran over and kissed him on the mouth. Culhane let out a few unprintable, graphic, and extremely homophobic phrases.

And then, to everybody's surprise, Rose Powell, who'd been standing there watching everything, hauled off and punched *him* right in the nose.

She looked at her own fist and said quietly, "He deserved it. For homophobia. Sexism. Racism. And for taking points off on the ballot because I have a nose ring and a purple streak in my hair. My dude. It's a whole new world out there. Time for you to catch up."

Culhane glared at us, blood dripping down his face, and then hunched his shoulders and left. The coach and his team followed.

"Ahem," said Joe Keller from the front of the room, a microphone in his hand. "I believe this all leads us right into today's final debate, for the Alabama state championship! *Resolved: Inaction in the face of injustice makes an individual morally culpable.* Please take a seat, everyone. We're going to get started in one minute! For real, this time."

MILLIE

In debate, we talk a lot about fallacies. These are ideas that might sound good or right on the surface but aren't actually logical or reasonable at all. There are a million different kinds of fallacies, and they weren't exclusive to the debate world. They were all over my own life, I'd realized.

My mom's view, that you either had to keep romance out of your life or be distracted, was a false dichotomy.[55] I'd assumed that because things went awry after I started dating Tag, that was somehow caused by me dating Tag. But correlation is not causation![56] The idea of not speaking up against Chatham's Lake, that I should grin and bear it lest it get worse, was a slippery slope fallacy.[57] Assuming that Tag couldn't be trusted because I'd had bad experiences with guys like the Chatham's Lakers was a hasty generalization.[58] Thinking that I couldn't be happy if I let my guard down was a post hoc fallacy.[59]

I didn't have to believe any of that. Not anymore.

I had to believe in myself.

We took our places behind the podiums onstage and flipped

---

55 Two alternative points of view are presented as the only options, though others are actually available.

56 Just because things happen in association with one another doesn't mean one caused the other.

57 The belief that one event inevitably leads to another until we come to an awful conclusion.

58 A conclusion reached without sufficient, unbiased evidence.

59 In full, *post hoc ergo propter hoc*, which means "after this, therefore because of this": "Since one event *followed* another, the latter must have been *caused* by the former."

a coin. I was the affirmative. "Ready?" asked Keller, holding his timer in the air. "Yep," I said, and he clicked.

I was ready to try something totally new.

"Has anyone out there heard of Mary Wollstonecraft?"

I got crickets. Tag gave me a funny look.

"She was a writer and philosopher who lived in Victorian England. She wrote the book *A Vindication of the Rights of Woman*. She died when she was just thirty-eight years old. But she left behind a legacy of writing and thinking and is now considered one of founding philosophers of feminism. She said that men and women should both be treated as rational beings and put forth the concept of a social order founded on reason. People didn't listen to her at the time. They considered her personal life scandalous, and her contributions to society were largely ignored for decades."

The crowd stared at me, perplexed. I cleared my throat.

"Mary Wollstonecraft stands as an example of what the patriarchy tries to do to women who don't follow the rules. It happened then, and it's still happening today. I was just locked in a closet by a group of male debaters who've had it out for me since I started as a freshman. A group of male debaters from this very school who wanted to keep me from winning this tournament. A group of male debaters who have been plagiarizing cases for years while the rest of us actually did the work."

Boos circled the room.

"I hope that makes you mad. It makes me mad, too. But that's hardly the worst thing that's happened to me in my time on the debate circuit. You're in the right place, don't worry. I just have something a little different to say than you might have expected. In some ways it gets at the heart of the resolution: *Inaction in the face of injustice makes an individual morally culpable.* But it's more than that. It's about why we do debate at all."

"Whooooo!" shouted Rose. "You go, girl!"

There was scattered applause. A lot of people still looked confused. I glanced at Tag, who had this inscrutable expression. But what he or anyone else thought didn't matter.

"The misogyny I have faced in my four years on the debate circuit is unacceptable," I said. "The sexual harassment of all kinds, from my fellow debaters and even judges and coaches; the crudeness and insults and shaming because I'm female; the other women I've known who've gotten bullied off their teams and off the circuit. Did you know that women are about four percent less likely than men to win debate rounds and two and a half percent more likely to stop debating on the national circuit after their sophomore year of high school?[60] Perhaps it's because they're being locked in closets and bullied." I looked at my audience, and they stared back at me. The judges were writing on their ballots. "Just one woman finished in the top sixteen in L-D at the 2016 Tournament of Champions.[61] Why? You can't tell me we're somehow just not as good."

I stopped and cleared my throat. "I stayed. And most of the time, I won. I've had a really great coach, some good friends, and my mom to help me. But I don't think any other woman—any person—should have to go through what I have."

I glanced at Tag. He was staring down at his podium.

---

60 From "Gender Disparities in Competitive High School Debate: New Evidence from Comprehensive Tournament Results Data," by Daniel Tartakovsky, May 9, 2016. http://vbriefly .com/wp-content/uploads/2016/05/Tartakovsky_Tabroom_Analysis.pdf

61 Ibid.

"Female-identified debaters are criticized for being too aggressive twice as often as their male counterparts—and when that happens to female-identified debaters, they lose seventy-five percent of the time. When female debaters are up against male debaters in that scenario, they lost almost ninety percent of the time. The win rate for female-identified debaters who compete in front of male-identified judges under the age of twenty-five is only thirty-one percent.[62] I've committed these stats to memory because I've seen them play out again and again. What does all that mean for female debaters when the same male judges are used over and over and over again at tournaments?" I looked over at Keller. "No offense to you, Mr. Keller. You're not the problem."

"None taken," he said, and everyone laughed.

"Actually, *everyone* is the problem," I said. "Whether we're doing it or we're complicit. I thought I had to work within the system to win. But sometimes, the system is just broken. I'm tired of worrying about who's going to try to punish me for saying what I believe. As Mary Wollstonecraft wrote, 'If we revert to history, we shall find that the women who have distinguished themselves have neither been the most beautiful nor the most gentle of their sex.' We should not have to be 'gentle' or 'beautiful' to be heard! This is a sport based on giving anyone who participates a voice, letting them use those voices, and judging those voices fairly and equally, based on the many differences we all bring to the table! We need to do better."

---

62 "Public Forum Does Need to Change: A Research-Based Evaluation. An Open Letter to the Leadership and Membership of the National Speech and Debate Association," by Rich Kawolics, Director of Speech and Debate, Laurel School, 2018. https://www.beyond-resolved .org/post/public-forum-does-need-to-change-a-research-based-evaluation

The audience, most of them, were applauding. Kargle stood up and yelled, "Go, Millie!" I took a few steps across the stage and then walked back, feeling the energy well up in my body, looking out at the crowd. My legs were wobbly. My hands were shaking. But it didn't matter. I didn't need to mark them with ink anymore, when I could say all this. "It's time for those of us who are women or nonbinary, or LGBTQ+, or people of color, or people who aren't rich or part of the Alabama good-old-boy network, to say what we truly believe, and it's time for the rest of you to listen. Really listen. It took me four years, but I've realized this much: Winning isn't about trophies, or championships, or even about playing the game. It's about doing the work to figure out what you believe, and then following through with it. That's what I want for the future of debate, and beyond. Sometimes, in order to win, you need to change the game. Because the rules as they are aren't rules you would have agreed to in the first place, given the choice. And I know we can do it. As Mary Wollstonecraft, feminist and the author of *A Vindication of the Rights of Woman*, wrote: 'The beginning is always today.'"

TAG

After she started talking, I hadn't been able to look at her. I was scared of what I might do in return. Cry or scream or run toward her, wrapping her back in my arms. Anything but debate.

I wanted to win, sure. My parents, who were somewhere in the audience, would be so bummed I'd given up this shot, especially when it was being offered to me right here on a shiny silver debate platter. She wasn't even arguing the resolution. The very basic burden of the debate. I could argue it and win. I tried not to think about Francine. Or how Principal Merwin would look at me in the halls.

But there were lots of ways to win.

I flashed to Millie's advice to Mason back when everything was so perfect: K.I.S.S.—"keep it simple, stupid" (or "keep it stupid simple"). I only needed to get out a couple of sentences. Mason would totally understand.

"I concede," I said. "What she said, it's not even debatable. It's just the truth."

The room went wild.

MILLIE

We got a standing ovation.

I scanned the room and found my mom in the crowd. She was hugging Coach Kargle and crying.

I tried to reach her, but I was surrounded by people. Everyone wanted to say something. To shake my hand. To tell me I was brave. I could barely move. I saw Tag on the other side of the room, looking at me. I waved at him, and he waved back.

Then Joe Keller was climbing up on the stage, a microphone in his hand. "Excuse me," he said. He put his fingers in his mouth, and a whistle came out. The crowd got quiet.

"Thank you for that rousing speech, Millicent. It's given us so much to think about. And I do hope"—he looked around the room pointedly—"we will all think. A lot. About what you said. Not just think—do."

People cheered, and he waited for quiet again.

"Now, the bad news," he said. "I've just had a call with the League. Unfortunately, the rules are clear: The only way to actually win state is to debate the resolution. You and Mr. Strong are both disqualified." The crowd booed. "I don't make the rules, I just got suckered into upholding them."

I looked at my mom, who was frowning and shaking her head.

"May I call on the semifinalists, Carlos Gonzalez-Claremont and Rose Powell, to debate?" Keller asked. "The actual resolution this time, please."

He looked out at the crowd. "Are Carlos and Rose here?"

Rose raised her hand. "I am," she said.

Carlos stood up. "Me too."

"Want to come up to the stage?" asked Keller.

Rose headed to the front. Carlos followed, straightening his tie, which this time had a series of smaller ties on it, with smaller ties on them.

"I'll flip a coin to determine who's affirmative and who's negative," said Keller. "No more surprises, okay? Call it in the air, please," he said. "Ladies first? Rose?"

"Heads!" she said.

"It is heads."

"I'll take aff," she said, and without a second to question herself, she cleared her throat and started to speak.

"What Millie said was right. It's happened to me, too. It's happened to all of us."

The entire room was quiet, and Carlos used that opportunity to say his piece: "If Millie doesn't win, none of us should. What she had to say is more important than debating the resolution—it *is* the resolution. She's doing what the rest of us are just talking about. And if Speech and Debate doesn't understand that, they're as dumb as a bunch of Chatham's Lakers." He gave me a big smile, and then turned to look at Ricky Yee, who grinned right back.

"I can see where this is going," said Keller. "Excuse me, I've gotta make another phone call."

There would be no winner of state in Lincoln-Douglas that year. And even though it wasn't what any of us wanted to hear, people were acting like it was a celebration. Tag's dad was going around inviting everyone to a nearby restaurant, talking about how his son had done this incredible thing, something bigger than winning, even. When he got to me he shook my hand. "Is this the young woman who sat at my kitchen table eating pancakes?" he asked. "You are an amazing speaker. You're just fearless!" Emily was peppering me with compliments and asking where I'd gotten my dress. I didn't want to tell her it was a Ms. Cheney Goodwill special, so I just shrugged and said my mom had found it somewhere. Mason came over and hugged me and whispered she was sorry about Millicent Calmerzzz. "It's okay; I'm glad it was you," I told her. Then Rajesh and Rose found me, both of them talking at the same time, before Rose was swept off for photos for the local paper for her role in backing me up. Carlos tried to reach me, but he got pulled into a conversation with yet another reporter. Francine came rushing over and said, "Honey, that may have been the most incredible thing I've seen in all my years as a debate coach." She looked weepy. "You know, I thought I had to just put up with that stuff for so long," she continued. "You make me realize how I can't keep quiet anymore, either. None of us needs to go through that ever again."

And then there was Kargle and my mom, both of them looking at me with these awestruck expressions, and I felt like I might collapse, like all the energy I'd put into the past few hours had finally just drained out and left me empty.

I looked for Tag.

From across the room, his eyes met mine. He was heading my way when a group of girl debaters caught up with me. "That was epic," they were saying. One of them wanted her picture taken with me, and then they all did. They stood around me posing, giving peace signs to the camera. "We go through so much of that shit, too," they were saying. "Thank God someone is finally saying something about it. Thank *you*."

There was an arm on my shoulder. "Millicent," the woman said. "Ladies, can you give us a minute? I think she needs a little space." The crowd pulled back, and I looked up at Angela Tennant.

"Wow," she said. "Just wow."

That's when it hit me. The full realization of what I'd done. I'd given up the scholarship. No Martha Linger. No full ride and then some to Alabama. I'd have to figure out a new way, cobbling together whatever bits and pieces of money I could get with financial aid. I sighed. I didn't regret saying what I had. But there were always repercussions.

"Can we talk?" asked Angela Tennant. "Give me a call once your head clears from all this, okay?" She slipped me her business card, and I put it in my pocket.

There was a reporter standing behind her, her phone in her hand ready to record. "I hate to interrupt but . . . can I have her next?" she asked.

◉

Mom and I skipped the party and headed home. We were both quiet; I guess she was thinking just like I was. On the way, I texted Tag—I didn't want to leave him hanging this time, too—and told him we wouldn't be there. **But thanks**, I wrote. **Minus not getting the scholarship, this is the best possible ending I could have hoped for.**

I'm here if you want to talk, or anything, he texted back. **I'll wait for you to get in touch first.**

Thanks. What else was there to say? Things were just different now. I couldn't go back to the girl I'd been. I didn't want to.

My phone kept buzzing with new messages, so I turned it off.

Once we got home, I slipped on sweats and was sitting on the couch next to Beau, who had his head in my lap. I was flipping through Netflix options and petting his soft ears when Mom came in the room. "Honey," she said, "can we talk?"

I put down the remote. "I know. You don't have to tell me. I should have just debated and won and gotten the scholarship. I've screwed up everything now."

"What? No!" she said, sitting down next to me. "You did exactly the right thing up there. It was what everyone needed to hear, and maybe more importantly, what you needed to say. I had no idea how much harassment you've faced. You and so many girls. I mean, I knew a little"—she frowned and I know she was thinking about the nude pictures Culhane had pasted to my door—"but barely enough. Honey, things need to change, and fast, in that world. Just like everywhere else." She shook her head. "There are these guys who are always hitting on me in the ER. Injured men! I'm like, Do you want me to break your other arm, too?"

I laughed.

"Not that I would." She sat next to me. "Millie, I loved your speech. I'm so proud of you. There aren't enough words to say it."

"But now we have to figure out how to get the money for college," I said.

"We will," she told me, and there were tears in her eyes. "But first: I owe you an apology."

"For what?"

"For not understanding. For not really listening. For dismissing stuff I didn't want to hear. Like with Tag. You really liked him, didn't you?"

I nodded. Again, that past tense, reminding me it was over.

"I just wanted to have a boyfriend and win debate," I told her. "I didn't think that was too much to ask. I wasn't going to drop out of school, or fail, or even lose everything—except then I did."

"You didn't," she said, smoothing my hair. "There are a lot of ways to win. You chose the bravest option. As for Tag, you're almost eighteen. I should have trusted you to make the decision for yourself, that you could date and excel at debate and school, too. I should have supported you more, and listened to what you were saying instead of getting scared."

I looked up at her and suddenly I felt like crying again. "Tag and I are over now, anyway," I said.

"Are you sure?" she asked. "I saw the way he looked at you at the tournament . . ."

"Yeah. I need some time for myself. Everything got so confused. I want to just be me for a while."

"Okay," she said. "That sounds really smart. I don't know if this is coming at completely the wrong time then, but . . ."

"What?"

She blushed. "Are you up for a visitor? Kenny offered to come over with some pizzas to celebrate. But if you want to hang out with just the two of us, we can say no."

"Mom, is this like a date or something?"

She turned redder. "Well, no . . ."

"It is! I can tell by your face!"

"I know you asked before, but . . . well, all those years ago?"

"Yeah?" I was dying to know.

"We broke up over the stupidest fight. It was really just a misunderstanding. He thought I was angry with him; I thought he was angry with me—I can't even remember about what, that's how silly it all was. We kind of stopped talking, and no one made the first move to apologize or reach out. Then I got pregnant with you, which of course was a total surprise, but to him felt like a betrayal, and it just seemed like there was no way to get back to what we had in those old days. But watching you debate, say what you really mean, well, it made me realize. I should say what I feel, too."

"And?"

"I told him that I still missed him. That I'm not sure I ever got over him, in a way. He was my first love."

"Oh my God. Mom. What did he say?"

She smiled. "He said he felt the same way."

"Oh my God," I repeated.

"So, what do *you* say?"

"What do *you* want to do?" I asked, poking her in the arm.

She shrugged. "Maybe those high school relationships aren't exactly ancient history after all. Maybe there's always a chance you can go back to something good and have it be even better. Or am I just being ridiculous?"

"Saying yes to pizza is never ridiculous."

She smiled and shrugged again. "I'm taking a cue from my wise daughter: I owe it to myself to see what might happen. To put who I am and what I feel out into the world, regardless of how much it might scare me. And to fight sexism and douchebags every step of the way."

I hugged her. "You got this."

"*We* got this," she said, hugging me back.

TAG

When we all got home, I sat down with my parents for another chat, but this time, I was the one who suggested it.

"I've been thinking," I said. "It's time I went beyond debate."

"Does this mean you're ready to start talking about college seriously?" my dad asked. "Alabama is a good school. I think you'll do well there."

"Well, no," I said. "I want to work for a year. Roberto says he'll make me his apprentice at Ciao! He's going to pay me fifteen dollars an hour. And I have this other idea. I want to organize an event. Actually, a series of them."

They both looked at me in surprise.

"There are so many people out there whose voices deserve to be heard, but nobody's listening. People who don't have a chance to do something like debate, who maybe don't have anyone who pays attention to what they think at all," I explained.

My mom nodded. My dad raised his eyebrows.

"I'm calling it Your Chance to Talk. Anyone who wants to can come discuss the stuff they're dealing with, the issues they think matter. People will listen with open minds. And we'll all eat delicious food because no one has a good conversation when they're hangry . . ."

"Do you know anything about planning an event?" Dad asked. "It's a lot of work."

"I started looking into it already," I said, pulling out the file I'd been putting together in my spare time. "I had a meeting with this city council member, Lila Johnston, and we've been emailing back and forth. She's given me a ton of suggestions, and a list of potential donors who might want to be involved in something like this. I already reached out to see if Ciao! will host it. They're usually closed on Sundays, anyway, and Roberto said yes so long as I pay for cleaning service afterward—he can write off the use. And I want to cook everything."

"Wow," said my mom. "Sweetie, that's really ambitious. And I love this idea for the summer. But we still think you should plan on going to Alabama on the fall."

"I respectfully disagree," I said. "Just because I don't want to go to college immediately doesn't mean I'm not taking my future seriously," I told them. "I have a plan. I can defer my admission to Alabama for a year, during which I'll apprentice at Ciao! and run my event series. Then I'll apply to culinary schools and compare what they offer to, say, majoring in hospitality management at Alabama, to figure out which is the better course for me."

"You know, Jill Fayne's daughter took a gap year, and she really learned a lot, working," added my mom. "Now she's going to Ole Miss and loves it. She's on honor roll! She says she needed that year to really focus and figure things out."

"Fine!" said my dad, raising his hands in the air. "A year. Then we discuss again." He sighed. "I can't believe the way you and Mason have learned how to use your debate skills against me for your gain."

"You wanted me to excel," I said.

He groaned, and then smiled. "And I gotta say: It's kind of awesome."

**HOPEWELL CROSSING SENIOR DELIVERS
FEMINIST SPEECH DURING ALABAMA STATE DEBATE FINAL,
LEAVING AUDIENCE IN AWE**

THE BIRMINGHAM HERALD

BY LORI LANGFORD

**UPSET AT ALABAMA STATE! TOP DEBATER
MILLICENT M. CHALMERS CHALLENGES COMMUNITY
TO DO BETTER FOR WOMEN, EVERYONE**

ALLTHEBAMANEWS.COM

BY THEODORA BRIDEY

**SCANDAL ROCKS CHATHAM'S LAKE BOYS' SCHOOL.
"IT'S BEEN GOING ON A LONG, LONG TIME," SAY SOURCES.**

ALLTHEBAMANEWS.COM

BY THEODORA BRIDEY

THE POWER—AND RESPONSIBILITY—OF HAVING A VOICE

THE PARK SCHOOL PAPER

BY TAGGART STRONG

PART FIVE

May

---

*Resolved: Secondary education in America
should value the fine arts over athletics.*
(Nationals)

MILLIE

Guess what: I did a kritik at Nationals. Just once. For fun. In octofinals I argued that because basic secondary education is not, in practice, equal or accessible for all people in society, a resolution that pitted fine arts against athletics was an insult to both students and educators—and beside the point. In fact, we should live in a society in which *both* are valued, but before that, education must be funded properly and provided to all in a way that was both fair and equitable. I got a standing ovation for that.

I made it all the way to semis, where I was proud to be beaten by a girl from Kansas City who might be the best debater I've ever gone against in my life. She won the whole thing.

I didn't see Tag there, but I was so busy, I didn't have much time to think about him at all, except at night when I'd wake up, missing him in the parts of my heart that couldn't sleep.

I was more popular, all of a sudden, than I ever could have imagined. News of my speech at state had spread far and wide thanks to the power of the internet, with an assist from local Alabama news. There was also a viral YouTube video, and this one had my real words in it. I got emails every day from girl debaters, and debaters who weren't girls, and even some women who weren't debaters who wanted to tell me what I'd said was helping them keep going. Sure, there was plenty of hate, too. But the love—that felt good.

So did seeing Chatham's Lake get banned for the entire next

year, and the students who assaulted us get suspended. Culhane was expelled from college after a Twitter blast from someone who'd been at the tournament told the world about what he'd done, and he and the coach were both fired. The school offered Kargle the job. He said no. He's got a whole new debate team at Hopewell Crossing now, including Brian's sister, Cleo.

Mom and Kargle are officially an item. When they're not behaving like teenagers, they're really, really cute. And she and I are spending more time with each other, with space for each of us to be who we need to be. It's a work in progress, but that's how things are with the people you love.

As for college money, when I finally called Angela Tennant after state, she told me that the Winners' Tournament had a spot for me—and if I won it, there was a pretty major scholarship attached to that. So, last week, I did just that. I'll be going to the University of Alabama on an almost-full ride in the fall, after teaching debate at Angela Tennant's Winners' Camp for the summer, which will give me the extra money I need and also seemed like a good way to keep changing the debate circuit for the better.

By most people's standards, everything was coming up roses.

But I kept thinking about flow-ers.

Dear Dr. Jefferson Wylie and the
Hopewell Crossing Board of Education, APPROVED

In the past four years of my career at Hopewell
Crossing, I have had the honor of working with
Millicent M. Chalmers, a truly exceptional student
who took it upon herself to compete in high school
Lincoln-Douglas debate even though there was
no team at the school. She came to me asking
for sponsorship and coaching after several other
teachers at the school turned her down, citing
difficulties in timing or lack of commitment to the
cause. She wrote her own cases. She practiced
diligently. And she won Alabama state three years
in a row—and at her fourth tournament used her
platform to do something even more powerful than
winning. (Please see the attached YouTube clip.)
She went on to place in the top four at Nationals
and to win first place at the prestigious Winners'
Tournament.

I have coached Millicent for four years, but she
has coached me right back, teaching me lessons
in fortitude, bravery, intelligence, and the ability to
succeed despite the odds. She has shown me what
it means to have a voice, and why it's important
to use it in the best way you can. That's why I'm
writing to you now.

Millicent will attend the University of Alabama
on scholarship this fall, won through her debate
success. I have a very small ask: I request that a

trophy case be set up within our school, alongside the cases displaying our various sports honorariums, to showcase her numerous trophies won through the years. We do this for football, baseball, and basketball—why not also for a girl who says what she believes, and who has the power to convince others that they may be able to do the same if they only try, and if others will only listen? So far, ten female students have approached me about joining the team. You can't convince me that's not because of Millie.

Respectfully,
Coach Kenny Kargle
Hopewell Crossing County School

To: MillicentMChalmers@MillicentMChalmers.com
From: ThisIsMasonStrong@TheStrongFamilyEmail.com
Subject: Important News

Hi Millie,

I miss you! I miss our talks about debate and everything. I wanted to invite you to this event Tag planned. We're all really proud of him. PLEASE PLEASE PLEASE think about coming? I want to see you! We all do.

I attached the invite.
PS He's cooking everything himself!

xoxoxoxo
Mason

YOUR CHANCE TO TALK

BECAUSE WORDS MATTER,
EVEN WHEN THERE ARE NO TROPHIES

WHERE: Ciao! Ristorante

WHEN: 5 P.M.–8 P.M., Sunday, May 23

WHY: Everybody's talking, but not everyone is listening. We want to change that.

WHAT WE'LL DO: Serve up a menu of delicious food (to eat) & some great speakers (to hear) & give you YOUR OWN CHANCE to talk about what's important to YOU.

WHAT TO BRING: Your own stories. An open mind. An empty stomach. And friends. All are welcome, as long as they agree to respect everyone present.

Special guests will include . . .

- **LILA JOHNSTON,** Birmingham City Council member, on finding her own voice as a youth

- **FRANCINE CHO,** speech & debate director at The Park School, on her experiences of sexism and racism on the debate circuit

- YouTube sensation/weatherperson **MAKENZIE STRATUS-CIRRUS,** on how they deal with the haters

- . . . and others

presented by Tag Strong & friends
please rsvp to tag@buildingstrongervoices.com

MILLIE

I asked my mom to drop me off about an hour before the event started. I figured if I got there early, Tag might have time to talk—and if he didn't want to talk, I could leave without drawing attention to myself. I walked in through the back and into the kitchen, just in case anyone was already there. I didn't want to get distracted before I did what I'd come to do.

He was standing there, his back to me, chopping something on the counter. There were his skinny legs in jeans. A T-shirt that I'm sure said something ridiculous on the front. And his pumpkin tie, looped around his neck haphazardly and hanging down his back, like he might have forgotten he even put it on.

I could barely breathe. It was like being in the supply closet again.

But about a million times better.

Also, everything smelled *incredible*.

TAG

I heard a noise and turned around. To my credit, I didn't scream or yell or jump or drop a million dishes to indicate my surprise that Millicent Chalmers was suddenly in my kitchen.

"Hi," I said. I took my glasses off and wiped them and put them back on again. *Not a mirage*, I confirmed to myself.

"Hi," she said back. "I hope it's not weird that I'm here."

"It's a little weird," I said. "But not bad weird. How are you?"

"I'm good," she said. "Things are going well."

"I heard," I said. "Semis at Nationals! And first at the Winners' Tournament! You deserve it."

She smiled. "Sometimes the repercussions aren't so bad, after all. I didn't get the Martha Linger, but I got enough money for college anyway. And Angela Tennant recruited me to coach the Winners' Tournament debate camp for the summer, too."

"Mason's doing that! That's the camp she and my parents finally settled on."

"I hope she's assigned to me," said Millie. "I'm teaching novices, so fingers crossed. What are you going to do?"

"I'm going to stay here. Literally, in this kitchen. I'm going to do an apprenticeship with Roberto . . ."

"Oh wow."

"I get to feed people really good food, and when I'm not cooking, I can keep working on Your Chance to Talk," I told her. I wiped my hands on my apron. I felt so nervous all of a sudden.

"That's such a cool idea," she said. "I'm glad you thought of it."

"You helped me. All the talks we had . . ."

Did her face look a little bit sad that I wouldn't be in Tuscaloosa, or was that just my imagination?

"Guess who's back together?" she asked.

"Rose and Rajesh?"

"No!" she said. "Wait, did they split up?"

"Yeah, because he's going to—wait for it—Harvard! And she'll be stuck in 'Bama for the next year finishing high school. But now I think they're going to try a long-distance relationship. And she kinda wants to end up at Amherst . . ."

"I always thought he'd get into Harvard in the end," she said.

"He debated it endlessly. But when you get into Harvard, in the end, I guess you go to Harvard. But—get this—he's decided he wants to be a music major! And his parents are supporting him."

"That's awesome," she said. "He's doing it his own way."

"Who were you talking about?" I asked.

"My mom and Coach Kargle!" she said. "Can you believe it?"

"I can," I said. "That seems right."

"I know," said Millie. "He's a good one." She came closer. "And, Tag, so are you. I needed some time to figure it all out. But now I know what I want. Really."

She took my hand, and she pulled me into the little supply closet where we kept flour and sugar and cans of tomatoes and olive oil and extra pots and pans.

I couldn't breathe for a second. She was inches from my face. And then she was kissing me with her soft lips, and her hair smelled like her lemon shampoo. I wrapped my arms around her, and we were holding each other as close as we could get, our hearts beating together in a supply closet of Ciao!, which would have been totally corny, except it wasn't.

She pulled away and looked at me. "Does your shirt say JUST DILL WITH IT?" she asked.

I nodded. "There's a pickle right here," I said, pointing. "It—"

She put her hand over my mouth.

"Shh. I have to get this out."

I nodded, pushing my glasses back up my nose.

"If that other closet was an ending, I want this to be a new beginning. For us. I'm trying to say what I really feel, and, well, I might kind of love you. I always did. Not kind of. Really. I *do* love you. Still."

My alarm went off at the worst possible moment. "My truffle mac and cheese bites!" I grabbed my oven mitts and went to check the oven. She followed me.

"Can I help?" she asked. "Do you need an assistant?"

"Just hang out with me. As much as you can before you leave to coach debate camp."

"And even then," said Millie.

"What do you mean?"

"Camp got moved to Birmingham-Southern, just down the street. Angela Tennant got an incredible deal from the university. I'm here all summer. But, for the record, Tuscaloosa and Birmingham aren't that far apart, either."

"I forgot to tell you something really important," I said.

"What?"

"I love you, too." I kissed her, putting everything true and real and important, everything I'd always wanted to say to her, into that moment. And then I stopped. "I just have one favor to ask."

"What?"

"If I give you a truffle mac and cheese bite, will you tell me what the *M* stands for?"

MILLIE

A few weeks later, I was all packed and ready to head to Birmingham for the first session of debate camp. Mom had the day off and was going to drive me and help me set up the dorm room where I'd be staying all summer. But first, I needed to make a stop at the library. I returned the Wollstonecraft book and tried to pay my overdue fine, but Mrs. Mendez wouldn't take the money. She gave me a hug and told me to come back whenever I could. "I'm gonna miss you and that Tag boy," she said. "Tell him that."

"I will," I said. "We'll come back and see you, I promise."

She smiled and handed me the book. "Keep it. I'll buy the library a new one."

On the way out, I passed the reference section, a place where I'd spent so much time researching to try to get what I thought I wanted, when what I really needed was to listen to not only my brain but also my heart, to find my own way to say all the things I really meant.

It wasn't my style to write in a library book, but I had Post-it notes. I opened up the big reference dictionary I'd used so often over the past four years, turning to the *M*s until I found what I was looking for.

MILLICENT M. CHALMERS

mav·er·ick

/ˈmav(ə)rik/

noun

noun: **maverick**; *plural noun:* **mavericks**

1. an unorthodox or independent-minded person. "a maverick among Connecticut Republicans"; a person who does not go along with a group or party

Similar:

individualist, nonconformist, free spirit, original, trendsetter, bohemian, eccentric, outsider, rebel, dissenter, dissident, bad boy

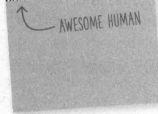
AWESOME HUMAN

AUTHOR'S NOTE

I was a shy kid. When I needed quarters to play video games or buy Lemonheads from the vending machine at the bowling alley where we went with my parents most Sundays so they could play in a league with their friends, I'd make my little brother ask so I didn't have to. I read books, hundreds of books, but raising my hand in class to say a few words was a whole lot scarier than plucking a four-hundred-page tome off the shelves and digging in. Then, in fifth grade, my family moved from the Chicago suburbs to Decatur, Alabama, for my dad's job. I realized I talked funny compared to everyone else, so I spoke carefully—and even less. In seventh grade, I tried out for chorus but sang so quietly no one could hear me. I didn't make the cut until my mom called and asked the choral director if I could try out again, this time a little louder. (He let me, and I made it that time.)

Eventually, I had a handful of good friends I talked to quite a lot. I'd learned how to swap out "you guys" for "y'all." I even had something of a southern accent. But I still didn't have the confidence to stand up in front of a large group of people and argue for what I believed in—until I joined the high school forensics team, which was coached by a woman named Ellen Langford, who cared about us doing our best and winning, but also about us, just as we were.

To be totally honest, it wasn't the desire to get better at public speaking that got me to join the team. It was wanting to get out of gym, which you could do if your seventh period was an extracurricular like debate. So I joined the team. And I was never the same after that.

Much of what's written in *That's Debatable* is informed by my own experiences from that time in the '90s when I competed in Lincoln-Douglas debate as a member of the Decatur High School forensics team. Unlike Millie, I never won state, but I did win second place one year, and I competed in Nationals as well. Like Rajesh, in my senior year, I was captain of the team, but there was no one like Tag around. We pretty much all played by the rules of the game, but we bent them, too: I remember one fellow debater using the lyrics of Young MC's "Bust a Move" to make a point.

There were no kritiks back then—at least, I'd never heard of them, and certainly, methods and techniques and styles have changed and will continue to evolve, with more conservative local regions adopting one way and the nationals circuit providing the option to do something else. But willingly dedicating yourself and many of your weekends, plus your summers (I went to debate camp twice, first in Alabama and then in Iowa), to this practice, carving out a social scene among people who wanted to work on writing cases and forming arguments about values and the important issues of our time: That's all very real. Of course, debaters have lives! But they spend much of their lives doing what they love, which is to say, debating. And also, getting to know one another.

Nearly thirty years after my time on the team, as I wrote and revised this book during the COVID-19 pandemic, I listened as our outgoing president tried to tell the world that his election loss was a lie, which was just the latest in a string of countless other lies.[63] I kept thinking about the words we use, and how we use them, and how sometimes arguing both sides is right, and sometimes it's absolutely wrong. Some things are debatable, and some things simply should not be, not anymore.

As I dug deeper into my characters and read about what was happening on the high school debate circuit as women stood up to speak out against the sexual harassment they'd experienced, I thought back to experiences I'd had back in the '90s. How certain male debaters, and even a few judges, had made me feel. What they'd said to me, and what I'd heard in whispers. What I had to wear and look like and how I needed to speak in order to win.

Back then, we had no #MeToo to express what was happening, so most of the time, whatever the hurt, we pressed on and tried to ignore and forget. We were afraid to speak out about something that might impact our chances to win, or we told ourselves no one would believe us, or other people told us this was just how things were. We tried to be stronger, but not speaking out about what's right, even when it feels like the only option, never makes you strong.

Now, thankfully, things are starting to be different. There are movements to change not only how we deal with things like sexual harassment, racism, misogyny, homophobia, transphobia, and other discrimination, but the very structures that created them. This is a long time coming, and we're only at the beginning, but I'm encouraged by new attention to the problems of the debate world, including the creation of student-led organizations like

63 https://www.cnn.com/2021/01/16/politics/fact-check-dale-top-15-donald-trump-lies/index.html

Beyond Resolved,[64] which advocates for all marginalized groups in high school speech and debate. I'm also glad that students like those at the Parkland, Florida, high school who had to go through one of the most traumatic experiences I can imagine, are standing up to say this is enough, the gun violence must end.[65] I am so proud of the teens of today for speaking their truths as both individuals and in groups. And I'm proud of the journalists who continue to bring matters of injustice to light through their work.

Joining the forensics team in high school had a huge influence on the person I am now. I started to speak, to write for myself, and eventually, to write publicly. I started to say what I believed— or what I believed I believed. Because, don't forget: Your beliefs should and will morph and change as you learn and discuss and experience. That's another extremely important part of growing up and, once you hit those adult years, of continuing to stay alive and engaged with society, while you also hold on forever to that kernel you know in your gut is true and right.

Debate as a practice isn't about saying what you *don't* mean; it's about shoring up your skills and argumentation and thinking to make a difference about what you *do* mean. It's about crystallizing that belief, and strengthening it, and really being able to fight for it. In that, its value isn't debatable, either. It's not just about winning: It's about making the world a better place, one fully informed point of view at a time.

I hope this book will help you do that, in whatever way you do. Because your voices matter far more than you may know.

---

64 www.beyond-resolved.org
65 marchforourlives.com

ACKNOWLEDGMENTS

When they say a book is a collaboration, they're really not kidding. Even though it's got my name on it, so many people were involved and deserve applause. So here goes: To the incomparable Joy Peskin, editor extraordinaire, thank you! A hundred million "you're the bests" (and I mean it!) to my literary agent, Ryan Harbage, who is calm, cool, and collected no matter the storm (or pandemic), and his colleague at the Fischer-Harbage Agency, Christopher Hermelin, who has superior taste in dog names. Thanks to creative genius and amazing human Eric Reid at WME (I owe you a lasagna!). To the whole team at Macmillan Children's, I am so grateful for your kindness, generosity, enthusiasm, and support.

To Quinn and Daisy, thanks for always answering my weird questions and for considering matters such as book covers and character names and musical choices seriously, or at least, for acting like you do. And for having such great taste.

To Ezra: I might be able to do it without you, but it would be truly horrible, and, honestly, why would I? That's just not debatable. To Gidget and Ramona, thanks for all the walks, and, yes, I have more treats for you. To Mom, Dad, Brad, Scarlett, Vivi, and Koko: I love you all so much. Thanks for letting me be the annoying writer in the family. Uncle Bill and Aunt Barb: Can you find the Simpkins?

This work would not have existed (or at least, it wouldn't have been very good) without my intrepid writing groups, who read and commented and deliberated again and again and gave support for matters small and large. To Beck Rourke-Mooney, Kerry McQuaide (who told me I could do it, regardless of the deadline!), Pamela Hoh, Trish Malone, Andrea Pyros, and Alisa Kwitney; to Maureen O'Connor, Glynnis MacNicol, Michelle Ruiz, Maris Kreizman, and Kate McKean; and, of course, to Casey Scieszka: Thank you for keeping me going. I love you all! (Are you ready for my next draft?)

Thank you to authenticity reader Shyamala Parthasarathy for her insightful, helpful notes, and to Dr. David Austern, a clinical psychologist at NYU Langone Health, for talking to me about trauma, how people might respond in a shooter scare, and what the psychological aftereffects of such an event might be. Thank you also to the journalist Emma Gray, who wrote the excellent piece "Competitive Debaters Are Ready for Their 'Me Too' Moment"[66] for *HuffPost*, and who read a draft of this novel and gave her thoughts.

To my BFF, Paige Orr Clancy, thank you for being the honorary debate nerd of my dreams (and Willa and Lillian, for reading!). My dear Camille Dodero and Steven Thrasher, the Zooms made it all go by a lot faster. Stela Xhiku, your website skillz rock, as always.

To Ella Schnake, who won Nationals in 2019 in Program Oral Interpretation for her incredible performance, "Debate Like a Girl"[67] (go to YouTube and watch it now), which helped inspire thousands of girl debaters and also my story, and who was kind

---

66 https://www.huffpost.com/entry/high-school-debate-me
-too_n_5f7217fcc5b6f622a0c2ab94

67 https://www.youtube.com/watch?v=li5HtExwEDc

enough to share her experience with me and give me feedback on an early draft of this book: You are awesome! Thank you so, so much.

To my former DHS Forensics team: Remember all those trips in vans to destinations where we'd do our very best to convince judges to vote for us, and, in the off times, have a lot of fun? I do.

Not least: Thanks to the writing community at large, which, like the debate community, contains multitudes and is not always perfect but is full of so many beautiful voices who deserve to be heard, and to whom we should be listening.